The Devil's Room

by Joe Fegan

"Joe Fegan"

The Devil's Room

ISBN-13: 978-1530086078
ISBN-10: 1530086078

Cover art by Anthony S. Markellis
Formatting and interior design by Ryan Robbins

Questions or comments?
TDR.inbox@gmail.com

First Edition

Printed in the U.S.A

This unworthy book is dedicated to the memory of a writer's writer, the prodigiously talented Glasgow novelist Campbell Black — dear friend, generous advisor *und fluchtling aus* Oswego.

(The Devil) cannot endure to be mocked.

— Sir Thomas More

Foreword

In 1986 there was a major change in the U.S. Internal Revenue code, and it caught many a taxpayer — and tax advisor — flat-footed. One such taxpayer was a college professor in upstate New York who had just begun to have major success in his second career as a novelist. As his books began to sell, the tax shelters his advisors had sold him began to crumble, and he found Uncle Sam taking more and more of his rising income. He'd never been to Ireland, but in 1990 a fellow writer told him about its miraculous tax code, which exempted income from creative endeavors — particularly writing. The tax-code change had many untoward effects, but perhaps none so strange as in the following tale.

One

Trelawny Smart, would-be expatriate and fugitive from the grasping tax laws of his native land, checked his watch and looked at the road sign through the Irish pub's misted window: Ballymorda. Wasn't that where they were supposed to meet? The estate agent, as they were called in this oddly familiar yet sometimes vexingly foreign land, had said he'd meet Smart at 1:30 in the pub at ... now what was the name of it?

He knew it was Bally something or other. But Ballymorda? Strange name, Smart thought idly, as he sipped his third Guinness of the afternoon. Here it was, 2:15, and still no sign of the realtor. Smart checked his pockets and found the fellow's card.

Fegan Fergus
Licensed Estate Agent, County Dergh
547 48735
"Fine older properties a speciality"

If he moved to Ireland, Smart supposed he'd have to relearn the language to some extent, melding Irishisms and Anglicisms into some new bastard version of American, his mother tongue. Would he recognize his own speech after 10 or 20 years in Eire? Would he soon begin to add letters to words like "rumor" and "specialty?" And then there was "yoke," the all-purpose Irish noun, meaning this thing or that or anything at all. He'd only been in Ireland a few days, but already he'd been yoked enough times to figure out what it meant. *How long will it take me to start saying "yoke,"* Smart wondered.

He waited a while longer, tapping his fingers as the furrows in his brow deepened. Then, lurching up from the low couch he was sitting on, he headed off toward the public phone in the corner. He dialed Fergus' number but got no answer. *He must be on his way,* Smart concluded hopefully as he headed back toward his seat.

Actually, Fegan Fergus was not more than 40 feet from Smart at that moment. He'd gotten to the pub early and had been waylaid by some friends and taken off to a side room for a game of cards. After several pints, Fergus had lost track of the time. He'd checked the crowded main room once for Smart, but Smart had gone to the public phone, so Fergus hadn't seen him.

Fergus simply went back to his mates, half of whom owed him money, and attempted to arrange things so that his debtors made good with his creditors, who comprised the other half.

At 3 o'clock Smart had had enough of reading *The Sunday Irish Times*, excellent sheet though it was, and decided he'd find another estate agent. "The hell with Fergus," Smart growled to himself a bit thickly as he drained another pint — his seventh of the day, counting the ones he'd had with breakfast. "I'll find someone else who wants to show me castles."

Smart headed a bit unsteadily toward the men's room, where two locals — Ballymorderers? Ballinamites? Smart couldn't imagine what these people called themselves — were engaged in animated discussion.

"Shite, Thomas, you had him dead to rights. You could have nailed him, but you let him get away. I could have used that money, man. Why didn't you call him?"

"It's not like that, Fegan. Not a'tall, man. I was just after a bit of settin' him up, like. He's fookin' dead where he sits but doesn't know it yet. By the time he realizes, it'll be too late. And as soon as he pays me, I'll pay you. Don't worry about a thing, so."

The two looked over at Smart and nodded as they washed their hands and combed their hair. "Pardon me," said Smart a bit stiffly to the one called Fegan, "but did I understand your name to be Fegan?"

"You did, sir. Fegan Fergus, estate agent, at your service. What can I do for you, then?"

Fergus had an engaging smile and merry eyes — the kind of face, Smart thought, upon which the map of Ireland was said to be written — and he probably wouldn't have understood if Smart had ranted and raved. And besides, Smart realized, he didn't really *feel* like ranting and raving. The seven pints in him — nectar of pacific gods, apparently — had had a mellowing effect. He held out his hand. "Pleased to meet you. I'm Trelawny Smart."

Fergus took Smart's hand and shook it warmly. "Would you be from the States, then?" asked Fergus. He was still smiling broadly, no hint of chagrin spoiling the choirboy features.

"Yes," said Smart evenly, smiling also. He looked Fergus squarely in the eyes. "I'm here to look at some property."

The briefest epiphany registered on Fergus' face. But he didn't miss a beat as he turned to his friend and said: "Thomas, be a good fellow and leave me and Mr. Smart, here, to our own devices, will you please? We've some business to discuss. Make my apologies to the boys, won't you? There's a good lad."

Thomas made his way back to the game, shaking his head and whispering "shite" to himself. What were the odds that Fegan would be able to recover from so grave a gaffe? A turf accountant by trade, Thomas began to make book for his mates moments after he reached their table.

"Well, Mr. Smart, did you have a specific type of property in mind, then? Or did you just want to get a feel for our inventory, so to speak?"

The famous author had to smile in spite of himself. The fellow had kept a potentially important client waiting for hours, but wasn't even going to acknowledge it, much less apologize. Blarney contained a large percentage of brass, Smart decided.

"Show me the best place you have, then show me the best value," said Smart.

"Very well, sir," said Fergus. "This way to my motor." Fergus took Smart's elbow and steered him out a side door to a late-model black Toyota parked next to the pub. Smart had been to England and had been exposed to driving on the right, but he still wasn't comfortable with it. He scanned the narrow two-lane road apprehensively as Fergus gunned the Toyota out into traffic, which thankfully was sparse. Everyone, it seemed, was at the pubs.

"And what prompted your interest in our wee country, sir, if I might ask?" Fergus inquired as he shifted smoothly up to highway speed.

"Taxes," said Smart.

"Say no more, Mr. Smart," Fergus said. "I understand perfectly. As a writer, you'll find a much better situation here, of course."

Smart didn't answer, but he smiled as he thought about the Irish tax code and its legendary exemption of income from creative endeavors. It was a writer's paradise, and he'd been a fool not to take advantage of it sooner. Many another novelist had decamped to the Republic from Britain or the States, getting the full enjoyment of their income and living like squires of yore with estates in the country and townhouses in Dublin. Rural Ireland — which was to say practically the entire country outside of Dublin and Cork — might be removed from modern life, but it had quick air connections to London, New York, Paris ... anywhere you might want to go, really. With the money he'd save on taxes, he could live like a belted earl and travel to boot. It was just a matter of finding the right house, which brought him back to Fergus.

"I scanned your catalog on the way over," Smart said. "Which house are you showing me first?"

"I thought we'd start with Moorside," said Fergus earnestly. "The views of the Shannon valley from the house are enchanting. And the owners have kept the place up quite well. They do want a good bit for it, though."

"Five hundred thousand pounds, wasn't it?" asked Smart. He remembered Moorside as being the most expensive listing in Fergus' catalog.

"Yes, and they're quite firm about it. Turned down a cash offer of 475,000 from a German fellow just a few weeks ago, they did. Got rather offended, in fact."

"Is the place really worth 500,000, Mr. Fergus?"

"Well, sir ... you understand my position. As an estate agent I'm legally in the owners' service. I would say, strictly between yourself and myself, that better bargains might be had, all things considered."

Smart looked about nervously as the Toyota careened around blind curves, nearly brushing against the hedgerows and stone fences that boxed in the roadway. If they suddenly encountered a walker or a rider, Fergus would never be able to avoid him in time. Smart buckled his seatbelt and gripped the safety handle.

One thing became certain as they drove, though: The heart of Ireland was a many-splendored place. Light glinted off sparkling blue and slate-colored lakes in the distance as the sun started to set, and here and there a gaunt castle turret — some connected to moldering ruins, some standing quite alone — thrust up out of the land like some phallic rejoinder to centuries of Catholicism. Thatched cottages, many of them vacant and run down, alternated with modern houses, some of a Mediterranean design that seemed incongruous until you the noticed the palm trees lining their driveways, and fields of grazing sheep and cattle. Here and there were manor houses, abbeys, convents, the odd wholesaler or erector's yard. They careened through tiny settlements so quickly that Smart didn't always see their names. The weather was dank this early-January evening, but Smart could easily envision a spectacular bloom in spring.

"Ever get any snow here?" he asked.

"Ah, a bit now and then. We had a thin white sheet around the holiday, but it didn't last. Arrived Christmas eve and gone with Santa Claus the next day, wasn't it?"

Smart smiled grimly as he thought of the winters in Tuscarora Falls, N.Y., home of Wadsworth College, where he taught Geology: They'd gotten five feet of snow the previous year, and were well on their way to reaching that again. He was sick of the maddening business of trying to carry on normal life in extreme cold.

"Well, Mr. Fergus, I wonder if we shouldn't cut right to the bargain, given the late hour and the fact that my schedule doesn't permit of much house-hunting here."

Fergus slowed the car and looked at Smart. "Well, Mr. Smart, I'd as soon show you Simpson Hall as Moorside, but Simpson Hall is in the opposite direction. It will take a bit of doing to get us there much before dark, I'm afraid."

"Still, I think 500,000 is a bit over my budget just now. It would be one thing if the owners were willing to deal, but if they're holding fast at 500 ... well, let me put it this way: The IRS — the U.S. tax collectors — have been having a field day with me."

"I quite take your point, Mr. Smart. But if we're to reach Simpson Hall before sundown I'll have to stop and find out the best route. I've never approached it from this direction before. I think there may be a shortcut, too, if memory serves. I'll head back and inquire at The Drowning Man, if you don't mind."

A few minutes later they pulled up to the gaily painted pub at the center of Ballymorda. It had been busy before, but now it was packed.

"I'm surprised to see so many people in a pub on a Sunday afternoon," Smart said as they moved across the crowded floor to the bar. "I thought the Irish were a God-fearing people."

"They have an almighty fear of missing a good time," Fergus said with a smile. "They get their theology on Sunday mornings, but they get their true religion — the stout religion, by way of St. Guinness — in the pubs on Sunday afternoons. It's the busiest time for Irish pubs, and quite often you'll see the priests at darts with the parishioners."

Smart headed for the men's room while Fergus had a word with the barkeep, a florid man with big, callused and scared hands whose business cards, stacked on the bar, proclaimed that he also installed plumbing.

Standing at the urinal, Smart thought about Moorside — an outsize Georgian manse with 150 acres and a full paddock and horse barn, not to mention a trout stream on the property and a gamekeeper's cottage — and wondered if he wasn't making a mistake in passing it up. But 500,000 Irish pounds — the equivalent of about $725,000 — would really stretch his finances. The IRS was demanding $200,000 and had placed a lien on a small house he rented to students, and although his last novel had fetched quite a sum at auction and a movie deal was pending on an earlier book, he didn't want to go too far out on the proverbial limb. On the other hand, he could solve all his money troubles if he could just buckle down and turn out an outline and perhaps a few chapters of his next thriller, which would be set in pre-Celtic Europe. Then he'd be swimming in cash again. Still, it probably didn't make sense to count one's financial chickens before their arrival. Maybe Simpson Hall would do.

By the time Smart got back to Fergus, the latter was sitting at the bar listening to a story that the barkeep, Seamus Gall, was telling about a plumbing job he'd done for a fetching widow that week. Gall's eyes glinted, as did those of his listeners, and although Smart was having a hard time picking up the nuances because of Gall's thick accent, he heard more than a bit of double entendre in this tale.

"So we're in her bath for a while, if you take my meaning, and then she says to me, she says —" here Gall paused for effect, and got a few anticipatory laughs — "Jaysus, Seamus, you're a handy man with a pipe, aren't you?"

The punch line didn't make all that much sense to Smart, but Fergus and the others roared, and Smart grinned in spite of himself. The mirth and bonhomie were palpable, inescapable. He also noticed, to his astonishment, that there was a seat open next to Fergus's and that three full pints of stout sat in front of it. Smart looked at the estate agent.

Fergus, who had laughed so hard there were tears in the corners of his eyes, motioned Smart to sit down and indicated the pints with an expansive gesture.

"I couldn't prevent 'em from appearing, Mr. Smart. As soon as I mentioned you were a writer from the States, well ... ."

He motioned again toward the three oxblood soldiers, which seemed to be waiting with something like reproach for Smart to address them. Smart picked up the first and began to drink, noticing as he did that an empty glass and two full ones were standing in front of Fergus as well.

So this is why they call it The Drowning Man, thought Smart. But their lack of progress didn't upset him. The Irish, it seemed, had made a science of enjoying themselves: Take each moment as far as it'll go, and the rest be damned! He set his glass down nearly empty and reached for his wallet. He put money on the bar for the next round and then proclaimed: "To Ireland!" as he hoisted another pint.

Two

The next time Smart checked his watch, it was 7:30 and dark as the proverbial pit outside. He found himself singing a sentimental Irish song with Fergus and many other fast friends around the bar:

"O Sinead, you're a lovely lass
but your pate lacks hair
and yourself lacks class.
With your bitching and moaning
you're a national embarrassment
And even the Pope's irate,
claiming sexual harassment."

Smart himself had contributed the last verse, an occasion for applause, and, of course, another round. How many pints had he tipped? The exact number was swimming about in the backwaters of his consciousness, but he couldn't pull it from the foamy current. There were four empties in front of him on the bar, but that was no real measure since Gall, the barkeep, had been steadily removing them between verses about the Irish singer and tales of his own amatory exploits.

Smart and Fergus had had a traditional dinner of bangers and mash — fat, tasty sausages and home-fried potatoes — at around 5:30, and Smart had assumed that the merriment would abate afterwards as the Irish yeomen headed home for a night of rest before resuming their workaday week of tending sheep and cutting peat. In fact, though, the revelry had only accelerated after supper, to the extent that Smart had asked Fergus at one point whether the next day was some kind of holiday. Informed that it wasn't, Smart had smiled in admiration of the Hibernians and ordered another round for the house.

As the evening progressed, the thought of prying themselves away began to seem more and more fanciful. Not that they hadn't begun the process of decamping several times, with good-byes all around and "Good luck to you, Mr. Smart!" ringing in their ears, but somehow they had never quite made it. It was as if The Drowning Man were some whimsical level of Hell in which doors kept moving just a bit out of reach and steps turned to level flooring beneath the feet, so that exit wasn't really possible. The barkeep always dealt Smart a new pint when he was about half way through the last, because it took several minutes for each cylinder of foam to resolve itself into what Smart considered the noblest quaff known to man. The transformation began at the bottom of the glass and worked upward; then a head of gossamer clay was added in a second operation at the tap.

Once, when Smart looked down at a fresh pint, he was astounded to see that Gall had used foam to write TS — Smart's initials — neatly on its head. He had called this to Fergus' attention, but the estate agent hadn't been impressed. "They all do that yoke, Mr. Smart. Now Lionel O'Rourke over to Ballycretty, he's been known to do folks' phone numbers as well." His smile was nearly as skewed as it was beatific. "Well, Mr. Smart, what's your pleasure then? On to Simpson Hall? I'd better call first, though."

"Oh, no you don't," said Smart. "If you go off to that phone there'll be 15 more pints by the time you get back. Let's just go, like thieves in the night. Otherwise we'll never get out of this place."

"Well then, I'll just settle up with Seamus, here ..." He reached for his wallet, but Smart waved him aside and put down enough money to inspire several more verses of the psalm of Sinead. He leaned over the bar and put his hand on Gall's arm. "Pour a few in my memory, Seamus. We've really got to go."

With that they made their way determinedly out to Fergus' car, which they had difficulty finding in the dark and crowded lot. "It's amazing," Smart mused a bit later as they raced toward Simpson Hall. "I may never see any of those people again, but they seemed like old friends — almost like relatives."

Fergus smiled and was about to reply when a large, dark animal sprang in front of their car on a tight curve. Cursing, he pulled the wheel over hard and stood on the brakes. They fishtailed and slid across the road, coming to a rest in a narrow, steep ditch that ran next to it. The impact was cushioned slightly by the thick grass that grew on the embankment, but Smart, who'd forgotten to put on his seatbelt, was stunned when his head hit the top of the windshield. The engine stalled, and the two sat in shock for a moment. Their seats were now angled about 25 degrees from level, which made it difficult to get out. Smart tried to open his door, but it was wedged shut.

Fergus, however, was soon out and walking around the car, cursing and kicking a low stone wall nearby. "That black bastard of a stinking sheep! I never saw the fooker till he was about in our laps!" Tearing his eyes from the twisted front wheels, he noticed that Smart was rubbing his forehead and groaning.

"Are you all right, Mr. Smart? My god, you've hit your head!" Fergus bent down and tsked a few times as he peered at Smart's skull in the weak light of the car's overhead lamp. "You've got a nasty bruise all right."

Smart cranked the window down and turned his face to the cold night air. "I'll live, Fergus. This head has endured worse." It was funny how you could be nonchalant about such an injury in a place like Ireland; in the States, you'd soon be on the phone to a good litigator. "But how bad is the car? Will we be able to get her out, or what?"

"Ah, it looks bad, Mr. Smart, I'm sorry to say. I don't think she's fit to drive now." Smart looked at Fergus and was surprised to see, just behind him, another man — a slight, stooped figure in a soiled down coat and ratty wool cap.

Fergus turned to follow Smart's gaze and started a bit. "Peter Pike! You scared the shite out of me, man! Did you see what that damned sheep of yours did to us?"

"Aye, Fegan. The silly fooker got away from me as I was penning them for the night and took it in his fool head to cross the road as you were coming. There was naught I coulda' done to head him off. It's a shame what happened, that it t'is."

The man named Pike moved a step or two out from behind Fergus and scrutinized Smart, who was still holding his head.

"Pardon me, Fegan, but who's this, if I might ask?"

"This is Mr. Trelawny Smart, a writer from the States who's thinking of locating in this area."

Pike turned to Smart and grinned a bit sardonically. "Welcome to Ireland, then, Mr. Smart." He stuck his grimy hand out for Smart to shake, an unexpected gesture given the circumstances. Smart grudgingly withdrew his hand from his head, although the pain was increasing, and extended it through the open window. He gave Pike's gnarled paw a quick shake, then put his hand back on the angry bump atop his skull, which he'd already christened Pike's Peak.

He scanned the little man again. Pike had a wandering eye and was somewhat bulbous of nose. All together, he looked as if life had slapped him around a bit.

"Thank you," said Smart. "Not a very auspicious trip so far, though." He looked meaningfully at Fergus, who cursed the errant sheep again. Pike, anxious to shift the focus of the conversation, asked where they'd been going "at such a speed" when the accident occurred.

"House-hunting is what we call it in the States, Mr. Pike, until your black sheep" — Smart had to smile at the irony of it despite his pain — "derailed us."

Pike looked thoughtful. "It's a funny t'ing, but the Missus was saying just now that she'd be sellin' the house."

Fergus pounced. "Selling Mordalee? Since when?"

"Well," said Pike, considering his words carefully, "it's lately she's been talking about it, so. I t'ink she t'inks she might do better on it now, if you know what I mean, what with the Germans all about. And she wants to move south, so she says — maybe to France or Majorca."

"Well, I'll be damned," said Fergus softly. Leaning down close to Smart, he added conspiratorially: "This business with the sheep could be a stroke of luck for you, Mr. Smart, despite your aching head. I've always thought Mordalee could make someone a very nice home, and at a very reasonable price. You'll see what I mean."

Fergus turned back to Pike. "Well, lead us back to the house if you would, Peter. We've got to tend to Mr. Smart's head, and we'll need to make some calls. And maybe we'll have a word or two with Lady Brimston."

It took some time to extract Smart's gaunt, six-foot, five-inch frame from the tilted Toyota, but Fergus and Pike eventually got him out without further damage to his head or the car. They walked along the dark road for a minute or two, then turned onto a dirt lane at the end of which Smart could discern a hulking black mass. It seemed almost too big to be a house.

Fergus walked on briskly in silence, lost in his own thoughts, but Pike was feeling talkative. "That sheep is a freak of nature, it is! Born of a white ram and a white ewe, and there's not a black 'un anywhere in its bloodlines. Strange how he came out coal black like that."

Fergus wasn't listening; his wheels were turning in a different direction. "Yes, strange," he said absently as he cut his pace to drop back next to Smart.

"Mr. Smart, this Mordalee is a gem in the rough, if you know what I mean."

Fergus seemed earnest enough, but Smart had to smile nonetheless. He could almost smell the set-up. Had someone written "Patsy" on his back at the pub?

"In the States, real-estate practitioners usually refer to such properties as having tremendous potential. What they actually mean is that it's an awful wreck."

He leaned in to catch Fergus' reaction, but the realtor didn't seem to take offense. "Oh, that it is, Mr. Smart, definitely. It needs a lot of work, no doubt. But unless I miss my guess about Lady Brimston, she knows that and is ready to deal realistically. She's been short of funds for some time now — running up accounts at all the village shops — even tried to sell an ancient tree on the property last year for firewood, before someone made her a loan. Forty pounds she was going to take for a glorious big birch right near the house. She's just about gone through all the family money by now, I expect."

Smart's ears pricked up a bit at this. Might he have stumbled — tumbled was the more apt word — onto a bargain? But he thought it strange that he should be hearing all this from Fergus, who was supposed to be working for the sellers. Certainly it wasn't in Lady Brimston's interest to have her financial straits detailed to a prospective buyer.

Fergus seemed to read Smart's thoughts. "The only reason I can tell you this," he said, "is that she hasn't retained me — yet. She's been playing coy with Mordalee for the better part of five years, but I'll bet she's in earnest now."

"Well," said Smart, not wanting to seem too keen, "her *bête noire* has made a visit unavoidable, so we might as well see what she's got."

From what he could see now, some 30 yards from the house, she had a vast, gloomy pile that looked like nothing so much as the set for a classic horror movie. He half expected to see Veronica Lake peering down with one eye from an upstairs window, and Vincent Price in a dressing gown at the door. But there were no lights on and no sounds from inside.

The moon had risen high off the horizon, and if it hadn't been for its strong light, the house might have been indistinguishable from the other shadows in the dark. A dim fluorescent bulb shone feebly just inside a stone shed that stood at right angles to the front of the house, and Smart could hear animals — sheep, he surmised — stirring inside it.

Pike stopped and turned to them. "I'll just go ahead, then, to let the Missus know you're coming."

Opening one of the building's huge front doors, which looked as if they had been designed for a race of giants, Pike slipped inside. Fergus took Smart's arm and led him off to the side. "Follow me for a moment if you would, Mr. Smart. Oh," he added somewhat belatedly, "and be careful where you step." Piles of manure dotted the lawn, which was scruffy and bare.

Fergus led Smart some 30 yards to a spot where they could get a good look at Mordalee. A Georgian manor of a style common in Ireland, it was as much colonial statement as dwelling. It had housed untold generations of a moneyed English family — the Brimstons — who had displaced the native gentry under the shield and rod of Britain. The Brimstons once had owned the surrounding countryside, and their seat bespoke power and perseverance, an enduring reproof to the gabbling, red-haired cottagers who dreamed of owning their own land.

"There's a bit of history for you, Mr. Smart," said Fergus quietly as they gazed at the house. "They built grand residences in those days to be centers of society. Mordalee once held 15,000 acres — all the land between Ballymorda and the earl of Dergh's estate in Dergh Town. Everyone in this area worked directly or indirectly for the Brimstons, who came over in the wake of Cromwell."

"But surely it isn't 17th-century?" asked Smart, who knew something of history and architecture.

"No, it was built for the most part in the 1780s. The first house the Brimstons built here was more a fortress than anything else. Once the land had been pacified, the English built grand homes to replace the forts — homes like this one."

Smart had listened closely for bitterness in Fergus' speech, but he'd heard none. Now, in the early 1990s, this apparently was all a quaint bit of history for Fergus, not a burning personal issue. How could they be so intent on killing each other just a few miles to the north in Ulster, Smart wondered, while here the past was viewed with an almost scholarly detachment?

"It looks anything but grand now, Mr. Smart. But it was a sight to behold in its heyday, I can tell you that. I saw a picture of it once at an auction in Dublin: flowering trees and gardens all about, arbors and walkways, carriages pulled up in a line out front." He sighed. "We can only imagine what it must have been like."

Smart looked at Fergus intently; he hadn't been expecting such a flourish from this country estate agent. He had to admit, though, that there was something — something what? Inspiring? Awesome? Intimidating? He couldn't define it, but Mordalee exerted a certain force.

Smart gazed at the decaying manse, which now was feebly illuminated by a few interior lights. Even in the dimness, he could see the house was in mortal need of repair. Windows were cracked or broken, tiles hung off the roof at odd angles, and a reeling, rotting staircase lurched off a wall in a pathetic attempt to meet a second-floor door. The woodwork probably hadn't seen a drop of paint in 30 years, and the stonework was a travesty of cavernous cracks and splits.

Smart scanned Mordalee again and again, each time noting some new atrocity: a window out here, a tilting chimney there, and a section of roof where the rainwater apparently fell straight to the floor. His eye paused at a particularly strange sight — an immense, leaded window that seemed to have nothing behind it, like an eye shut from the inside. He turned to ask Fergus about it, but the estate agent had vanished.

"Over here, Mr. Smart." Fergus had moved to the corner of the front and side walls, and was motioning Smart to join him. "Lady Brimston has invited us in."

Three

Smart followed Fergus into the foyer with a feeling of destiny. It wasn't exactly *déja vu;* Smart certainly had never seen anyplace like Mordalee before. But it felt momentous somehow to cross the wide marble threshold — like crossing the Rubicon. Pike, who was holding a chipped decanter of water, led them into a large room off the hall and motioned for them to sit in massive chairs that may have been expensive when new, but now looked like rummage.

"The Missus will be with you gentlemen shortly; she wasn't expectin' callers. There's refreshment on the sideboard, if you don't mind helping yourselves." Pike gestured to a few bottles and glasses on a huge but badly stained and scratched buffet. He set the decanter on it, then left the room, and Fergus immediately made for the whiskey. "She's got bourbon here, Mr. Smart — Old Granddad. Care for a spot?"

"Well, why not? My head couldn't feel much worse than it does now. You'd better dilute it a bit for me, though." Fergus nodded sagely, adding about a thimbleful of water to the glass.

Smart looked about with a mixture of appreciation and despair. The room was undeniably grand. It measured some 40 feet by 30 feet, and its tall, leaded windows were inset with drapery cabinets. Window seats lay beneath them. But the parquet floor was broken and discolored in places, and several large basins stood about, apparently to catch rainwater. The plasterwork was bowed outward in places, which gave the walls and ceiling an odd, pregnant look.

On the floor was a threadbare and torn Persian carpet. Illumination came from an odd variety of sources: A tall, Tiffany-style floor lamp in one corner, which had mismatched bulbs in two of its three sconces; a trashy-looking lamp from the '70s on one end table; and brass sconces on either side of the fireplace. One had a candlelight-style bulb in it; its mate didn't. They were lissome Art Deco maidens and probably collectible. The white tile fireplace itself, however, was another matter: It apparently hadn't been used in ages, and Smart noticed some debris in the hearth that suggested the habitation of rodents or birds in the chimney. "Probably bats in the belfry, too," Smart said aloud.

"What's that, sir?" asked Fergus as he handed Smart his drink.

Before Smart had a chance to reply, the double doors at the opposite end of the room opened to reveal a fantastic apparition.

Lady Brimston, all of five feet tall in high heels, was eye-catching nonetheless, like a classic car. Smart guessed she was at least 75, but she apparently was yielding nothing to advancing age. Her hair was dyed a deep auburn, and she wore it in a long and girlish bob. In fact, she might have been Scarlet at the ball, except for the crow's feet and wattles. She smiled broadly as she progressed elegantly toward them, her great, luminous eyes never leaving Smart's until she turned abruptly to Fergus.

"Well, Fegan, it's been quite some time since you came to call at Mordalee."

"Yes, Lady B., I'm afraid I've been remiss," said Fergus, smiling as well. "But," he added ruefully, "you know how business is: It doesn't always take one where one would rather be."

Smart looked at Fergus briefly, afraid his ears were deceiving him. Was this 30-something bucko actually flirting with the old lady? No, Smart concluded; it was too preposterous; he was simply playing along.

Or was there something enchanting in the heady floral scent that had wafted toward them with her ladyship's approach? A particular flower, yes, but which one?

He turned back to Lady Brimston, who had extended her heavily veined, porcelain hand to him. "And who," she asked Fergus while looking directly in Smart's eyes, "is *this* distinguished-looking gentleman?"

Smart smiled in spite of his headache and realized he was blushing, something he hadn't done in ages. He felt anything but distinguished-looking, what with a red welt on his forehead and offal on his shoes, but he was aware that his height had always lent a certain distinction, gratuity of nature though it was.

"This, ma'am, is Mr. Trelawny Smart, whose books you may have read. He's a novelist with a good following in the States. And elsewhere, too, I expect," Fergus added hurriedly.

Smart found himself kissing Lady Brimston's hand. He'd never done anything of the sort before, but it seemed perfectly natural now. He realized the scene must have looked like an outtake from a Britcom on PBS, but there was something fascinating about this aged but determined coquette and about the faded grandeur of this room … he felt himself being carried away.

"It's a pleasure to meet you," Smart said somewhat stiffly.

"The pleasure is all mine, Mr. Smart. I'm afraid I haven't read any of your books, but I shall ask Peter to pick some up for me next time he's in Dergh. What sort of books do you write?"

At this point in their conversation, of course, she should have been apologizing profusely for the damage done to his skull by her sheep, but somehow none of that seemed relevant. Instead Smart, against all odds, found himself telling Lady Brimston that his *oeuvre* had come to be known as "cave thrillers" because he had mated the whodunit with painstaking paleontological research.

"How *interesting*, Mr. Smart! What an exciting life you must lead. And what a fascinating Christian name you have — Trelawny. Any relation to the great Victorian adventurer?"

Smart was astonished. He'd never met anyone except a few literature professors who'd heard of his relative and namesake, Edward Trelawny.

"He was distantly related to my mother, whose family came from Cornwall. I'm surprised you knew the name. "

"Well, you shouldn't be. There are a lot of us poetry lovers about, and any true poetry lover must love Shelley. And anyone who loves Shelley would have to know — and revere — the name Trelawny. After all, we couldn't really *know* Shelley the man without him."

Smart was charmed, and he noticed out of the corner of his eye that Fergus was, too. So, this superannuated Circe was trying to ensnare them, eh? Well, so what? Let the old girl weave her spell. He was enjoying himself.

They spoke for a while longer about the ancestral Trelawny, how he had shipped out on a man'o'war at the age of 13, married an Arab princess at 19, become a privateer and then a squire, an adventurer and a guerrilla chief, a biographer of the poet and then a celebrated literary lion in his own right, the terrible old man of the Romantics. He'd roared through a long life like a tornado, and Smart sometimes regretted that he'd been born a latter-day Trelawny rather than the earlier one. Lady Brimston dwelt especially on Trelawny's brief but transfixing friendship with the tragic young poet.

"One wonders, Mr. Smart, what Shelley might have written if only Trelawny had followed his better judgment and prevented him from taking that small boat across the bay — the very boat Trelawny had given him, and could never forgive himself for ... ."

Lady Brimston, it turned out, had read the Romantics at Edinburgh and Trinity College, and had fancied becoming a professor of literature at one point, although she had never finished her degree. Smart usually found professional scholars the most tedious of God's creations, but this failed academic was anything but tedious. There was a nobility of spirit, a vital honesty about her, notwithstanding the wig, the makeup layered like an ancient stream bed, the bridgework that kept her smile together and the corset that strained beneath the provocative dress to keep her ample charms in place.

She was talking to Fergus now, who seemed to have forgotten their business at the house. Smart understood: How could you bring such a creature back down to earth once she'd launched on a flight of fancy?

"Well, Fegan, I just don't know *what* they're teaching in school these days, but if your niece is bored with literature, send her over to me. I'll give her a taste for the classics, and it will be my pleasure more than hers, because it's a blessing to introduce a famished mind to the great books."

Smart had followed her and Fegan over to a long sofa, where he and the estate agent seated themselves at her insistence, although she mainly kept her feet and refilled their glasses more than once.

"Do you fancy bourbon, Mr. Smart? I know Fegan here does, because he left Mordalee last time awash with my supply. But I find it so much ... well, more mature than the Irish whiskies. And I don't drink Scotch on principle, although the single malts are excellent."

Lady Brimston, it turned out, had been jilted by a rakish Glaswegian named Thomas Black while at Edinburgh, and when she had returned to Ireland to repair her heart, she'd sworn off all things Scottish. "Wouldn't even have a Shetland or a Scottie dog," she said, downing more Old Granddad for emphasis.

The conversation flowed effortlessly. After Shelley and Trelawny, they spoke of Byron and his inglorious end. "A cad, but a divine cad who deserved better than to choke on his own vomit in a Greek hovel," she said a bit recklessly, speaking of long-dead figures as if they'd been school chums. Here Smart protested gently; he wasn't at all sure about the choking business, and the house, according to his information, wasn't exactly a hovel, even if it wasn't a palazzo of the sort Byron bought and sold like so many timeshares.

That had brought them to the subject of Greece, and Smart was reminded of his youthful adventures there, when he'd gone as a graduate student to study rock formations and retrace his famous relative's steps. Like Trelawny, he had found himself pursuing a fiery Greek maiden; unlike him, he had been pursued in turn by her inflamed kinsmen. Their talk then had meandered to the plains of Troy, and Schliemann and his golden artifacts and the University of Berlin and the war, which Lady Brimston had spent as a nurse and spy in Malta — so she claimed, and who was Smart to doubt her? — and on and on.

At length Lady Brimston excused herself to "make micture," as she put it, and Smart and Fergus found themselves alone. Suffused with good feelings and practically sloshing with bourbon, they sat grinning stupidly at each other. Finally Fergus broke the fat silence.

"I wonder if she means it, Mr. Smart: The bit about sending my niece over here to get an education in the classics. It would seem Lady Brimston is certainly the person to repair that part of her schooling."

Smart agreed, noting that her ladyship had a most remarkable intellect and a rare *joie de vivre* that couldn't fail to impress a young girl.

They were deep in conversation when Lady Brimston returned. She joined in as if she had overheard what they'd been saying from the lavatory, and reiterated her invitation to Fergus to bring Moira, his niece, to her anytime. She would waive tuition, she said with a smile, if Fergus would but help her sell her house. They all laughed, and Smart realized that it was the first anyone had mentioned of their putative business at Mordalee.

Fergus was about to pursue the subject of the house when Pike entered, looking a bit put out. He seemed to Smart to be dolefully eyeing the much diminished bottle of bourbon on the sideboard as he spoke up: "Pardon me, ma'am, but it's getting late and I must take my rest if you don't mind. I've been out trying to get that black one back, but it's no use in the dark. So unless you'll be needing anyt'ing else ... ."

"Not at all, Peter. You may retire, and thank you. I didn't mean to keep you up. It seems we lost track of time, doesn't it? But that's what happens when the chemistry is right, as they say."

Pike nodded toward Lady Brimston and said "g'night, then, gents" to Smart and Fergus. He was about to retreat when Lady Brimston raised her hand. "Just a minute, Peter." She turned to Smart. "That bruise on your head looks nasty, Mr. Smart. Is it still aching?"

He put his hand up to his head and grimaced slightly, aware that he'd probably drunk too much. The alcohol had anesthetized him at first, but now it seemed to have lost its effect.

"Peter," said Lady Brimston, "why don't you take Mr. Smart out to the headache stone before you retire?"

"*Now*, ma'am?"

"I know it's late, but if our guest's head hurts, it's the least we can do. And I've never known the headache stone to fail, have you?"

Pike scowled, but kept his peace. Smart was flummoxed. "Headache stone? Sounds like something out of science fiction."

"Oh, quite the opposite, Mr. Smart, quite the opposite. It's sorcery we're talking about, not science and not fiction!" She laughed gaily. "And it should be a particularly good remedy for a man with your affinity for antiquities."

Fergus spoke up: "Lady Brimston's property includes a village site from the old days. By which I mean the *very* old days — the Stone Age."

Smart was intrigued. "But a 'headache stone?' What does it do?"

"Well, it really doesn't *do* anything, to be sure. It's just a large rock with shallow depressions hollowed out on top, which the ancient inhabitants used for grinding up grains and medicines," Fergus said. "But legend has it that touching your head to such a stone is an infallible cure for the headache."

"And ours has never failed to my knowledge, Mr. Smart," added Lady Brimston. "Why not let Peter show you the way? It's not far."

Smart was about to demur, thinking that the whole idea was a bit too farfetched, when it occurred to him that a walk in the night air might cure his headache. "I'm game," said Smart. He looked at the herdsman. "If you'll just lead the way, Mr. Pike ... ."

"All right then," Pike said, "but let me get a lantern, Mr. Smart. I'll meet you at the front door, so."

He left the room, muttering softly to himself and shaking his head, while Smart turned to Fergus. "What about you, Fegan? How's your head?"

"Oh, fine, Mr. Smart, just fine. I've used the stone myself, however, and can vouch for its curative powers. But I think I'll stay here while you're out with Peter and discuss things with her ladyship, if you don't mind. Then we can talk when you get back."

"All right," said Smart. "I'll be back in a bit, then — with a head cleared for business."

He walked to the foyer and stepped out into the cold night. Pike soon joined him with a kerosene railroad lamp. "This way, Mr. Smart. And mind where you step, sir." They set out across the yard, and Smart looked up. Above them stretched a deep night sky within which hung one of the most brilliant moons he had ever seen.

"You almost don't need that lantern with all this moonlight," he said to Pike's back, but couldn't catch his grunted reply. Smart attempted to make contact again. "How far is it, by the way?"

"Only a few hundred meters, sir. It's among those tall trees yonder." Pike gestured with the lantern toward a copse at the far end of a field of low grass and scrub.

Smart felt himself stepping on hard piles of sheep dung, but they presented more of a danger of tripping than of fouling his shoes. He looked at the horizon and saw a few stars struggling gamely to shine through the bright moonlight. It was an illuminated night — stunning and magical — and Smart was glad he'd chosen to take this odd hike with Pike. If they happened to see a banshee or a faerie council on their way, Smart thought, he wouldn't be particularly surprised. After all, it would be only another strange part of a very strange day.

Here he was at this improbable place, with its fascinating lady of the water buckets, its grand salon and headache stone, its errant sheep and leaky-eyed shepherd. And he felt certain that, if the terms were right, he'd end the day as squire of Mordalee and a happier man, by far, than he'd been in a long while.

"This stone, now," Pike suddenly began, "it's been there for ages — no one knows how long, but the best guess would be thousands of years. Maybe millions. But at least the people who used it for a table — for that's what it was to them — were here thousands of years ago. You see that building?"

Smart followed Pike's arm with his eyes and noticed, for the first time, that the copse of trees was growing up through a stone structure whose roof must have fallen through ages ago, judging by the trees' size. The building was small, with a few narrow openings for windows and a door.

"That was a church, Mr. Smart. It was built here to ... well, to snuff out the past, so to speak, to replace the old with the new when Christianity came. But as you can see, sir, the past has a way of reasserting itself."

"I'm not sure what you mean. Are you referring to the trees?"

"Yes, the trees. The legends have it that the trees are the spirits of the old priests, the devils who made sacrifices here before the coming of the saints. The church couldn't contain them, so it seems."

Smart looked at Pike, a bit surprised at this disquisition on the war for ancient Ireland's soul. He wondered if Pike wasn't glad, in his secret heart, that the druids had held their own. "Is it safe to go inside?"

"Oh, sure it is, so — the walls won't come down. But just watch your step, because the roots are tangled underfoot."

Smart and Pike stepped gingerly among the roots and listened to the wind as it whistled and sighed through the bare branches overhead. The lantern threw garish shadows inside, while the moonscape outside seemed peopled by its own more subtle cast of apparitions. There really wasn't much to see in the tiny ancient church — walls of coarse cut stone and the trees that seemed fit to burst them.

They left through the narrow doorway, and Smart wondered how long it had been since worshippers had filed out this way, having prayed and chanted to keep the old ways at bay. A thousand years? Five hundred? Had Cromwell's bloodstained men wondered, too?

Just outside Pike paused, handed the lantern to Smart, and gestured to a small boulder half sunk in the ground before them. "There, sir — that's your headache stone. Just kneel down and put the part of your pate that aches against that hollowed-out part there and close your eyes. Your head will clear directly. In the meantime, if you don't mind, I must relieve myself."

Pike walked to a dark place between the chapel wall and a large tree growing outside, leaving Smart with the lamp.

Smart looked down and was a bit disappointed to see that the wondrous rock appeared to be just an ordinary-looking piece of granite — ridged in places and flecked with quartz. He wasn't sure what he had expected it to look like, and he felt a bit foolish for his disappointment. Knowing how hard such rock is, though, he marveled that the ancients could have worked it. There were two smaller depressions and one that was about as wide as a man's forehead. *Ah, yes,* thought Smart: *the first aspirin.*

He looked for Pike and could see his back. His hands were to the fore as he waited patiently for relief. Smart knelt on the cold damp earth, wondering whether the Irish had another cure for the arthritic knees that headache stones probably caused. He put the lamp down next to the rock, feeling increasingly foolish. But he'd come this far, and his head was throbbing. Glancing again at Pike, whose stance hadn't changed, Smart placed his hands on the rock and braced himself, then lowered his forehead to the indented space. The fit was nearly perfect.

Smart closed his eyes, and his mind focused on the clacking of the leafless branches as the wind rubbed them together overhead. A strong gust came up, suspending the sound for a few moments, and Smart had the sensation of being swept out of himself, as if his soul might go kiting off. The cold stone seemed to cradle his forehead, and he felt a mystical kinship with the suffering hundreds — maybe thousands — who'd knelt there before him.

The tension suddenly went out of his arms as the stone seemed to absorb it. He could feel himself smiling, but he wasn't sure what about, except that the pain was vanishing. He knelt with his head to the stone for an unknown period — it might have been 30 seconds, or it might have been five minutes. Then he heard something — a rustling in the grass nearby — and smelled a slight rankness in the night air.

Lifting his head from the rock and picking up the lantern, he saw a large, black ram. It was standing on the other side of the rock and staring as if it was going to ask Smart just what the hell he thought he was doing. Gingerly, Smart began to stand up, which made the sheep bleat once and bolt.

"Mr. Pike," said Smart, "I think we've found your damned sheep."

Four

The flight to JFK from Shannon was long and tiresome, and as usual when traveling by air, Smart hadn't been able to sleep. He'd flown first class, of course, but with his long legs there was still no way to get comfortable. When the attendant had asked if she could get him anything, he'd given her a sour grin and said: "Bring back the Zeppelins."

At Kennedy he took a bus to Manhattan and then grabbed a train to Rensselaer, across the Hudson from Albany, where Libby would pick him up. He sat in the bar car now, halfway between Ireland and oblivion, too lagged to sleep and too tired to read, munching a salted nut occasionally and sipping a bourbon in honor of Lady Brimston.

He'd gone back to the house that night of the sheep knowing that he would become lord of Mordalee, whatever it took, and had made an offer after a cursory inspection the next day. The whole procedure had been a farce, and he knew it. Try as he might, he couldn't bring himself to see the old pile's true liabilities. He simply wanted to own it, and would do so come what may.

So he'd clucked and nodded as Fergus had discreetly pointed out this and that disaster; the central heating he'd have to install, the 20-odd chimneys that would have to be repointed or completely replaced in some instances, the weak steps in the wide main staircase, the roof work, the drainage, on and on, a catalog of woes.

And then there was that strange compartment on the second floor — the Devil's room, Fergus called it — which he would have overlooked entirely if the estate agent hadn't made a point of showing it to him. There was a quaint story attached to it — something about a long-ago Lord Brimston, a stiff-necked Orangeman, who'd gone to town one day and encountered the village priest. The priest, trying to be defuse the situation, had engaged him in conversation and suggested that they sit down at some point and discuss their differences over a game of whist. Brimston reportedly had replied: "I'd rather sit down with the Devil, Sir!"

To modern ears, Fergus had pointed out, that might not have sounded like much of an affront. But to a man of the 18th century it was a grave insult, and the incident might have led to a deadly duel had it not involved a man of the cloth. But it did, according to local legend, lead to an encounter with the Devil, who had taken offense at being thus compared to a priest and was waiting to greet Brimston in the large upstairs room when he got home.

As he was telling this tale, Fergus opened the door to reveal a tiny, oblong nook. It was so small that it could be taken in with a glance, and neither of them entered. This, Smart realized, was the odd room he had spied from the outside; it stood out because the interior wall was only a few feet behind the window.

Smart had chuckled and made a joke about giving the devil his due, but the estate agent hadn't laughed. He seemed to take the whole matter seriously and said he just wanted to be sure that Smart knew "all the facts" about the house before he bought it. Then he'd turned and led Smart to the next room, a garret of sorts under the eaves that Smart thought Libby might fancy as an office.

At the end of the tour, he'd made an offer of $170,000, and Lady Brimston had accepted it. There had been no bargaining, no give and take — just three satisfied parties, and they'd sealed the deal with more bourbon. Smart had been planning to ask for a rebate in view of the freeloading, cloven-hoofed boarder he'd have to put up with, but he'd forgotten to say his piece. He wondered idly what plans Libby would have for the Devil's room, once she got over laughing at the tall tale.

It had been surprisingly easy to buy Mordalee. Now, of course, came the hard part — persuading Libby that the move to County Dergh, a place about 125 miles from Dublin and about a thousand light years from New York, would be a positive one for all concerned, even her six armadillos. He winced when he thought of them; they were her pride and joy, and he knew they were non-negotiable. She had been an armadillo fancier from the age of 10 or so, when she'd found a few orphaned 'dillo whelps while walking near her family's ranch in Abilene and had nursed them back to health. Now their descendants inhabited a special greenhouse Libby had had built for them in back of their house in Tuscarora. She had begged off the trip to Ireland because one of them had seemed sickly, although she'd called to say it had been a false alarm.

The armadillos could present a real problem — he could just imagine the reaction at Irish customs as they came off the plane at Shannon — but they probably wouldn't be fatal to his plans. After all, they were disease-free, so far as he knew, and wouldn't thrive if they got loose in Ireland's cool and wet climate. So they'd probably be allowed to import them after quarantine.

Smart tried to think of what else might ruin the deal. Libby wasn't really dependent on his earnings, although she'd become more accustomed over the past several years to spending his money rather than her own. But she formerly had worked as a college aid administrator, and once had bought a condo in the L.A. area that had nearly doubled in value by the time she moved on and sold it a year later. "It was like winning the lottery," she'd joked about it, "without even buying a ticket." She'd also inherited quite a tidy sum when her father died and much of the family land was sold off. Every once in a while she'd demonstrate her financial independence by underwriting some surprise extravagance, but in general she'd accepted the idea that he was the main breadwinner and financial factotum.

She also loved horses but didn't own any just now, thank God. Having grown up on a ranch, she could ride like a hussar. It was her equestrianism that had drawn them to Tuscarora Falls — arguably the horsiest town in the country in August, when the thoroughbreds ran. But Smart felt the equine equation was as much an asset as a liability when it came to the move. After all, Ireland was at least as horse-crazed as Tuscarora, and Dergh had its own hunt, something Tuscarora didn't. Smart knew this would have a powerful impact on Libby: In fact, he'd taken the precaution of buying her a bright red hunting outfit before leaving Shannon.

Luckily, Smart thought as a wry grin lit his face, they didn't have much in the way of family and friends to hold them back. Libby's three sisters were scattered geographically, and they weren't all that close emotionally, either. She had some chums from college, but they, too, had gone to the four winds and rarely found time to get in touch, much less reassemble. Libby's mother still lived on the ranch outside Abilene, and they made the trek out there once a year to visit the old girl and hear her tales of woe. They could still visit her, Smart thought; or at least Libby could. He would try to beg off from now on. She would stay for two weeks instead of one, and when she got back to Mordalee she'd be twice as glad to get away from her mother as she usually was after her visits.

Smart had been a singleton, and both his parents were dead. He and Libby had friends at Wordsworth, but no one they couldn't live without. His leaving would anguish the dean — a gimlet-eyed inquisatrix who seemed to detect sexism in every male utterance — but she would get over it. Nor did he feel any particular loyalty to the college, which was a high-priced repository for the children of the trust fund set. You simply couldn't help but feel the basic unfairness of life as a Wordsworth professor; every week you worked for less than what your average student might spend on a weekend's skiing.

He had to admit, though, that the constant grinding of his face by his students had been a powerful motivator. Would he have started to write in earnest if it hadn't been for the rich young twits who provided a daily lesson in the joys of limitless funds? Probably not, he acknowledged. He might have been content to earn a piddling salary and supplement it occasionally with money from oil companies, which he helped analyze drilling data.

The *Montrealer* slowed suddenly, and with it Smart's train of thought. He'd be home soon, and he hadn't even told Libby he'd bought Mordalee, although he'd promised her "big news" when he saw her. She would be furious and curious in equal parts when she came to pick him up, Smart figured. Not telling her had been risky, but he'd felt that if he gave her the opportunity to quash the sale, she would have done so. Better to present her with a *fait accompli*, he'd reasoned, and then try to make it up later. But how? What if she were adamant about staying? He didn't want to think about that. He knew he couldn't live without Libby, but he also felt he couldn't live without Mordalee. Somehow he'd have to bring the two together.

The train came to a stop at Hudson, a shopworn if picturesque little city about 30 miles south of Albany on the river's edge. Smart walked to the deck between the bar car and the coach and peered at the station, forlorn under its heavy mantle of snow. At least that was one thing he had going for him, Smart thought: Libby was not a skier and regarded the long and ferocious northern winters as he did. Of course, the sodden and miserable Irish winters were no bargain, either, but they could spend a lot of time in the Mediterranean, Smart figured, on the money he'd save in taxes. When you added it all up, that's what it mostly came down to: taxes. A whole lot less to pay in Ireland. And therefore a whole lot more to spend. He trusted Libby would see this positive calculus.

It was dark by the time the train pulled into Rensselaer, which was such a depressing place that it had the almost magical effect of making Albany, just across the river, seem a bit like the Emerald City. Smart pulled his baggage off the overhead rack and waited to exit as the packed coach slowly emptied. Outside in the garish mercury lights of the station he could see her — tall and striking, looking beautiful, as she always did, and somewhat annoyed. *Uh oh*, he said to himself.

But Smart felt confident; he had gotten his second wind and would be glad to escape the capsuled torpor of the train. And he was truly happy to see Libby, the woman who'd taken him home from the lost and found 10 years ago. She had forced him to cut back on his drinking, put some starch in his backbone, and let him know that she wouldn't take any shit. And — unlike several of his former significant others — she had meant it. Smart had used her strength to arrest his steady slide into chaos, and he would always be grateful to her.

Physically, too, she was a striking woman — almost six feet tall in heels, with large brown eyes and shoulder-length blond hair. She wasn't exactly beautiful, at least in the classic sense — her features were too irregular — but she often drew the admiration of men, and, more tellingly, of women. This had impressed Smart, who knew how exactingly women catalog and discount each other's goods.

She hadn't seen him yet and was looking away, toward the other end of the platform. Smart snuck up on her, put down his bag just as she turned to him, grabbed her around the waist with both hands and pulled her to him. "You look scrumptious, lady," he said as he nuzzled the warm flesh of her neck. "Let's be off before your husband shows up."

"Trel, you idiot!" Flustered, she pushed him off; Smart usually didn't get physical in public. She was flattered by it, but suspicious, too. She knew it must have something to do with the "big news" he'd been so coy about.

She let herself be kissed, although she didn't return Smart's ardor. She would play it cool, Smart surmised, until he came clean. And maybe after that as well: horrible thought. "My, aren't you the ice queen tonight?" Smart said ruefully as he picked up his bag and slipped one arm around her back. "One would almost think you felt some loyalty to that gallivanting man of yours."

"Have you seen him?" Libby asked tartly. "The last I knew he was in Limerick, babbling about some revelation he'd had."

"Oh, yes," said Smart. "A revelation it was. But let's not talk about it till we get to Sandro's, OK?" Libby held her peace as she got in the driver's side of their Grand Cherokee. Smart put the bag in the back, then climbed in beside her. He was silent, but she found his fixed grin unnerving.

"Well, you look like you ravished all the redheads in Ireland. I certainly hope you didn't, because otherwise Sir Smartie may have to be re-circumcised."

Smart loved it when Libby referred to his member, although he didn't much go for threats to truncate it. Libby had an awful temper, and Smart knew he could be at the center of a tempest at any moment. "Not at all, not at all. Nothing like that, my dear baroness."

She didn't respond immediately, seemingly intent on guiding the car up the river to Troy and Sandro's. Finally she took the bait. "Baroness? Is that some kind of a hint?" She looked at him more skeptically than angrily, a nuance Smart found heartening.

"You'll see, my dear, you'll see. But let's wait till we've sat down. I've got too much to tell you on an empty stomach."

They rode on for a minute or two in silence before Smart broke the ice by asking how things had gone in his absence. She filled him in with quotidia, playing her cards close to the vest until the exact nature of the game became apparent.

Sandro greeted them at the door, as was his custom. He was a huge man, dark and cask-shaped but springy on his feet. Sandro was the *maestro del cucchino* in addition to being the greeter in chief, and after he had ascertained their mood — too frosty by half — he had seated them near the fireplace and gone off to give instructions for their meal, which would begin with a cordial. Sandro's regulars rarely ordered; he simply supplied them with his own inspirations. The food was always sublime, so Smart often didn't even bother to ask what each particular dish was called. Libby, for her part, had long ago given up trying to duplicate Sandro's masterpieces at home. She used to ask how he'd clarified a sauce, or exactly what spices he'd used in a pizzaiola, but Sandro would deflect all flattery and wheedling with a Mona Lisa smile and a few mumbled self-deprecations.

When they were seated and alone, Smart took both of Libby's hands in his and nuzzled them, a burlesque of an adolescent in heat. She smiled in spite of herself, but was far from ready to surrender. She pursed her lips slightly and looked him straight in the eyes.

"Well, Romeo? Wherefore hast thou been, and whatfore hast thou done?"

"Glad you asked, my only love. I've been to a very different sort of world, a place where magical realism seems to be the order of the day rather than a literary affectation. It's ... well, it's hard to explain. There's something very different about Ireland, though."

She didn't respond, since she didn't feel that he'd told her a thing as yet. She sipped her cordial, keeping her eyes on his all the while. "Yes? I'm waiting, Trel."

"Well, I'll just come out with it, then. I've never been much good at fooling you anyway." (*Not for want of trying,* he thought to himself.) "I've bought you a county seat."

She blinked and arched her eyebrows. "A county seat, Trel? Did I ask for one?"

Smart ignored this sally. "You'll ride to hounds as Mistress of Mordalee, *ma chere*. You'll be the center of all social life in Ballymorda and beyond, because the Earl of Dergh is a doddering old widower who simply won't be able to compete."

She paused a moment while all this sunk in. He knew there was a part of her that saw herself as the heroine of a bodice-ripper, who would relish the idea of setting the social tone for the surrounding countryside and ruling all its women and, through them, its men. But she wasn't quite ready to give herself these airs yet.

"Trel, are you telling me that you want me to move to Ireland? I don't know anything about Ireland, except that it's a hell of a distance from everyone and everything that means anything to me."

"Except me, my dear. I became an Irishman, I'm afraid, on my first day there. I've got to go back, and you've got to come with me."

Just then Dante, the waiter, arrived with their appetizer, a steaming turreen of spicy minestrone, a provincial antipasto and fresh, warm bread. He poured two glasses of Mon'Tedisco, a beguiling red, and left the bottle behind after promising to return shortly with their first course. Libby had withdrawn her hands from Smart's, smoothed her napkin on her lap, smiled distractedly at Dante and said nothing.

Smart, who looked like a man who'd been interrupted in the act of proposing marriage, applied himself to the bread with vigor, tearing off two pieces and buttering one for Libby.

"You've got to agree, dear heart. I know you'll love it there. In fact, I guarantee it. If you don't, we'll move wherever *you* want next. But you've got to give it some time. And by that I mean at least a year or two."

Libby was still too stunned to speak. She cautiously tasted the steaming soup, nibbled on the bread Smart had given her, and drank some wine, which finally thawed her voice. "So you've committed us, is that it?"

She hadn't proceeded to the indictment, much to Smart's relief. If he played his cards right, he thought, he could have her fully on board before the cannoli.

He took her hands again, being careful not to hold them over the steaming soup. He looked long into her eyes before speaking. "It was beyond my power to resist, Lib. You'll just have to take my word for it until you can see it. It's astonishing — the people, the land ... ."

"The tax structure? Trel, I'm not sure I want to uproot myself in order to evade taxes. Now why don't you just pay up and forget about Rick Diamond? We lost some money — a lot of his other clients did the same — and we should just learn from our mistakes and go on. I don't feel a need to move across the Atlantic."

She'd skewered his balloon, but Smart wasn't giving up. He knew part of this was just ritualized resistance, an assertion of her place in the scheme of things. And he knew that if he acknowledged that place — perhaps even genuflected toward it, given the scope of his crime — he might get a pardon.

"It's not just the taxes, Lib. Really. I mean, let's just put that aside for a moment, although losing the income tax could easily save us $100,000 or more per year. That's a hundred thousand, Libby — enough for a lot of living, traveling, fun. But let's leave it aside anyway. I admit that I landed in Ireland with a chip on my shoulder against the IRS, and that I was mainly looking for a tax shelter.

"But what I found was something else entirely — a sort of land that time forgot. An educated, English-speaking, agrarian economy with post-industrial overtones. You know, you can watch someone trundling by in a dogcart, and then the next vehicle to come along has a wireless phone in it. Jumbo jets take off over the smoke of peat fires, and penniless, wild-eyed bards hold forth for the price of liquid refreshment in every pub." He hadn't seen any bards himself, but he'd had it from Fergus that they existed and that they held forth, especially when there were American tourists about.

"You sound like the Irish Tourist Board, Trel. Are you writing copy on the side to make up some of what you lost to the IRS?"

Here was the crucial juncture in their conversation, as Smart knew. She'd thrown down the gauntlet, and he certainly was tempted to pick it up and whack her with it. But to do so, he realized, would be a foolish waste of energy, because he'd already won. She was looking for a tiff now only by way of salving her pride, because she'd accepted — not without conditions, he was sure — that they soon would be lord and lady of Mordalee.

Smart assumed a look of aggrieved piety and forbearance and said: "You're a truly vicious old cunt, you know that?" Libby shrieked like a schoolgirl sharing a raunchy joke, and stomped hard on his foot under the table. "And you're every mother's worst goddamn nightmare! How the hell did I ever end up with you?"

Smart smiled through the throbbing of his toes, hoping none were broken and realizing that he'd gotten off easy even if they were. They sipped wine and nipped into their food with gusto, eyeing each other appreciatively all the while. The meal began to take on some of the aspects of foreplay, and Smart made free with his knees under the table, which Libby didn't discourage.

He talked at length about Ireland, about Fergus, the house, Pike, the sheep, the headache stone and the old church, leaving out only his extreme simpatico with Lady Brimston. There was no need, after all, to spoil the mood they were working on. And besides, he hadn't exactly been smitten by the old lady — it had been more along the lines of a kinship of spirit. But he couldn't deny that if he'd encountered her ladyship 20 years before, he might have fallen for her. In her day, he felt sure, she had been a siren.

But so was Libby. With her full breasts, long legs, reasonably taut bottom — given the fact that she was in her mid-40s — gift for ribaldry and undying love of sex, Libby was quite a package. She had the mannish trait of being able to turn on instantly, like a microwave, with high heat and great intensity. She never got headaches near bedtime and rarely said she wasn't in the mood. Which was fine with Smart: He thought of her statuesque body as a temple of Venus, and of himself as its high priest. He'd discreetly strayed off the sacred precincts in favor of a luscious coed now and then, but never with the idea of giving up his vocation.

Even more sexy was her ability to empathize. He loved how she laughed at his stories of the pubs, clucked when he told her how badly Mordalee had been neglected, perked up at mention of easy air connections to London, Paris and Rome, and admitted that although she was reasonably happy in Tuscarora, it wasn't necessarily Mecca for her. "The most important place for me," she said, rubbing his leg with hers and looking down to address his crotch, "is where you are, o elastic fantastic Sir Smart."

"Lascivious lady!" Smart nearly shouted. "You'll be the death of poor repressed Ireland." He was beginning to feel quite good now, and he hadn't even told her about the hunting outfit yet. Wait till he got her to put that on — and then take it off.

An hour or so later they pulled into their own driveway, and Libby went in the house to put on the lights and check on her beloved 'dilloes while Smart garaged the car. It felt odd to be in a place at once so familiar and so strange, now that he'd decided to sever all connection with it. He couldn't say that he didn't have a certain feeling for the house; their move here had been a big step up after living in the dumps of his struggling years. They'd put quite a bit of energy and money into making it their own, but now Smart was ready to move on. Eight years in Tuscarora, with its brutal winters and its August parade of upper-class twits, was enough.

In the kitchen Smart poured himself a nightcap — Irish whiskey, which he'd bought before his journey to help prepare for it — and began to feel just a bit unsteady on his feet. It wasn't surprising. He was 52, and he'd traveled five time zones that day. Still, he wasn't about to postpone the ravishing of a willing Libby. He quickly tossed back the drink, then bounded up the stairs.

A few moments later they were both in their bedroom, and Smart opened his suitcase. Libby sat on the side of the bed, and he made her close her eyes before he took out the hunting outfit and placed it in her lap. "You can look now, o goddess of the hunt — and of my heart." She let out a little yelp of delight. "It's beautiful, Trel. Really classic!"

It had cost a fortune, which she could tell just by feeling it, and she loved the bright scarlet color. "Go in the bathroom and put it on," Smart encouraged her. "Just the hunting togs. Nothing underneath. Then come back and we'll see about chasing that sly fox into his lair."

"You old horny toad, you!" Lib giggled as she hurried off to the adjoining bathroom, anticipating how the fine wool would feel with nothing under it. Smart, waiting for her to return, changed into his silk bathrobe, then lay back on top of the bed.

Libby had to struggle a bit, tugging on the breeches and straining to button the tunic across her breasts. "You were a bit optimistic on the size, dear," she called to Smart. "It'll either have to be taken out a bit, or you're going to have to give me one hell of a workout!"

She waited for a randy riposte, but heard none. She undid several buttons on the tunic, checked the effect in the full-length mirror behind the door, and then sallied into the bedroom. She turned to Smart with a flourish: "Talley ho, Sir Smart — come hound me out of this scarlet sheath of sin!"

Smart was facing her and smiling, but he didn't respond. His eyes were closed and his breathing was slightly irregular. He was dreaming of Mordalee.

Five

On St. Patrick's Day the phone rang, a major triumph. But Smart never did find out who was trying to reach them, because the connection had been severed almost before it was made. But the fact that the phone had rung at all had been a marvel, a glimpse of light at the end of the long tunnel of repairs and renovations. It seemed to offer proof that their connection to the trunk line at Dergh might be proceeding.

They'd been without service for weeks, so this possibility had huge import. But the phone disconnect literally had been the least of their woes; when they'd first gotten to Mordalee in early February, they had almost turned around and headed back to Dublin. The weather was miserable — cold, dank and wet — and the house was, too, because it had no heat. Vermin had moved inside, and water was pouring through the peaked sieve that served as a roof. The ancient kitchen stove had been balky, so they couldn't even cook. "Let's order a pizza," Lib had said reflexively, but of course there were no pizzas to be had and no phone with which to call.

They'd spent that first night huddled in a vast, cold second-story bedroom, listening to the creaks and drips and the wind sighing both outside and in, the rustlings in the walls and the closings and openings of doors as the air pressure fluctuated. They had brought a few bags of nuts with them from the plane and some tea and crackers from the airport shop, and that had been their first supper as Lord and Lady of

Mordalee.

Fergus had left a message at the airport that he would meet them at the house to help get them settled in, but he was nowhere to be seen when they arrived. Smart wasn't altogether surprised; he knew the estate agent's intentions were noble, but no match for the lure of the brew. But since they had no phone, he couldn't call round to the pubs to locate Fergus and ended up lugging in their bags himself. There really wasn't all that much to carry, since the bulk of it was scheduled to arrive over the next few days by truck.

By the time the truck — and Fergus — arrived two days later, they were cold and almost literally starving, since the electricity had failed and they'd run out of cash due to an oversight on Smart's part. But Fergus, true to form, brought a sunny smile, a crock of stew, a gallon or so of stout and a few bob to lend them "until they got their accounts straightened round."

Libby had been prepared to tear out Fergus' liver and eat it while he watched, but she had found herself disarmed. "I told you that would happen," Smart had chided her after Fergus left. Libby, bemused in spite of herself, had had to agree. "He's a charmer all right. Are they all like that?"

Smart said he thought a very large percentage of the Hibernians were like that, and that they, as outlanders, would have to adjust. It wasn't that the Irish weren't a serious people; it was just that they were most serious about their pleasures. And their pleasures, often as not, seemed tied to the pubs. It wasn't all drinking, though; there was a pleasure in companionship and in the life of the mind that seemed oddly lacking in what Smart now ironically thought of as "the old country." Who in 20th-century America really cared about literature? About ideas as abstractions to be considered in and of themselves, with no hope of profit?

Smart had to laugh whenever he thought of his encounter with

Doc Gilchrist in Dergh, to whom he'd gone the day after he'd sealed the deal with Lady B. His head no longer ached after his application of the stone, but he thought he should have it checked out anyway. So Fergus had borrowed a car and driven him to the office of the good doctor, who had kept him waiting at least a half hour before admitting him to his surgery, such as it was. The room smacked more of a professor's nook than a medical office: Books were everywhere, few of them about medicine, along with yellowed charts and posters from the health ministry on the dangers of excessive drinking and smoking. Gilchrist, a short, thick man of about 60 who had the heavy, flaring eyebrows of an owl, gave Smart's head and eyes a cursory look before pronouncing it "A mighty bump, but only that, and one that will soon subside with no application of medical science."

Smart had thanked him and was about to ask what he owed when Gilchrist had asked if he was the visiting writer he'd heard about. Smart had allowed that he was the very same, assuming Gilchrist had heard of Trelawny Smart. Gilchrist's grave and preoccupied demeanor had brightened suddenly, as if some secret of his soul had been unlocked.

"Mr. Smart," he'd said, "I'm a great admirer of yours. I can't buy your books hereabouts, of course, but I do send over to Dublin for them as your English publisher brings them out. It's a wonder how you blend geology and mystery. You must go to Mayo, Sligo and Clare and some of the wilder places in the west to see the rock formations. The Burren, which looks like a lunar surface, will be a great inspiration to you, I've no doubt."

They'd discussed his books — about which Gilchrist seemed to know more than Smart himself — at great length, and the doctor had poured them both some Scotch and had dismissed two other patients with an admonition to come by later if they still felt poorly.

"It's all in their heads, Mr. Smart, all in their heads," he'd confided after shooing the second one. "Both what they used to call hypochondriacs, before that term became politically incorrect. I'd refer 'em to a witch doctor if we had one here in Dergh. Now about that last book of yours … ." After an hour or so, Gilchrist had said he was due in hospital but would love to continue their talk at some other time. Smart said he would be moving to Mordalee soon and looked forward to seeing the doctor again. They'd parted very amicably, and he was half way down the main street, near the earl's castle, when he realized he'd forgotten to pay. He ran back and knocked on the physician's door.

"Why Mr. Smart, you're winded," Gilchrist said. "Did you forget something now?"

It had taken him some time to realize why Smart had returned, at which point he refused to accept payment and professed amazement at Smart's alarm. "I did nothing but have a pleasant chat with you, so why should I charge you?" he said in the manner of one precluding all further argument. But he was glad to accept Smart's invitation to dine at Mordalee as soon as it was ready to receive guests. It had been a sort of social fig leaf for Smart, who hadn't the slightest concept of when that might be. But he hadn't been able to get the smile off his face for the rest of the day.

There were other encounters of this sort; the canny priest who had driven a hard bargain for the rectory piano after hours of pleasant chat and brandy; the on-again, off-again negotiation with Pike, who went to visit relatives up north when Lady B. had decamped and wasn't sure when he might come back to Mordalee or under what terms; the postman who delivered a commentary along with the mail, some of it demonstrating a knowledge of Smart's affairs that would have provoked paranoia in Tuscarora, but seemed quite harmless — even benign — in Ballymorda.

But in general their first days in Ireland had been hard, as Libby hadn't hesitated to point out, although she'd generally kept her good humor: no hot water, no hot food until they got the new stove installed about a week after they arrived, no baths except at local inns when they couldn't stand the cold and the smell of themselves anymore; no respite from an unending round of supervising the tradesmen who gutted and painted rooms; no connection to speak of with the outside world, except through the pages of *The Irish Times,* which Smart bought on Sundays and allowed himself the luxury of reading despite all his undone work.

The Dublin sheet was wonderfully literate and not nearly as parochial as he had expected, as if its writers' perspectives varied in inverse proportion to the size of their country. Odd, thought Smart, how so many American scribes seemed to have an inversely proportional view as well.

The Smarts had allowed themselves a weekend or two in Dublin in the area of Trinity College, near the Liffey and the nightlife. It wasn't Manhattan and would never be confused with London or Paris or Rome, but it had flair, and you could understand the natives with a bit of practice. They had dined at an amusing little Indian restaurant, O'Rajah's, and had gone to see a rock band named Danny and the Scabs afterward at a grotto called Cullinane's Insane.

The Scabs were four freckled, red-haired backup singers who did a more than passing gloss on the Motown sound and choreography while Danny, a very fey West Indian lad, shimmied his way through Supremes covers with a reggae lisp. They'd gone to an Italian bistro the next night, and though the food wasn't quite the equal of Sandro's, it was much better than they had expected to find so far north of the Po.

When they'd gotten back to their room, Libby said: "You know, Ireland has every right to be a boring little country, but somehow it isn't." And Smart had had to agree: It was tiny, out of the way, famously wet, with an interminable and vicious little religious war on its border. Yet you couldn't help but enjoy it. The night before, for instance, he had noticed that Dublin TV put the "Late, Late Show" on at 9:30 p.m.

And there was no "Late Show" to precede it. It was as if the Irish had made a national commitment to puckishness.

"It has something to do with the water, I think," Smart had deadpanned. "They filter it through hops and malt and such, and the result is a very risible land."

In the end Pike had returned, just in time to forestall the sale of the sheep and the goats and resume his rightful place in a corner of the great house, lending a hand with most jobs but seeming to take a dim view of it all. Of course, he and Libby had had to determine sovereignty within a week of Pike's return.

It had begun innocently enough; Pike had suggested that "the Missus" consider selling the "armydillas" to the zoo in Dublin rather than trying to keep them at Mordalee, which clearly wouldn't sustain them. Libby suspected immediately that Pike was trying to get out of the job she'd set him of building a greenhouse in the courtyard, and she had been correct. But the main reason for Pike's reticence had eluded Libby. It wasn't that he was lazy *per se,* although he was not a man to volunteer for unnecessary travail. It was more that he considered his own expertise in animal husbandry limited to certain species, and armadillos were not among these. Ask him anything about sheep, goats, swine, kine and fowl, about draft horses and the racing breeds, about dogs and the animals they hunted, and he was your man. He didn't, however, cherish the idea of tending to strange half-turtle, half-anteater things. Of course, he had too much tact to come right out with any of this.

"The zoo would love to have them, Missus, and I'm sure they'd do poorly here, especially in the winter. They're not used to this kind of cold and damp, I'm quite sure."

"Let's give it a try, Peter. Don't forget, we kept them in Tuscarora, which is in upstate New York."

"Considerably below this in latitude, though, I believe, Missus.

We're much farther north here, although we don't get the snow."

"You really shouldn't worry about them, Peter. They'll do fine. Once the greenhouse is set up, they'll get all the heat they need, and that's really the main thing. We can put a propane heater out there on the really cold and overcast days. Besides, they sleep most of the winter."

"But the zoo could care for them just as they need, Missus. Who knows if we'll be able to get what armydillas eat? Is it ants and such, then?"

"No — they eat anything green, Peter, and there's no shortage of greenery in Ireland. Now, have you ordered the glass and the chain-link to cover the floor?"

Pike had mumbled something and beaten a tactical retreat at this point, determined to prevail, if possible, in the rematch. Libby, for her part, had seen that although she was the acknowledged lady of the house, giving orders and seeing them executed might be two different things, especially with the likes of Pike. She had discussed it later with Smart.

"Of course you're in charge," Smart said, "but I think we have to remember that Pike has worked for the Brimstons all his life, and his parents worked here, too. This place is really more his than ours, no matter whose name is on the deed, and we'll need to keep his feelings in mind when we make changes."

Libby's eyebrows lowered menacingly. "Whose side are you on, Smart?"

This peremptory challenge had caused Smart to wince. Lording it over a manor, he was beginning to realize, might not be all that different from faculty politics.

"Yours, of course, my dear," he'd said, looking earnestly into her eyes and squeezing her hand. "But it would be far better to have Pike's active cooperation than to push him into opposition. Why not have the carpenters build the greenhouse and set Pike to doing something else, like repairing the fencing for the sheep? Then after he gets to know Pookie and the rest, he may come to feel differently toward them."

"Pookie is such a sweetheart — I've got to call tomorrow and see how they're doing in quarantine. It's really ridiculous, considering how healthy those animals are. I wish we could get them out early. I don't like being without my babies for such a long time."

"I know, love. They'll be fine, though — I told the customs people there'd be something in it for them if they made sure all your pets made it through OK, and they said they'd do that. So don't worry about it. And let's give Pike time to adjust, OK?"

She was silent awhile after that, sipping sherry and staring at nothing while he fiddled with the controls for the satellite dish that had been installed that day, another major milestone in their return to the 20th century.

He was deeply engrossed in the programming when she said, as if from the midst of a dream: "There really is something different about this place, Trel. Do you suppose it might have anything to do with the Devil's room?"

Six

Libby's comment had taken Smart by surprise. He hadn't given the Devil's room much thought before then. He put down the instructional manual and sat back in his wing chair.

"What do you mean, Love? What would that have to do with anything?"

"I don't know. But you have to admit that the room is strange. I mean, I've never seen a house with a walled-off room before."

"Oh, come on," Smart needled. "Lots of houses have rooms that are blocked off for one reason or another. Sometimes a house is just too big — which may be the real reason why the room was closed."

"It wasn't, Trel, and you know it. They kept most of the room in use; only a small part was sealed off. But it was the part next to the window. What made them do that?"

Smart didn't say what he thought: Someone had seen — or thought he'd seen, which was much more likely, given the Irish affinity for strong liquor — the Foul Fiend here at Mordalee. It almost seemed plausible, given the other odd things about this land and about this house in particular. You really couldn't just laugh it off, although that probably was the appropriate thing to do.

"I think these people have very vivid imaginations," Smart said quietly. He didn't need to elaborate for Libby who "these people" were; they'd gotten into the habit of referring to the natives somewhat elliptically, like missionaries in Papua discussing the quaint customs of their headhunting flock. "But why do you think that room would have any effect on ... on what, exactly? What did you mean?"

"I'm not sure. It's just ... odd. Pike's odd. I mean, look at his life — sheep. No wife, no family, just the sheep and the stout."

"Well, that's not so odd for Ireland. Apparently the old bachelor tradition is still very much alive and well here. But OK — Pike's odd. So what? What's that got to do with the room?" He couldn't quite bring himself to say "the Devil's room." It had seemed so silly. They'd laughed about it back in Tuscarora, and Libby had said she'd pack a copy of *The Exorcist* for when they moved in. But now that they were here, it didn't seem quite so funny.

"I don't know, Trel. It's just a strange old house, I guess. And Lady Brimston and all the Brimstons, from what I've been able to learn, were quite odd as well."

Smart said nothing, thinking about the story they'd heard from Rose, who did the washing and cleaning once a week. Her first day on the job she'd sat down with them after work for tea while waiting for her husband to pick her up.

"It's an eerie old house, it is," she'd said apropos of nothing. Then she'd launched into a tale about ghost horses — how she and her young daughter had heard a sound like the thundering of hooves coming around the corner of the house. The sound had been so loud and so realistic that her daughter, then six, had asked: "Who's riding horses, mommy?"

But Rose had known that no one at Mordalee rode horses, and none were being boarded in the rundown stables. She had heard the sound again and again — "It sounded like a foursome on horseback — the drumbeat of the hooves, the sound came in waves, over and over, as if they were just about to come around the corner of the house. But there was no one there when we looked, keeping to the side of the house lest we be run down. No one there."

She'd added that her daughter had not wanted to come back to Mordalee, but she, Rosie, didn't mind "sich manifestations" as long as she didn't have to stay overnight. That's where she drew the line, she cheerily informed them, as if they might start importuning her to stay.

Libby had looked at Smart and Smart had looked at the charwoman, trying to determine if they were being subjected to some quintessentially Irish hazing or initiation rite. But Rosie's smile had remained fixed, and her gaze gone into soft focus. She hadn't seemed to be telling the story for effect.

Then there was the strange flight of the change. Smart had been lugging a pocketful of both American and Irish coins about with him for the first three days at Mordalee, too wrapped up in disasters to focus on the unnecessary weight the U.S. coins represented. On their fourth night at the house, Fergus had come by and offered to take them to The Drowning Man for supper and a pint or two. Smart, changing pants, had separated out the American coins and put them in a pile on the night table near his side of the bed, meaning to exchange them at the bank in Dergh.

They'd spent a raucous evening with Fergus and some of his friends, coming home at 11:30 or so. But when Smart was putting his slacks away in the wardrobe he happened to look beneath a chair that was a good 10 feet or so from the night table where he'd put the coins. There on the bare floor were three quarters, looking for all the world as if someone had examined them while sitting in the chair, then dropped them on the floor.

At first this impossibility hadn't completely registered with Smart. He bent down, stared at them, picked them up and pointed out their location to Libby, just back from the bathroom. "You must have dropped them, Trel," she said. But Smart didn't remember dropping any coins. And it was something you wouldn't easily forget, because the house had a way of amplifying sounds — falling coins on the bare floor, within the twelve-foot plaster walls of the room, would have sounded like a fusillade.

To make his point, he took a few coins from the pile and dropped them in careless fashion on the floor, simulating what he might have done while changing his pants. The coins made a racket, and none of them rolled more than a few feet away.

They'd looked at each and smiled, as if to say: "Who knows?"

There were other oddities as well. Light bulbs had a way of burning out days after being installed, and pictures sometimes fell off hooks and went clattering to the floor at night. One hook — albeit a thin one — had been straightened, almost as if someone had pulled the picture off it.

But the strangest thing was when Smart had awakened in the middle of the night a few weeks before with the sounds of an argument ringing in his ears. No lights were on, and Libby was sleeping soundly. A man and a woman seemed to be having a tremendous row, and Smart's first waking thought was that he should intervene to forestall violence. But then, awakening more fully, he realized that there was no one else in the house except Libby, who was asleep, and Pike, whose room was off in a corner of the first floor. And this altercation was going on overhead.

Smart had stepped gingerly into the hallway, turning on its dim light and moving toward the sound. When he got to the door that led to the attic — a dark and musty place he didn't much feel like visiting, even in daylight — he realized that the shouting was coming from the top of the stairs. He opened the door, expecting to see a light on above, but there was none. Only darkness — and a sudden silence.

Smart had had the distinct impression he had interrupted a domestic dispute among the dead, and he felt no need to mediate it. He'd shut the door to the attic stairs and gone back to bed, shaking his head and thinking, absurdly, of the Cowardly Lion's refrain: "I *do* believe in ghosts! I do, I do, I *do* believe in ghosts!"

He'd lain awake for a while after that, listening for more sounds from the attic, but it had stayed quiet — preternaturally quiet, still as a tomb. Normally, the old house made an astonishing variety of noises at night, with its flapping shutters, creaking windows and the opening and closing of doors from changes in air pressure. Even the new heating system was far from quiet, and the plumbing was known to make gross sounds. But that night, in the wake of the hair-raising argument Smart had heard — he couldn't recall any details, only its hysterical intensity — the house had seemed to hold its breath.

In the morning he hadn't said anything to Libby, not wanting to alarm her. But she had mentioned at breakfast that she hadn't slept well. In fact, she'd had something of a nightmare in which she and Smart had argued ferociously.

Pike had heard the shouting match, though. He'd mentioned in an offhand way the next day that he was tired, having been awakened from a sound sleep. He'd looked meaningfully at Smart then, perhaps expecting him to confess that he and Libby had had a tiff. But Smart said: "It woke me, too. Awfully loud, but Libby managed to sleep through it. No sense in mentioning it to her, I think."

Pike had looked surprised and a bit skeptical at first; then he'd nodded, apparently satisfied that Smart was telling the truth, and whistled softly. He said: "I've not heard that much noise from the attic in quite some time, Mr. Smart." Then he touched the beak of his cap and went off to his sheep.

Smart had had no direct experience with former persons. He'd always been skeptical of ghost stories from the day his grandfather, a bluff Cornishman, had told him of the night he'd stayed in a haunted castle and seen nothing but scurrying rodents. His grandfather had concluded that talk of ghosts was so much nonsense, and Smart had always felt the same. And as a scientist, he had always dealt in quantifiables — chemicals, elements, molecular structures, the plodding research that led to the slow but steady accretion of hard knowledge. The geological world — anything but occult — held no hint of ectoplasm, and the only evidence of the dead it contained were the fossils he sometimes came across in the field.

But he'd had a strange, disturbing dream once. He still thought of it occasionally, although it had occurred maybe 20 years ago, when he was in his early 30s. He'd not been given to nightmares, and this one hadn't exactly been horrifying, either. But at a certain point in the dream, he'd looked at a screen door. It was the outer door of his "dream" house, and it wasn't unlike the screen door you might find on any older home. But this one had a *chiaroscuro* face on it, all dark and darker places in the mesh but distinct nonetheless. He couldn't see exactly what the eyes were looking at, but he knew they were staring at him. Smart woke up that night in a cold sweat, marveling at it. What strange recess of his mind had produced this portrait of the face of evil? He gradually became aware that someone was staring at him. It was Libby.

"Trel? Earth to Smart — do you read me? Please copy, over."

Smart smiled sheepishly but didn't respond immediately. He'd never told her of his dream and wasn't sure he wanted to discuss the subject now.

"Sorry, love. Just lost in reverie there for a moment or two. Well, what do you want to do about the Devil's room? Should we advertise for boarders in the Stephen King fan magazine? Tear down the wall and put in a skylight? Hang a huge crucifix over the mantel?"

She was smiling now, but there was still something troubling her. "Do you think we could tear down the wall, Trel? Maybe we should."

Smart thought about this option. From a strictly mercenary standpoint, the idea of opening a bed and breakfast for geeks and weirdos was clearly the best. But maybe it wasn't all that practical. And he didn't want to share Mordalee with Stephen King fans anyway.

"Well, why shouldn't we tear down the wall if we want to? We own Mordalee, don't we?"

Libby didn't answer directly, noting instead that they probably wouldn't have been able do such a thing in Tuscarora without approval from the historical commission, a pack of purists who wanted to preserve the town in a bell jar. The conversation trailed off, and they went for a stroll before supper. In the end, neither Libby nor Smart wanted to deal with the question of who really owned Mordalee.

Seven

A few mornings later Smart went to Ballymorda to inquire about getting a contractor to remove the wall in the Devil's room. He had only been joking about the skylight, but the idea of rejoining the blighted alcove to the rest of the house had seemed a good one, and he thought he'd solicit a bid or two and see how much it would cost.

His first stop was at The Drowning Man for a word with Seamus Gall. The ruddy barkeep — who looked, Smart thought, like a leprechaun on steroids — was at his post, washing glasses from the night before and setting things to right before the midday trade. He began to pour a Guinness as soon as he saw Smart walk in, although it was only 10 a.m.

"Ah Seamus, you're a wonder," Smart said as he pulled up a barstool. "A genuine psychic, you are. A man has only to think 'refreshment' — not say it — and you begin to pour."

"To tell you the truth, Mr. Smart," Gall grinned, "it's what 95% of me customers seem to want, no matter the time of day. So maybe I'm less the wonder and more the creature of habit."

They made small talk as they waited for the foam to turn to beer, and Gall mentioned that it was lucky he had the pub to fall back on, because his contracting business had been slack since Smart had finished his plumbing renovations at Mordalee. "You wouldn't have any other projects up your sleeve now, would you, Mr. Smart?" Gall asked hopefully.

"It just so happens — there's your mind-reading again, Seamus — it just so happens I do have another job to let out, if you'd be interested. Or maybe you can recommend someone who can do things with a bit of finesse. This would involve renovating a room."

"Well, plasterwork and such really isn't my forte, Mr. Smart, but I'd be glad to stop out to Mordalee and look at it with you. If I felt it was over my head, I'd recommend someone good to you."

"I know you would, Seamus. It's that walled-off room, the one Fergus called the Devil's room, of all things. Are you familiar with that tale?"

Smart had been addressing his stout rather than Gall, but when he looked at the bluff publican he was surprised at the change that seemed to have come over him. He'd blanched, and his smile had gone fixed and cold, more of a grimace. Mechanically drying glasses and wiping the counter, he didn't answer immediately.

Finally he said: "Aye, I've heard that story. I'm afraid I wouldn't be your man for that sort of job, so. All thumbs when it comes to framing and plastering, as I said."

"But what about a recommendation then, Seamus? You said you knew of someone. We've been very pleased with Shaughnessy's work on the roof — do you think he'd be the one for this job?"

Gall didn't look directly at him, and suddenly seemed pressed for time. "No, I don't think so, Mr. Smart. Not in his line at all. He's your man for the big outside jobs, but not the fine work inside. You might have to go to Dergh for that, and I'm not so familiar with those people."

Smart found this hard to believe; he knew for a fact that nearly everyone in Ballymorda was related, by blood or marriage or both, to someone in Dergh. Indeed, Doc Gilchrist had told him that the entire county was one extended family, if you weren't too strict about your definitions. The idea that Gall, a publican and contractor, wouldn't know of a plasterer in Dergh was almost ludicrous. But clearly Gall was preoccupied with something. He kept checking his watch as Smart, nonplussed, took another tug at his stout.

Soon Gall left the bar and went into the back room. Smart continued to drink, waiting for Gall to return, but he never did. This was very unlike him — usually he was the soul of sociability.

Shaughnessy the roofer walked in just as Smart was finishing his pint, and gave him a loud greeting. "Mr. Smart, you're a fine sight of a morning at The Drowning Man, so you are sir. What brings you out at cock's crow, so to speak?"

Smart explained that he'd come for a word with Gall about a job, but that that worthy had disappeared without a trace after begging off. Very odd behavior, Smart felt compelled to note.

"That it t'is, yes," Shaughnessy agreed, leaning over the bar and craning his neck to see where Gall might be concealing himself. "Very unlike Seamus Gall," said Shaughnessy. "I said, VERY UNLIKE SEAMUS GALL TO LEAVE A CUSTOMER HIGH AND DRY AT THE BAR!" Gall still failed to appear.

"He seems to have gone out of the building," Smart remarked.

"Impossible, Mr. Smart. He wouldn't do that at this hour. He must be in the basement or taking a call or tapping a kidney. But if he's being a boor, I'll just help meself so, and leave him the tariff but no tip, seeing the lack of service today." With that Shaughnessy stepped behind the bar and deftly poured himself a pint, returning to the customer side to wait for it to stop foaming.

"Now then," Shaughnessy said as he lit a cigarette, "what's the job you have in mind? Gall may not care for honest work, but I do."

Smart laughed; they both knew Gall was as hard working a man as was to be found in Ballymorda, his gallivanting with local wenches notwithstanding.

"Well," said Smart, "we're thinking of redoing that room off the top of the stairs — you know, to the right of the landing. You were working over it when you redid the roof. There was a nasty hole near there, if I remember correctly."

Shaughnessy, startled, looked Smart in the eye. "Not the Devil's room, now, is it?"

"That's the one. We'd like to take out that silly wall and open up that space. It'd make a nice big guest room, I'm thinking."

Shaughnessy — known for being talkative — was silent. He stared hard at his pint, as if trying to speed the transformation so he could drink it down and be done with it. But Guinness takes several minutes before it can be drunk, and the two sat in silence for most of that time as Shaughnessy fidgeted. Finally Smart spoke: "Well, what do you think? I know you're a roofer, so if you don't want to tackle it, could you suggest someone? What about that fellow from Kirklally who was out a few days for plastering while you were there — what was his name?"

Shaughnessy didn't answer; he was staring so intently at his glass that Smart thought he might not have heard him. He was about to speak again when the roofer said: "Horan? He does good work but not that kind of work, I don't think."

"That kind of work? What do you mean? I thought it would be exactly his kind of work." Smart was beginning to feel irked. What was it with these people? They complained of being short of work, then spurned the work you offered.

"Horan is a good plasterer and a good Catholic, Mr. Smart. I very much doubt he'd have a hand in taking down that wall. Nor would I, sir, for all the money in the United States of America."

Smart was stunned; he was not only being turned down, but insulted as well. This was the first time he'd encountered the infamous Irish "begrudgery" he'd been warned of by Doc Gilchrist, who'd said there was a dark side to his countrymen. Smart felt a hot rejoinder welling up, but before he had a chance to reply, Shaughnessy stood, drained off his pint, and made quickly for the door. He turned before he got out, though, and seemed to repent a bit.

"I'm sorry, Mr. Smart, if I've been short with you. But you'd be well-advised to think long and hard before taking down that wall. It's not sacred — the opposite, really — but it's our history. And I don't think you'll find anyone in this town — or in this county — to do the job for you. Good day, sir."

With that the roofer left the pub, and Smart found himself alone in The Drowning Man, a place where there usually weren't enough seats for the patrons.

He shook his head, dazed. What had he said? Were they all so foolish as to think that the story about the Devil had been anything but a myth? Or was this a subtle kind of rebuke, a putting in his place of the rich American who'd come in and usurped the Brimstons? He found it hard to believe the latter; there hadn't been a trace of it in all his dealings with the locals up till now. In fact, people seemed to go out of their way to make his acquaintance and let him know that he and Libby were welcome among them. They'd even gone to the local church once or twice, but had stopped when they'd noticed that they were the only congregants who didn't rise to take communion. He and Libby wanted to fit in, but they weren't quite ready to join the Catholic Church to do so.

Smart shook his head again, not quite believing that Gall had actually left the building and wasn't coming back. He took money from his wallet and laid it on the bar. And, like Shaughnessy, he didn't leave a tip.

Eight

Libby could hardly believe Smart's tale of rejection and abandonment at the hands of Ballymorda's construction establishment. "Incredible," she said, shaking her head. "You'd almost think they really believe this stuff about the Devil. What do they think will happen to them if they take the wall down?"

Smart didn't answer immediately; he had picked up the paper and was skimming a story about the disastrous condition of Aer Lingus, the Irish state airline, which looked as if it might go belly-up without massive new subsidies. The republic's finances seemed to be imperiled as a result, something Smart found vaguely disquieting. But why should it bother him, Smart thought, since he wasn't responsible for the republic's finances?

"Trel?" Libby looked at him expectantly. Lately these out-of-body experiences of Smart's were becoming more frequent, Libby thought.

"Hmmm? Oh, right, Shaughnessy. I don't know what they think, my love, but they may be afraid that the foul fiend would be riled somehow. Why else would they refuse the job? They probably don't want to find out if someone they very much don't want to meet would be offended enough to protest in person."

"Oh, stop it, Trel. These are 20th-century people. Shaughnessy has a car phone and an air hammer, for Christ's sake. Gall has satellite TV in his bar — 300 stations if you include all the German porn. I just can't believe they'd buy in to that sort of hogwash."

Smart said nothing, but he thought of the change that had come over Shaughnessy and Gall as soon as he'd mentioned the plan. Clearly they would rather have made coffins for their own sainted mothers than take down the wall to the Devil's room.

"Maybe they think it's something like Pandora's box," Smart mused. "You know — once you've taken down the wall, you've opened up Ballymorda to all manner of visitors from the netherworld, uncontrollable forces. They may see it as a kind of portal that had better be left closed."

Libby, who had been mending a piece of saddlery with a long needle and coarse thread, put down what she was doing and stared at Smart. "I can't believe this, Trel. You sound like one of them. Portal to the netherworld, eh? That sounds like an idea for a low-concept horror flick."

Smart accepted this rebuke without comment. He was sure he was right, though; they had been telling him not to open up a channel to hell. And he had seen the same reaction from Pike when he'd broached the idea to him in a general way after talking to Gall and Shaughnessy. Pike, too, had turned grave and distant and had said he didn't think it would be a good idea to go tearing down that wall, which might be a load-bearing wall.

Smart had smiled, thinking that even Pike would have to reverse himself and acknowledge what was obvious for all to see: It was an excess wall, without a hint of load-bearing function, that had been erected only to close off a small section of a large room. But Pike hadn't returned his smile or even taken note of it, hurrying off down the hall and tossing over his shoulder that he might have cause to visit his relatives again in the near future.

Would Pike move out if they tampered with the wall? Smart guessed that he might.

"Trel — focus, please. What should we do about this? It's not such a complicated job — we could probably do it with Peter's help."

"Well, I suspect Pike won't want any part of that, my dear," Smart said amiably. "After all, if he begged off on housing for your 'divilish armydillas,' I can just imagine how he'd react to the idea of flinging wide the gates of hell."

She'd had to smile at that in spite of herself. Since the armadillos had been released from quarantine, she'd noticed that Pike went nowhere near them if he could possibly avoid it. She had caught him contemplating them once or twice from afar, though, as one might regard some freak of nature that could turn nasty.

"So what do we do, Trel? Tackle it ourselves? I can just imagine you in there with a crucifix in one hand and a plaster hawk in the other." She permitted herself a discreet guffaw at Smart's expense, then impulsively leaned close, giving him a good look down the long declivity between her breasts — a sight that always had predictable effects on Smart's easily roused libido — and kissed him on the forehead. "I think you'd be a cute contractor, Sir Smartie. Or is it more of an erector you'd be, now?" She smiled just a bit wantonly.

Smart realized with a start that she was propositioning him. And why not, since they hadn't had a romp in more than a week? But although he felt a momentary flush and stirring in his groin, he didn't feel like pursuing the matter just now. He simply wasn't in the mood. But he didn't want to seem to be spurning her offer completely, so he gave her rump a meaningful squeeze and grinned salaciously, as if to say: "Later."

She looked at him quizzically and tousled his hair, slightly disoriented at this unlooked-for reticence. Apparently, Smart wasn't rising to the bait this time. *How odd,* she thought. Then she straightened up and put on a more serious face. "Well, I guess we don't have to settle this business about the wall right now. I mean, it's not as if we lack living space in this old pile. And we haven't exactly had busloads of visitors since we got here, so we can't say we need guestrooms."

Smart nodded, reminding her that they'd gotten a letter from Vanouse MacDonald, a Wordsworth colleague, the day before in which the malacologist had said he might be dropping by in the summer for a week or two, since it looked as though he would be taking part in a teaching program at Trinity College in Dublin. He hadn't been sure that the job was in the bag at the time of writing, but he'd noted that Trinity had seemed keen on having a tenured American mollusk expert, and there weren't many to be had. "So iron laws of supply and demand would seem to be working in favor of the shell answer man," Van had concluded.

Smart was looking forward to seeing Van, with whom he'd spent many a night carousing back in Tuscarora, but he was a bit worried about it as well. It could be a disaster if Van managed to arrive just as he was getting his novel in gear. He hated to be rude, but sometimes his muse insisted on visiting at the same time as friends — and she had to take precedence, especially given the fact that he'd made no progress since before the move.

Smart wasn't too worried, though; he'd never had any hesitation about writing once he'd discovered, at the age of 40, that he was a scribe at heart. He'd been strictly a geologist before that, laboring diligently on his master's degree and then making steady progress toward his doctorate. But one day he'd read something about a fellow academic — a civil engineering professor in the Northwest — who'd tried his hand at a novel and shattered all previous sales records his first time out of the box.

Smart had found the book — *The Culverts of Klackamas* — unreadable and embarrassing, but inspirational nonetheless. After all, he'd reasoned, if this sophomoric dreck could make someone fantastically wealthy, why shouldn't he, Smart, give it a try? He'd closeted himself with a typewriter and a bottle of scotch, but had consumed surprisingly little of the whisky as a novel quickly took form. The first three chapters — some 40 pages — had virtually written themselves, the words spilling out of his imagination and onto pages about as quickly as he could type, and he'd gotten an advance on them from a reputable publisher almost immediately. The last 200 pages hadn't come quite as quickly, but he'd gotten the book done in five months. Within a year or so it had achieved respectable hard-cover sales — about 15,000 copies — and Smart had found himself transformed overnight from unknown geology prof to literary lion. But he had enjoyed the change. It had provideded him another route out of himself, something he was always keen to find.

That first book — *Son of Stone* — had become something of a cult classic, eventually selling close to 100,000 copies in paperback. It also became a low-budget movie that helped launch the storied career of Helmut Hulkenberger, a huge Swabian with a thick accent who'd seemed an especially unlikely choice to play the cultured hero Smart had created. Yet Hulkenberger pulled it off, combining topographical musculature with a droll, almost whimsical quality, and the movie made money even before hitting the video stores.

Six novels had followed in relatively quick succession, the last four being the adventures of a neolithic sleuth and proto-metallurgist named Nagap. Nagap, who mined gold and lapis in the western reaches of what is now Germany and decorated his loinskins with small bright jewels (thus becoming the earliest rhinestone cowboy, by a clever critic's reckoning), had been an instant hit, giving the protean Hulkenberger yet another vehicle for his relentless rise. They'd filmed the first of these sagas —*The Mines of Nagap*— several years ago, and negotiations had gone on for some time about doing a sequel. But Smart wanted much more money this time out, and so did Hulkenberger. There matters had rested for more than a year.

Smart had begun to feel a bit becalmed. Gradually he became convinced that he needed to write The Big One, the blockbuster that would catapult him into the first rank of popular novelists and ensure his place on Easy Street — if not in the study of Western Literature — for the rest of his life. He'd been paid a very substantial advance six months ago without having to produce so much as an outline, but strangely the words hadn't filled the pages as easily as in the past. In fact, Smart thought wryly, if he continued at his current pace, there was a good chance he'd have to ask for a second advance. This time, though, they would certainly require an outline.

"How are you doing with your garden, my dear?" Smart asked distractedly. He got no reply, then craned his head around the room and noticed that Libby had left. He slouched down in his seat a bit and hoped she hadn't been too put out by his lack of ardor; maybe he would rouse himself to give her a good roll in the hay tonight. It was unprecedented, he knew, for Trelawny Smart to lack for desire. Were the Irish authorities putting saltpeter in the water supply at the behest of the church? He smiled, knowing that the church had no objection to marital penetration as long as it was unsheathed. It kept the people busy, and it kept the church in people.

Smart thought again of the wall: THE WALL, as it was beginning to loom in his mind's eye, a marquee in huge glyphs of hewn stone, cracked monoliths like the lettering for the old Technicolor epics of the '50s and '60s. Could he get Charlton Heston or Anthony Quinn to come out of semi-retirement and play the lead as the fearless Irish contractor (sad thought that The Duke was no longer around) who took down THE WALL, damn the consequences, in order to lift the hapless natives out of their backward-looking funk?

Maybe Hulkenberger would get the part, Smart thought. Who cared that the accent was all wrong? A hammer in the Devil's eye, a witticism as he repulsed blood-red lasers of pure evil with a handy crucifix made of twisted rebar rods, and the masses would love it. Smart got up and put his hands in his back pockets, thinking idly about the casting for *the Devil's room* and, of course, the sequel: *Satannic Suite* or some such drivel. Nothing he could come up with, he realized, could possibly outdo the shameless hucksters of Hollywood, who would gladly market pus if only they could get it onscreen.

He walked over to the radio and flipped it on, stopping at a powerful signal from across the sea in Glasgow: A retro-rock station with an all-Stones format. As Smart listened, marveling at Scottish enterprise, the earnest deejay explained that while the station was "pootin' the mean focus" on the Stones, they also would play "relay-ted" music, *i.e.,* the Animals from the period when they had contested the top of the British charts with the Stones, Howlin' Wolf, Willie Dixon and other American mentors, the Beatles to provide counterpoint to the Stones' limited psychedelic offerings, etc. Smart shook his head: Was it true, as some said, that the '90s were merely the '60s standing on their head? If so, he thought, he might not have the stamina to relive those wild times. Or maybe he'd get a second wind and get wilder than ever before. Could he take that sort of abuse anymore? He was in reasonably good shape, but he certainly wasn't the physical specimen he'd been 25 years before. Who was, with the possible exception of Hulkenberger?

As he walked out of the room, the deejay turned up the volume on a song he hadn't heard in ages: "Ah can't GIT no … sat-tis-FAC-tion …"

Nine

Smart avoided the Devil's room for the next week or so, attempting to focus all his energies on writing. But though he sat for hours in his study and made clacking sounds with the keyboard — deceiving Libby into thinking he'd finally broken the creative block that had plagued him since their arrival at Mordalee — what he mostly did was play computer games. A few false starts had taken shape — one of them 12 pages long, but a dead end in the final analysis — and he thought he'd finally hooked on to the Nantucket sleigh ride of a new book several times. But at the end of the week, all he had to show for his prodigious tapping was a rather paltry "Space Conqueror" score.

He couldn't touch the source of his malaise, but if experience was any guide, it wouldn't take much more of it to send him careening down the path toward dissipation — long afternoons and longer nights in the pubs, crawling on his belly toward the next pint, until Libby would have to lock him up, figuratively but almost literally, for his own good. He didn't want to go through that cycle again, and he knew that Libby, for her part, was getting apprehensive about it. Each time in the past had seemed a little worse than the time before, a bit less tolerable to her, and she didn't want to be in the situation of questioning the foundations of their relationship, which is where his boozing always took her.

Smart stared at his computer screen again. There were no words on it, only the maddeningly repetitive sworls of "Space Conqueror," with its infantile theme music playing again and again. *What idiot gave computers the means to make noise?* Smart wondered as he clicked the sound off.

Not wanting to leave the room and admit defeat to Libby, Smart opened the *Accumulate!* personal-finance program on his computer. He scrolled to the latest entries for his checking and other accounts, which were kept up to date automatically via modem. The pattern was the same as it had been over the past three months: bills being paid against lower and lower balances; a lot going out and very little — the odd royalty check — coming in. He was far from a pauper, it was true, but at this rate his fortune wouldn't last out the year unless they started economizing drastically. Oh, Libby would love that. She'd been promised the life of a country doyenne, and now he'd have to tell her to start clipping coupons and limiting those leisurely chats with her mother in Kansas.

No problem, Trel, she'd say, voice sweetly dripping venom. *I'll just take in a bit of washing to help make ends meet.*

Would he have to sack Rose and Pike? He certainly hoped it wouldn't come to that — he liked them both, despite their lack of couth or perhaps because of it, and he knew that such an action would have repercussions among the burghers of Ballymorda.

Pike had gone north as promised to visit his sister's family in Sligo, whether because he thought Smart was about to start tearing down the walls of hell or for other reasons Smart couldn't divine. In any case he'd been glad to see Pike go for a while — he didn't draw pay while away. But that modest relief for Smart's checkbook was almost overshadowed by the imminent demise of the state airline, which had flown into a crisis and would require massive infusions of cash.

The airline had compounded its own woes by throwing a riotous holiday party for top management in Ibiza. The bash, replete with sloe-eyed island babes and a chartered 747, had struck a special chord of infamy with the public and especially with the church — aching to get the focus off its own pedophile priests for once — and was now universally referred to as "Aer Flingus" in the tabloids and on TV. There was dark talk in the Dail, Smart had read, that in a crisis of this magnitude *everyone* — every resident of the Republic, no matter his naturalization status or previous exemptions from taxation — would have to pitch in.

Of course Smart had called his local member, Dicky Hickey — "the Smiling Thief of Ballycreef," Pike always called him — and Hickey had assured him that revocation of the writers' tax exemption was not in the cards. "It's just idle talk among the dregs of the House, Mr. Smart," Hickey said. "The exemption for writers is a sacred thing to the Irish, so don't worry about it, is my respectful advice, sir."

Smart had been partially mollified until he'd picked up *The Irish Times* the next day. On page 1 was an article under the heading: "Can we still afford to exempt wealthy writers from income tax?" The article noted that foreign authors were reaping millions from the tax exemption, while Aer Lingus crews were being axed right and left and the tourist industry in the west of Ireland was threatening to implode. "A fiscal catastrophe is what awaits this country if all sources of revenue aren't tapped in the present situation," the article concluded, noting with sour satisfaction that the recent European recession and rising interest rates also meant that many "tax-fleeing" authors wouldn't be able to pick up and leave the Republic easily because their "fancy houses" wouldn't sell.

Smart had tried to place another call to Hickey, but a young- and pert-sounding aide who answered the phone at his Dublin office and took Smart's name and number said the member wasn't available. "He's in committee," she told Smart, as if that settled the matter.

"When will he be out of committee? I'd like to talk to him as soon as possible about a very urgent matter," Smart said.

"I quite understand," said the aide. Then the line went dead. When Smart attempted to redial, Hickey's line was busy. And neither the lawmaker nor his assistant called back. Furious, Smart resolved to vote against Hickey at the first opportunity. Then he realized that, as one of those un-naturalized "tax-fleeing" authors living in a "fancy house," he couldn't vote. *But I can support his opponent,* Smart thought triumphantly. His glee faded when he recalled that he wouldn't be able to support anyone much longer unless he made some money.

Ire at Hickey and the whole Paddy establishment drove Smart back to the keyboard once again, where he not only closed down the "Space Conqueror" program but wiped it off the hard drive, thus scoring the ultimate winning game. It was a hollow gesture, of course, because he still had the disk and could re-install the game anytime. But wiping out the universe felt good anyway. *If only wiping out Hickey and his lot were so easy,* Smart fulminated.

He was too distracted to write, and since Hickey had eluded him, Smart sought an easier target: Fergus. He'd find out from him the true state of the Irish real estate market. Not that he was considering selling Mordalee; but it would be a good idea to know what was what, "just in case." He rang up Fergus' office, only to get a recording to the effect that the number was no longer connected. Cursing his own stupidity, Smart dialed The Drowning Man and was immediately put in touch with the estate agent. Checking his watch (it was 11 a.m.) and clucking to himself, Smart asked Fergus what he was doing at the pub so early in the day.

"Doing?" said Fergus. "What the fook *would* I be doing here? Who is this, me Mom, now?" Smart heard raucous laughter in the background. Fergus was in rare form and playing to an appreciative house.

"It's Trelawny Smart, Fegan. Remember me?"

"Smart is it? Is this some awful fooking joke? Don't get smart with me, now ... ." There was more laughter in the background and rallying cries.

As Fergus ranted on, Smart was of divided mind: One part of him wanted to put the phone down, drive directly to The Drowning Man, take Fergus out behind it and slap the living shit out of him; the other part wanted to congratulate the estate agent for his phenomenal insouciance, his utter refusal to knuckle under and play the role of adult. How many realty agents spoke this way to clients in the States? Precious few, Smart thought, in this age of franchised "McRealtors" and customer-satisfaction surveys. He had to admire Fergus for thumbing his nose at money, ambition, propriety ... even at Smart, the noted author. He'd put thousands of pounds in Fergus' pocket, but that seemed to count for naught with him.

"You're completely knackered, obviously," Smart said. "I'll try again when you're more coherent."

"Coherent, is it? From the Latin, I believe: *co,* denoting two, and *here,* as in sticking together. So I'm not sticking together, says you. Well, there've been times in my life, I may as well admit it, when I've been more coherent, as you say, but what's so great about coherency? When we consult Plautus, we find that the virtues of sticking together are sometimes overrated. In fact ... ."

Smart hung up, shaking his head. Would he ever learn the true state of the Irish real estate market from Fergus? *No,* he thought, *but I might learn the state of the Roman villa market from Plautus.*

Still shaking his head, Smart got out the County Dergh directory and dialed the number of Mulhearn, a competitor of Fergus' and a noted abstainer. The news wasn't good, although Mulhearn tried to put the best face on it. The market had more or less dried up, the estate agent said, adding soothingly that the condition was "no doubt temporary." The flood of German money had suddenly become a trickle, Mulhearn said, noting that "even over the last three months, the difference in sales is striking. Only those willing to reduce their asking prices considerably have been able to sell lately."

Chastened, Smart thanked Mulhearn for his time and hung up, eyeing a nearby bottle of the Macallan's scotch that Libby like to tap from time to time. She got slightly giddy — and unfailingly randy — after but a sip or two of the peaty single-malt, but she always stopped drinking just then. Unlike himself, Smart thought ruefully. He'd never seen Libby truly drunk, whereas a taste of whisky for him too often would be a passport to the land of dislocated senses and forgotten responsibilities. It was a fun place to visit, but the consequences on return were too awful to contemplate. Above all, he couldn't stomach Libby's unspoken misery and embarrassment when she came to bail him out of whatever mess he was in. On the other hand, he thought wistfully, the Macallan's was such fine whisky that it left you virtually without a hangover, no matter how drunk you got.

Smart turned away from the bottle with a huge effort, then faced the computer screen and stared at it. After two or three minutes he began to write:

At dawn on the day before the 10th moon, the elders of the Wolf Clan gathered up the sacred pelts and fetishes and sought the counsel of Nagap, he who makes the stones flow, royal whelp, sachem and lawgiver, light of all the clans of Urboiea. Nagap took their gifts as ceremony dictated, with smiling eyes. But his heart was heavy.

He hated such portentousness and generally ditched it as soon as the plot got going, but his readers seemed to expect it at the beginning of each book, so he duly supplied it. *Can't disappoint Nettie Nemec,* he thought grimly. Nettie was a housewife in Fulton, New York, who was a big booster of Smart's. She was always writing him and threatening to start a fan club, which the publisher had encouraged but which Smart found inexpressibly depressing and had so far managed to quash.

Gradually the familiar surge of excitement and dread overtook him as another Nagap story began to take over his mind. It was a hopeless addiction, writing fiction; you felt such liberation as the words poured out and a wispy little universe of your own device began to take shape, growing fuller and more comprehensible with each stroke of the keyboard. Yet he knew that each effort, so splendidly begun, could end in miserable failure with a mass of thousands of dead words, hundreds of pages that all the king's editors and all the king's toadying critics and back-scratching, ladder-climbing writers couldn't put right again. What if it all didn't hang together?

Coherent: from the Latin, I believe. Smart again shook his head in an involuntary tribute to Fergus the facetious, whelp of the bogs and provider of low comedy to the thirsting red-haired multitudes. *Maybe Fergus is in his cups because he hasn't a prayer of ever selling a house again,* Smart thought. In that case, he'd have to buy him another drink as soon as he sobered up. Some realities — and some realties — were too grim to face. But he'd buy Fergus stout, Smart vowed, not whiskey.

He smiled as the keyboard sang, page after page issuing from his mind by way of his fingers, each building upon the last and leading inevitably to the next. Libby, who'd heard the fevered clacking music as she'd passed outside Smart's door, left him alone, returning at the end of the day with supper, which she left on a tray outside his door after knocking once. It was quite possible he wouldn't stop even for sustenance, she knew, growing gaunter as the words flooded out and the pages piled up. But when he got thin and the stack got fat it was an excellent sign, signifying another imminent birth with all its attendant joys: fame, money, travel, the childlike satisfaction Smart derived from seeing a goodly selection of his books lined up on some retailer's shelf. And while he was writing, she knew, he wouldn't be drinking.

Ten

For 30 pages or so, Nagap — reluctant but brilliant warrior, ardent lover, prince of troglodytes — strode the Earth again, fashioning molten metals into cunning shapes, inventing the missionary position in order to enhance penetration by way of oral contact, resolving bloody disputes among his less-evolved cohorts and in general laying the foundation for the flowering of Celtic culture which in fact would not occur for another several thousand years.

Smart was transcendent, mixing paleontological savvy with deft plotting, strewing corpses wantonly about the primeval landscape, sketching a spare yet nuanced portrait of the multifaceted caveman. It was coming along quite well — a virtuoso performance, until it all ended abruptly at page 31.

Smart had come up to breathe, as it seemed, tearing himself away from his desk for a 10-minute coffee break. He was excited, beside himself, his eyes a bit glazed from peering simultaneously at a computer screen and the interface between the Stone and Iron ages. He was considering a host of new directions for Nagap, including an encounter with an alien (perhaps an emissary from Ur or an even more ancient Indo-European city-state) who would attempt to introduce a rudimentary system of taxation to Nagap's people. Nagap would of course resist, sending the alien and his loathsome concept packing and making the Neolithic ages safe for capital formation. He'd also make Nagap a navigator this time out, the inventor of the schooner-rigged corracle, and he'd have him plunge down the Rhine and meet and vanquish a tribe of femmes fatales who would prefigure not only the Lorelei but ball-busting modern feminists as well.

Libby was out, so he made coffee just for himself rather than for the two of them, as was his custom. Normally he'd use such a hiatus to shed some sparks, touch her with his creativity and receive her enthusiasm and encouragement in return, but now he'd have to keep it bottled up. He'd just begun to steam some milk for cappuccino when he heard the screeching of brakes outside in the courtyard behind the kitchen. A car door slammed, and a man let out a howl of pain and rage.

"Fookin' bloody shite! Ah, what a fookin great stupid whore I am, Jaysus Christ preserve us! Bloody damn door, shite!"

Outside Smart saw Fergus' new car — a sporty, late-model Rover with four-wheel drive — and the estate agent himself, hopping and cursing and holding one hand in the other. His face was red, whether from the unseasonably cold wind that was blowing down from the Slieve Bloom or the shock or booze Smart couldn't tell. *Probably all three,* he thought.

Smart went out. "Fegan — what the hell did you do to yourself? Are you going to need a doctor?"

"Slammed the bloody fookin' door on me fookin' small finger is what, Mr. Smart. Now I'm not sure if there's anything left of it." The estate agent continued to hop and wince, but Smart noticed that he seemed oddly out of sync with himself, as if he was capering in a stop-action film.

Smart hurried over and put an arm around the realtor. Eventually he got him to reveal the wounded digit, which was intact but very ugly. The tip was now a purplish-black tumescence, and the nail was cracked and covered with dark blood. "Looks awful, I'm afraid," said Smart, guiding Fergus into the house. "We'd better put some ice on it right away."

Fergus protested weakly: It was really nothing and would mend itself without further bother, etc. But he let himself be led into the kitchen nevertheless, moaning and sucking in air between his teeth. Smart put some ice on a thin kitchen towel, then gathered it into a kind of sack and smacked it on the tabletop a few times. Then he gingerly positioned the shattered ice around the swollen finger and cautioned Fergus to keep it in place while he got something to ease the pain. Shaking his head, Smart went into the parlor and poured a shot of the Macallan's for Fergus. The estate agent brightened appreciably when he gave it to him.

Smart grinned, encouraging Fergus to drink. "There you go, sport. You're a rough one on the old digits, aren't you? If you're going to waste one, though, I suppose that's the one to waste."

Fergus drained half the glass in a deep draught, then sat down heavily. "Thanks, Mr. Smart. I'm very much obliged to you, although you shouldn't have taken the trouble. Especially in view of the fact that I ... ."

"You were a bit of a turd on the phone, eh? Well, let him who is without sin cast the first stone, is my motto. I've done more than a bit of cutting up in bars in my time, although I must say that I usually don't get into it quite as early in the day as you seem to."

"I don't know what came over me this morning, Mr. Smart." There seemed to be genuine wonder in his voice, as if he'd seen the blue robe of the Virgin of Ballymorda rather than a neon Guinness sign. "If me poor mother over in Tralee heard of such carryings-on, she'd box my ears."

"That same recourse occurred to me," Smart said smoothly. "But in the end I decided that's your mother's job, not mine. And besides, self-righteousness is at least as ugly a sin as dissipation."

There was a silence as Fergus appreciatively finished the whisky.

He turned away as Smart carefully opened the cloth sack to examine the finger. The bleeding had stopped, and the swelling, though still bad, seemed to have been arrested by the ice. "You'll live," Smart said. "But I don't know if you'll thrive, what with pissing off customers like that."

Fergus looked deeply abashed as he set the glass down. "I wanted to apologize to you for that, so. There's no excuse for it, really. Was there something you needed when you called before?"

"Well, I'm concerned about this taxation business — you know, all this talk in the Dail and the press about taxing everyone, even the dead saints in the ground, and part of what had me going was the slowdown in the real estate market. Buying this house and remodeling it put quite a crimp in my liquidity, and I was wondering how much I could unload it for in a pinch. Not that I'm *in* a pinch, mind you," he added hastily, seeing Fergus regard him closely. "But if the damned politicians hit me for a bailout of the airline, I may have to think about moving again."

Fergus looked uncomfortable as he searched for just the right phrasing. "Well, things have slowed down a bit, I'm afraid. Quite a bit, actually." He paused, then finally spat out the whole truth: "There's not a damn thing moving, in fact."

"So Mulhearn told me," Smart said. Fergus started.

"You wouldn't go to that sanctimonious whore now, would you Mr. Smart?"

"Well, if I had to list in a hurry and you were too busy entertaining your drinking buddies, I might," said Smart. Fergus knew he had that coming, so he looked at the floor as he waited quietly for Smart to continue. "Mulhearn was quite obliging, if not very encouraging. He said prices have fallen off sharply over the past few months, and that sellers are having to discount steeply in order to move properties like this."

"A temporary thing, I'm sure, Mr. Smart. Why just yesterday the mark rose against the pound, and if that keeps up the Germans will be back in this market in a flash. They're very nervous about all those poor people to the east and south of them, you know — they see Ukrainians and Balts and Poles and god knows what-all pouring across the border some day as their economies collapse. They actually see Ireland as a sort of pristine haven, not only from their neighbors but from themselves, in a way — their history, the whole 20th century."

Smart didn't reply. He readjusted the ice around Fergus' finger, then invited him to the drawing room for another Scotch. Smart was somewhat anxious at first to get back to his study, but he didn't want to be blunt about asking Fergus to go. So he listened politely as the estate agent discoursed on the ebbs and flows of eurodollars and how the new EC structure would affect Irish property values.

Time passed, and with it the Macallan's, and before Smart knew it the day had dissolved. Fergus left at about 5 p.m., promising as he went to have the finger checked by a doctor. "Not Doctor Gall, Fegan. A real physician, now!" called Smart as Fergus climbed carefully into his car.

Smart went to the lavatory and was about to return to his study when another car pulled up — Libby's burgundy Peugeot. Out she stepped with a smiling, red-haired matron. She was Mrs. McCaughey, Smart learned, the local vet's wife, and she would be dining with them tonight while her husband was assisting with a difficult case — a prize mare with twin foals, reverse presentation — over beyond Dergh town. Libby had met her in the nearby Top of Tipp shopping mall, one of the first of its kind in Ireland, where Dr. McCaughey had abandoned her to answer the call of his beeper.

Before Smart could excuse himself, Libby had politely but firmly planted him in the drawing room opposite Mrs. McCaughey — Bess, as she insisted she be called — and asked him to stay with their guest while she "threw a few things together for supper." Smart had heard this phrase before — it meant that Libby, who usually left the cooking to him, planned to attempt something elaborate and difficult. This in itself was fine with him — she was an excellent cook when she was in the mood — but it meant that they wouldn't be dining until 7 or later, and that he would have to play the good host until then and probably long after.

In the event this wasn't as onerous a task as it had first seemed, because Bess was a prodigious conversationalist, cocking her head slightly to one side like a bird to make sure she caught every word and never letting things lag. Her brother-in-law, as it turned out, was distantly related to Pike, and her husband was on close terms with Dicky Hickey, about whom Smart wanted to know more. Was their representative in Dublin, as Pike maintained, a smiling thief?

Bess said she had no direct evidence one way or the other, but she did subscribe to the popular axiom that despite their modest pay, no Irish politician ever left office poor. She added, however, that she wasn't too worried about Hickey because he probably didn't have the ingenuity to be a really good thief. "I don't begrudge them something for their pains — answering the phones at odd hours when someone's hit a roving cow on a back road somewhere and such. A bit of boodle I can accept," she said judiciously, "seeing as that's the way of it. It's *gluttony* I can't abide in a politician, so."

The evening passed very enjoyably. Libby's beef Wellington was a smashing success, and the Bordeaux Bess had brought proved its perfect complement. She kept them regaled with a great deal of local history, much of it personal but none of it slipping into the category of mere vulgar gossip. Finally, at about 10 p.m., Bess said she must be getting home. Smart waved his good-byes from the courtyard, then made his way slowly back to the kitchen. It was late, and he was very tired. The creative energy he'd felt earlier in the day had largely been replaced by a torpid feeling of bonhomie which, if it didn't produce pages, at least was a vast improvement over his recent malaise.

He tidied up the kitchen, not wanting to leave a mess for Libby, who would be worn out by the time she returned. Then he considered making himself that cappuccino he'd set out to have earlier in the day. He decided to make two this time — Her Nibs would appreciate a pick-me-up when she got home. He added a bit of amaretto to the frothy coffee for good measure. *You might as well go all out when scoring points,* he thought.

He heard the car pull up outside just as he was about to return to his study. He almost kept going, although hitting the keyboard didn't seem all that appealing now. He paused just outside the door and looked into the dim room at the computer on his desk. There he was: Nagap the Invincible, the Hamlet of cavemen, roaming in the gloaming, just a few feet from him. The story was another potential hit — perhaps the breakthrough that had eluded him so far. You never knew, once you got to setting things down on paper, what might emerge. But he decided he could wait until tomorrow to find out.

He turned back and met Libby at the kitchen door with her cup of cappuccino in his hand. Smiling, she took the cup in one hand and stroked his back with the other. She was feeling expansive despite her fatigue.

"Oh, thanks, Trel — you're a doll. Wasn't she neat? I'd heard she was indispensable if you want to get the full picture of what's what and who's doing it to whom around here, but who knew she'd be so ... what? Droll? Sparkling? All of the above? She was delightful, I thought."

Smart grinned. "She's an Irish type, I think — a storyteller by birth. These people really seem to relish that sort of human contact. You see a lot of that in the pubs, but the pubs have no monopoly on it, apparently."

"There's something special about it," Libby agreed. "It must be what comes of living on a small island and not being totally immersed in television. Or maybe it's the fact that they're all the same ethnic group — family, in effect." Smart said he wasn't quite sure about the ethnic angle, but he was sure that whatever it was, the Irish seemed to have no shortage. They returned to the drawing room, where Libby draped one leg over Smart's knees, rather suggestively, as they sat on the couch and sipped their coffee. Smart felt pleasantly aroused, and he rubbed her thigh in lazy circles higher and higher on her leg. She smiled at him over the rim of her cup as he got close to the apex.

He felt undeniably horny tonight. It had something to do with the success he'd had earlier in his study, something to do with the good company and with the feeling that he'd broken through at last, squared the circle, begun to make a success of this Irish venture. He was about to tell her about the latest Nagap tale when a small motion of Libby's reminded him forcefully of Lady Brimston. It was just the way she smiled dreamily for a moment or two; he remembered how Lady B. had done that when talking about her errant Glaswegian, Thomas.

"You know," he said, still languidly stroking the inside of her thigh, "it was in this very room that I fell in love with Lady Brimston and decided to do the only gallant thing and take this house off her hands." He expected a playful riposte from Libby, but instead she turned solemn, shifted uncomfortably and sighed heavily.

"Bess told me something on the way home that I probably ought to tell you, Trel. It's not happy news, though."

"What is it?" asked Smart, bemused. "Pike comes from a long line of ax-murderers? The armadillos have to get their shells stamped by customs?"

"No," Libby said quietly. She took a deep breath and looked down at her cup. "She said she'd been very close to Lady Brimston at one time, apparently when the Brimstons kept a stable full of horses here."

"She was close to Lady B.? What's so awful about that, my dear?"

"Nothing, of course. But she said she'd heard from Featherstone,

Lady B's solicitor, that ... ."

"What?" Smart asked quietly. But he had a premonition. He didn't really want to hear the news from Featherstone, but Libby took a breath and pressed on.

"She said Lady B. died a few weeks ago, right after moving into her little villa on Minorca."

Smart felt shattered. He sat in silence, digesting this information for a moment or two. "Lady Brimston is dead? Was she sure of that? We just got a post card not two months ago ... ."

"I know, Trel. I told her that Lady B. said she was in good health and spirits, that the sunshine agreed with her after so many years of bog and fog, as she put it. But Bess said that it must have happened quite recently, because Featherstone had told her of it a few weeks ago."

At first Smart was too stunned to reply. Finally, he spoke: "Lady Brimston dead ... I can't grasp it. She was so vital, despite her age. What did her in?"

"Bess said Featherstone was vague, but it apparently was something sudden, like a heart attack or a stroke. She said she'd gotten the impression that it was all over quickly, anyway. No suffering."

Smart looked beyond Libby at the double doors through which the former owner of Mordalee had swept into this room when he'd first met her, looking like a faded movie star who had somehow achieved immortality — perhaps through sheer willpower. Could she really have died? "I knew she was old," Smart said slowly, "but it still doesn't seem possible."

"I'm sorry, Trel. I knew you'd be upset."

Smart nodded absently. He had stopped stroking Libby's thigh, and she removed her leg from his and took their empty coffee cups to the kitchen, where she pottered for a while with the dishes.

Smart thought of the magical evening he'd passed in Lady B's company: the bourbon, the literate but cozy chat, the intelligence and charm that had made him nearly forget a mild concussion, the trek out through faerie country to the ancient headache stone. It had happened less than half a year ago, but it already seemed like an episode from a stranger's life, an interlude he'd read of somewhere and marveled at from within the predictable confines of his own stale existence. He was about to pour himself a scotch when he caught himself.

"In memory of Lady Brimston," he said out loud, "no more scotch will be consumed in this house. At least, not tonight." He tumbled some bourbon into a saloon glass and drank a salute to the late mistress of Mordalee.

Eleven

The next morning, Smart awoke with riotous laughter ringing in his head. He looked up wildly, half expecting the sound to be coming from the ectoplasmic residents upstairs, but in fact it was all coming from inside his own skull, as he gradually came to realize. It had been a dream, but the only element of it he could recall was the laughter — loud, harsh, mocking, penetrating, inescapable, building to a peak of scorn and derision. He had been holding his ears in his dream, trying to shut out the noxious noise, and he had the persistent sense now that his ears hurt, although they didn't.

Shaking his head, Smart got up and looked out his bedroom window hesitantly, as if to see whether the world had changed in any significant way since he'd gone to bed the night before. Physically it hadn't, of course — outside were the same fields and the same cows, the same old trees clotted with squawking black rooks, the same ancient, ruined castle gatehouse moldering among the brambles on the edge of his property. But the knowledge that Lady B. was dead had indeed changed Smart's world somehow.

The weather seemed to stew and sulk in sympathy; the skies were sullen and low, and the wind brought the scent of rain and a bit of chill. Smart put on his heavy Turkish robe and made his way slowly down the wide steps to the kitchen, shaking his head again as he tried to recall what all that awful laughter had been about. He couldn't remember anyone or any sort of story from the dream — just the caustic mirth, and the feeling that he must escape it or shut it out to survive.

Libby had left some coffee in a pot for him, and Rose, bustling in from the washroom, told him there was a mess of eggs, ham and toast in the oven's warming compartment. Libbby, she said, had gone to Dergh town on some errand regarding her creatures, by which Rose meant the armadillos, and had said she would be back later in the day. Rose herself would get lunch ready for him and finish up the washing and ironing before leaving at noon, she told him. Smart thanked her distractedly before sitting down at the tiled harvest table that filled most of the kitchen and tinkering with his breakfast. Mostly he drank coffee — the whole pot within a half hour or so, and then more that he brewed himself — and tried to place that laughter. What had unnerved his unconscious self about it, he came to realize, was its familiarity, the fact that it had seemed to well up from some subterranean source within his very being — yet it was not his own laughter. It was as if someone, he thought uncomfortably, had sublet his soul.

Eventually he gave up puzzling over the dream and resolved to do something to take his mind off it. But he didn't feel like writing today, or at least not at this moment. The skies had lifted a bit since he'd awakened, so he decided to have a stroll about his estate, like a proper squire. A few minutes later, clad in a tweed hunting jacket, gabardines and green wellies, he ventured out the front door and down the gravel path toward the dirt drive that led out to the county road. He was thinking of nothing in particular, just taking in the scene and breathing the outdoor air, now more than a little heavy with the scent of growing things. The winter had been harsh, by Ireland's lights, but now all nature seemed to be producing buds, flowers and shoots in a fierce green competition.

As he walked under a great old oak that had only the day before burst into leaf, a flock of rooks exploded from among the branches, their black wings flapping heavily and their beaks clacking as they cawed and scolded, making a commotion that very nearly scared Smart out of his wits.

"Jesus Christ!" Smart exclaimed. "Goddamn stupid birds!" He'd moved his arms over his head instinctively to protect himself, and now he lowered them somewhat sheepishly, glad no one had seen him quail at this aerial ambush. It was odd, how they'd been silent until he'd gotten right underneath them before they'd burst out of the branches like choirs of the dead, seemingly in their hundreds. He checked his sleeves for shite, as the Irish said, and was thankful to find none. The flock was flapping heavily toward another large tree, and soon was contending noisily with the tribe that occupied it and circling to see if they would yield. Smart shook his head again, making a mental note to have a word with Pike about trimming the rook population at Mordalee if that were at all feasible. *Fucking dirty birds is all they are,* he huffed to himself as he walked on, *a bloody foul nuisance.*

Looking down as he strode, imagining the shotgun reports of a great, satisfying slaughter of rooks in the fall, when the leaves were off the trees, Smart noticed a curious hoof print in the soft earth. It was cleft, like a goat's, but it was much larger than that of any goat he'd seen — almost the size of a man's foot.

What the hell could have made this? he mused to himself, bending down on one knee to examine the print. It seemed to have been made by a giant ungulant, something like the baluchitherium of the Ice Age — a creature Napag had hunted and served to his Stone Age confreres *en croquette* with a piquant slug sauce — but there was no such animal in the fields and forests of central Ireland. He heard a snuffing sound behind a tree some 20 yards ahead, and thought he saw a flash of black fur as something bolted off into a thicket of yew and brambles beyond it. He ran up to the tree, half expecting to see the black ram Pike had lost that fateful night five months before, but there was nothing when he got there but a rank odor. Smart sensed that something was watching him; he slowly scanned the trees and bushes all around but saw nothing. "Hmm," he said. "What's going on here?"

It was as if his own patch of Irish sod was trying to confound or mock him somehow, trotting out loud birds, giant livestock, vanishing voyeurs and who knew what else to make him doubt his wits. He retraced his steps, meaning to have a look at the giant hoof print again, but when he got back to where he thought he'd seen it, the ground was unblemished.

"I'm losing it, no doubt about that," Smart muttered to himself. He bent low to examine the earth more closely, feeling increasingly foolish and irritated, but gave up after a moment or two. Straightening up and casting another look around, he walked quickly back to the house. The solution, he decided, was simple: He would displace the morning's strange events by focusing on Nagap.

Once ensconced in his study, he made a great show of getting ready to write — sharpening several pencils, even though he hardly ever used them, and straightening papers on his desk. Then he turned on his computer and waited for it to boot up, checking his notes from the day before. But they wouldn't do much good, he realized, because he'd outstripped them by the end of the day. No matter. "After surviving a plague of rooks," he said out loud, "it's a good day to wing it."

But by the time he read to the end of the page he'd been working on, he found he was clueless as to how to proceed. Indeed, the writing from yesterday looked alien, like hieroglyphs or graffiti some hacker had left on his computer overnight. *Jesus Christ!* he thought. *What's up with me today?*

He stood up, but forced himself to take a deep breath and sit back down. *I'll just read from the beginning,* he thought. *Get myself back into it.*

But what he read seemed a grotesque parody of what he thought he'd written the day before. It made no sense; its awkward prose embarrassed him; and he found himself wishing, by the end, that he'd never created Nagap. Still, he didn't want to give up — he'd definitely been on a roll the day before, and he couldn't just let that feeling fade away. There had to be something redeeming in the pages he'd written, he told himself, so he forced himself through them again.

This time he didn't make it to the end. In fact, he felt physically ill by the 10th page or so. He was aghast: How could he have written such dreck? He shut the computer off without bothering to save, half hoping that when he turned it back on the offending blather would be gone, or perhaps transformed into the novel he thought he'd been writing.

But when he'd composed himself enough to reboot his computer a few moments later, he couldn't bring himself to go back to Nagap. He played *Onan,* a kind of mental masturbation game in which one was prompted to personalize canned sexual fantasies, but he stopped when it occurred to him that the program's writing was better than his. He hastily switched to *Lord of the Universe,* but he inadvertently dropped his spacecraft's cloaking device and was obliterated almost immediately.

Smart was cursing his luck when he began to feel a mind-boggling headache coming on. *Christ, no!* he thought. But there was a bright side to a headache: It made work impossible, thus giving him an excuse for not producing. He took a double dose of pills nevertheless, not wanting to venture out to the headache stone on such a weird day, and waited for them to take effect. He heard the back door slam as Rose left, and he felt a bit of relief knowing that he was alone.

At least there would be no one to witness his humiliation, he thought. Not that Rose normally would have known about it. But if she'd stayed around, he might have felt compelled to blurt it out to her, and her embarrassed clucking would only have made things worse.

"What can I do?" he said out loud. *Seems I can't do a damn thing lately ... can't write, can't take a walk, can't sleep, can't dream, can't even get it up for Libby.*

That was a truly disturbing thought. He'd never had trouble performing for any woman, least of all Libby, and he knew that she was beginning to notice his indifference to her. But he just wasn't feeling any desire, that was all there was to it. They'd seen some laughing high-school girls in the village the other day, all budding breasts, creamy thighs and candy-apple cheeks, a sight that usually would have made the sap rise, but he'd felt nothing. Libby, always sensitive to his sexual moods, normally would have chided him for his attraction to jailbait, expecting that she'd end up with the fruit of his lechery later, but she'd said nothing. *Trying to spare me,* he thought. But sooner or later, he knew, she would vent her frustrations.

He dreaded that, because then he would have to put up or beg off, and he wasn't at all sure he could put up. He just didn't feel it — he was sexually becalmed, and since he'd never been that way before, he had no idea what to do about it. "Am I just getting old?" he asked a mirror in the hall. But he didn't look that old — his longish, unkempt hair was still mostly black rather than gray, and his face had only a few lines about the mouth. He checked his eyes, but they were a clear blue, if somewhat bloodshot — in any case, not the rheumy eyes of an old man.

What could he do to break out of this awful funk? He thought of calling Doc Gilchrist, but the good doctor wasn't a shrink, and Smart didn't feel he knew him well enough to talk about everything that was ailing him in order to get a referral. Besides, he hated the idea of shrinks. Everyone knew they were often crazy themselves, and who were they to go spelunking about in your psyche, dredging up embarrassing irrelevancies and making tendentious sounds as they put you in this or that diagnostic bag? Smart felt that he could analyze himself as well as any psychologist, using the one infallible tool of analysis at anyone's disposal: honesty.

He'd always found that when he confronted himself with ruthless candor, he could bring about change. Now, though, honesty seemed to be of no use, because he couldn't even put his finger on what was wrong.

Then he thought of something: the Devil's room.

Twelve

Maybe he couldn't resurrect Nagap today, but he sure as hell could get rid of that little abortion of a room. He jumped up — it felt good to have a focus for his frustrations. He practically ran out to Pike's shop in the barn to scrounge up a sledgehammer, crowbar and saw. He'd never been the handy type, but he didn't think it would require any great skill to take down a wall and a doorframe. *Just bash away is all you have to do,* he thought happily as he bounded upstairs with the tools. Wouldn't Libby be tickled to see it gone for once and all?

He burst into the upstairs bedroom and let the tools fall to the floor in a resounding clatter, then tried the door that led to the Devil's room. He'd always imagined himself opening it gingerly, as if to be able to close it quickly again in case something foul started to seep out, but now he simply flung it open. The fact that it was unlocked didn't surprise him; who, in Ireland, would open a door into a room with such a name? He laughed as the door swung wide: Past residents had probably kept jewels and valuables here, knowing no thief would enter. Now, however, there was nothing in the room. It was just a small, walled-off space — about 12 feet wide by maybe three feet deep. It looked very much like the room it had been cut off from, except that the bedroom's walls had been repainted.

The Devil's a man of simple tastes if this is where he hangs out, he thought. The air in the tiny space was stale and musty. He ran a hand over one wall, which was a pale ivory color. These walls might have been the very bones of the old house, and he tried to imagine the wonders Libby would work with the expanded space. He flicked the husks of ancient bugs off the windowsill and thought of how different the house would look from the outside once this great blind eye was opened again. Smiling, he went back into the main room and grabbed the sledgehammer.

About three hours later, covered in plaster dust but otherwise happy, he brought the tools back to Pike's shop and headed for the shower. *Pike can clean up when he gets back,* he thought. *The main thing is, the Devil's room is gone.*

When he got out of the shower he went to the living room, taking a pad and pencil with him from his study so he could concentrate on getting Nagap back on track. He didn't bother to change out of his bathrobe, half-hoping that the sight of him in it — combined with the news of what he'd done — would inspire Libby to reach inside its folds and get things going. She'd been known to take matters into her own hands when the mood struck her, and he smiled when he imagined her reaction to his handiwork upstairs. For the first time in weeks, he felt a frisson in the area of his crotch.

Such thoughts, however, weren't conducive to re-plotting Nagap's reprise, so he put the pad and pencil down and poured himself a bit of scotch. Then he went over to the radio and turned it on, tuning it to the Glasgow all-Stones station. He remembered with wonder that he'd entirely escaped the nor'easter of a headache that had been coming his way. He'd taken pills, true, but they usually did nothing to avert the Big Ones.

Must be the beneficial effects of a job well done, he thought, remembering how easily the wall had crumbled under his determined blows and how satisfying it had felt to bring the door and frame down intact. Pike, he knew, would find a good use for it, after crossing himself repeatedly and muttering darkly to himself.

"This is Lord Kenspeckle," the deejay said in a staticky growl, "the rajah of retro rock. You'd better have some sympathy for this dark fellow who's up next. Can you guess his name?"

A moment later, Smart found himself singing along with Mick Jagger's voice:

Please allow me to introduce myself,
I'm a man of wealth and taste.

The name of the song was just beginning to form in his mind when he heard a loud sound from upstairs. It was, unmistakably, a large piece of furniture being moved. Then another loud furniture sound, then the sound of a door closing.

"What the hell was that?" Smart blurted out. He turned the radio off, then jumped to his feet, eyes wide. There was no one else in the house, and the ghosts in the attic weren't active during the day and didn't move furniture anyway. Besides, the sound had come from the top of the stairs — the bedroom that had led to the Devil's room.

Pike must have come home early and let himself in while I was in the shower, Smart thought. Or maybe it was Libby — but she would have shrieked for joy by now. It must be Pike. He put on some clean clothes in the laundry room off the kitchen, not wanting to deal with Pike in a bathrobe. Then he climbed the stairs, listening for more noises but hearing none. *Pike must be stunned,* he thought to himself. He smiled. *He'll be a while getting over this.*

He concluded that the noise must have been Pike moving the tall, heavy doorframe across the floor, or propping it up against the wall. In any case, he was prepared to be firm with Pike. There would be no going back. It was, after all, a *fait accompli,* and the hounds of hell had not come bounding out.

But when he got to the top of the stairs and looked through the open door of the bedroom he was astonished to see the inner door and wall exactly as they were before he attacked them. He blinked, shook his head, and looked again, but the scene was the same. the Devil's room had somehow regenerated itself.

Smart was rooted to the steps, his hand clutching the banister for support as he felt reality slip into something amorphous and unfamiliar. He had taken down the wall and the door, yet there they stood, pristine. They didn't look as if they'd been repaired, even if that were possible; they looked as if they'd never been touched. Smart sat heavily on the third step from the top and twisted his body so he could keep his eyes on the bedroom. *I'm losing my mind,* he thought. *This proves it.*

He wracked his brain. Could he have fallen asleep after taking those headache pills and dreamed the whole business about knocking down the wall? *That must be it,* he thought, as implausible as it seemed. But then he looked down at the floor between the bedroom door and the stairs. He saw a set of footprints made of plaster dust — his own footprints. He was just beginning to consider the implications of this latest shock when he heard a noise from behind the closed door. It was the sound of someone moving a chair.

Smart got up shakily and hesitated, uncertain whether he should move toward the closed door or away from it. Finally, though, he decided he had to find out what was going on in the Devil's room. He approached the door slowly, keeping his eyes on the doorknob as if he expected to see it begin to turn of its own accord. But it didn't, and he stood for a while just in front of the door, listening. There was no sound. After a few moments, he opened the door.

"Ah, Mr. Smart," a man's voice said, "I thought you'd never come. Have a seat and let's get started, shall we?"

Thirteen

Lauretta Smale's gorgeous lips parted slightly in an ironic smile as the paunchy little man behind the lectern called her name. It was her turn to go to the head of the Holiday Inn conference room and be sworn in as part of the Special Section of the IRS, but she couldn't help thinking it was a little like being inducted into the Girl Scouts. She'd been a scout for only a few months when she was eight — the chasm between the nonstop outdoors adventuring she'd envisioned and the prosaic reality of troop meetings and cookie sales had been one of her first great disappointments — but she could see herself sticking with the IRS for as long as it took to nail Trelawny Smart.

As she made her way to the dais to become Special Agent 38, several of her male colleagues were unable to prevent their longing eyes from roving over the stunning contours beneath her short red sheath dress. She was only 20 years old, but her features had a sensual, sophisticated cast that made her look older and self-assured. She was tall — at least six feet in heels — and she moved with the lithe grace of a big cat.

The dashing Agent 23, like several other male trainees in her class, had done his best to get something going with her, but she had parried his interest with adamant professionalism and maddening politeness. All the young men in their unit and even some of the old married bulls had attempted to penetrate her impressive reserve, or so it seemed, but all had failed. So at least 23 didn't feel frustrated at losing her to someone else. No one had been able to make time with this bombshell, who, he concluded, was reserving her charms for an unknown but spectacularly lucky man.

Lauretta had been looking like anything but a bombshell on the day, five months before, when she had shown up at Billings Community College to check her grade in the accountancy final. She had been pushing to finish several papers and a bio lab that week, and she hadn't slept or showered in ages. Her thick chestnut hair had been matted and piled under a grungy beret, and she had hung back behind the thronging students before going up to see her posted grade — an A — because her sweatshirt had gone gamy on her. The grade, especially given how little time she'd had to study for the exam, was gratifying, and for a moment it hadn't mattered that she really didn't know quite why she had chosen to major in accounting. Then an official-looking notice, stuck on the bulletin board next to the section that contained the grades, had caught her eye:

— ATTENTION ACCOUNTANTS —

The Internal Revenue Service needs your help in the battle for tax fairness.

It was the fairness angle, cleverly inserted by some copywriter trying to tap into youthful idealism, that had snagged her interest. By the time she'd read to the end, though, she realized that the ad wasn't about redressing social injustices, except in the very broadest sense. The IRS was out to nab fugitive tax cheats, and it was putting together a flying squad of mostly young agents who could go anywhere and do whatever it took, within the law, to bring them to justice. The rewards of this job, as the ad's text made clear, went far beyond the warm glow of avenging law-abiding taxpayers by nabbing rich scofflaws. In addition to offering an attractive starting salary, the agency was prepared to sweeten the pot with a 40% commission on any funds turned over to the government. In some cases, the ad went on, this could amount to hundreds of thousands of dollars. But it was the accompanying list of miscreants, each with an outstanding judgment next to his or her name in parentheses, that really caught her attention. The name "Smart, Trelawny ($200,000)" took her breath away and almost made her faint. Her father, the great writer and cad who'd been the bane of her poor mother's existence, a tax cheat! *Now* she knew why she'd taken accounting.

Within a few days she'd shown up at the local IRS office, dressed for success in a dark business suit she'd pawned her stereo gear to buy. She'd also taken the time to research the problem of tax cheating, and had watched her interviewer smile and nod approvingly when she noted that the billions that were unlawfully diverted from the U.S. Treasury each year represented an unconscionable loss for those deserving programs — like Medicare, Headstart, Food Stamps — that were constantly being squeezed for funding.

Her single-minded rectitude along with her excellent grades had deeply impressed the IRS recruiter, who had signed her up with uncharacteristic speed and then put her through a crash course in code enforcement and the delicacies of luring outlaws out of hiding without actually "entrapping" them. She had learned that while she could "play" a suspect as long as it took to arrest him (almost all the agency's "Top 100" cheaters were men), she was expected to abide by the rules so that any convictions resulting from her efforts would stand.

"We're not interested in dragging someone into court on a tax charge and then having the case blow up in our faces because his rights were trampled," one earnest-looking instructor had told her. She didn't have to volunteer her identity as an IRS agent to a "perp," he added, but if asked, she was expected to tell the truth. "You mean, just like a vice cop on TV?" she'd asked.

"Exactly," he replied.

The trick lay in avoiding being asked before she was ready to lower the boom. And the key to that, an avuncular ex-FBI agent had told her after class one day, was role-playing. "Choose a credible role and play it to the hilt," he had said. "Seem to be exactly who you want him to believe you are, at all times, and don't let a shadow of doubt creep in. Then, when he least expects it, nail the bastard!"

Fourteen

Smart stared into the tiny room — which wasn't tiny anymore. And it wasn't the bare-walled space he'd opened up just a few hours ago. The room looked huge to Smart's astonished eyes — at least 20 by 30 feet — and it was richly furnished. A crystal chandelier sparkled over a gilt Louis XIV desk at its center, and in one corner stood an antique globe in a carved mahogany stand. Fine oriental carpets covered the floor, silk draperies framed the gleaming sills and mullions of the windows on the opposite wall, and an 18th-century marble fireplace with an elaborate wood mantel punctuated the wall on Smart's right. A set of brass implements and a bellows stood next to the fireplace, and ornate andirons laden with kindling and logs were set up in the middle of the hearth. But there was no fire.

"Oh, right — forgot about that," said the voice, and flames leapt instantly from the logs.

Smart turned toward the source of the voice — a medium-sized, middle-aged man with deep-set eyes and dark hair going gray at the temples. He regarded Smart with a keen, businesslike gaze.

"You're surprised, of course. I hope you like what I've done with the room. But have a seat, Mr. Smart, have a seat."

The man gestured to a plush chair across the desk from him. Smart was too numb to respond.

"Come, come, Mr. Smart — if time is money, as you Americans are so fond of saying, then we're both getting poorer. Do sit down and let's begin."

Smart shook his head and closed his eyes, but when he reopened them the scene hadn't changed. The man was still looking at him expectantly, and he had begun to tap a pencil on the blotter in front of him. Smart lurched toward the chair and sagged into it.

The man took a slim gold case engraved with the initials EFM from the vest pocket of his dark, pinstriped suit and removed a business card. He then rose slightly from his seat and extended his left hand across the desk to Smart, who shook hands mechanically. The man had a firm but cold grip, Smart noticed. With his other hand, the man placed his card face up on the desk. It read:

E. Finister Malcott
Life Accountant

The man laughed. "Don't meet too many life accountants, do you, Mr. Smart? It's a different sort of profession, I'll grant you that. But very important. Someone's got to keep track of it all."

"Who are you?" Smart said.

"It's no mystery, Mr. Smart — Malcott's the name, life accountancy is the game. I've come because there are some problems with your accounts."

Malcott, if that really was the man's name, stared at him steadily. *He never seems to blink,* Smart noticed uncomfortably.

"What are you doing in my house? And how did you ... ?" Smart's voice trailed off. How did he *what?* Clearly, the whole thing was impossible. The man must be a professional illusionist.

"As I said, Mr. Smart, I came to help straighten out your accounts. And as for the remodeling ... well, I took a lease on this room a long time ago and was a bit ashamed of how drab it was. I think business should be transacted in a conducive setting, don't you?"

The man's air was cordial, Smart noted, but his voice was strangely flat.

"What do you mean you have a lease on this room?"

"From a former owner. Not the most recent Lady Brimston — it goes back long before her. Leased in perpetuity. Check your deed, Mr. Smart. It's all there."

Smart hadn't gone over the deed line by line, but he'd paid a local solicitor to do so, and the man hadn't flagged any such provision.

"I'll wait if you want to get the deed now. But I assure you there's no need. It's a valid lease."

He said this with such finality that Smart decided not to press the point. He could check the deed at his leisure, after all; the main thing was that the man had set up shop in his house here and now, and Smart wanted to get to the bottom of it.

"This whole scene is impossible," Smart said.

"Oh, you writers are a skeptical lot," Malcott said, smiling thinly. "But how can it be impossible, Mr. Smart? You're sitting on a chair, after all. You see me behind this desk, and you hear me talking to you. I can assure you that this scene, as you put it, is at least as real as certain other elements of your life."

"What do you mean?" Smart growled. "What do you know of my life? We've never spoken before."

"But that's my line of work, Mr. Smart. It's my business to know things about people. For instance, I know you have a daughter. Do you remember her? Perdita, the little lost girl of your forgotten years."

Smart felt the expansive room collapse upon him. He shut his eyes, massaging his temples with his fingertips, his mouth half-open in shock. *Perdita!* How could Malcott — or anyone, for that matter — know about her? Perdita wasn't even her real name. It was the name he'd given her in his mind, and he'd never spoken it to anyone else.

"Her given name was Lauretta. Such a pretty name."

Smart stared at him.

"Oh, yes, Mr. Smart, I know quite a bit about you. Everything, in fact."

He gazed evenly at Smart as he said this, and Smart began to feel himself being pulled into the dark centers of Malcott's eyes, like a man stumbling toward an abyss. He gripped the desk for support and forced his own eyes shut. *He knows about Lauretta,* he said to himself. *It's impossible. But he does.*

"You haven't kept up with little Perdita, have you? Unfortunately, her mother passed away a year or two ago, and she's on her own, doing whatever it takes to get by. You know how they are at that age — they think they're so much more mature than they really are. They desperately need parental guidance, but of course she has none now. And she's just joined up with a rather disreputable group that specializes in separating people from their hard-earned money. A sad story."

Smart couldn't breathe for a moment. *My little Perdita a gang member?* He looked down at the floor, his mind reeling, and found himself noticing a strange thing. Instead of claw feet, the desk and chair legs had split hooves.

"Who the hell are you?" he finally shouted at Malcott. "Why have you come here?"

"You know very well who the 'hell' I am, Mr. Smart. You opened the door to this room — my room — so whom did you expect to find inside? The truth is, you need help. And I can provide it."

Fifteen

Smart sat in his study several hours later, nursing a scotch. Luckily, Libby was still out. He didn't know what he'd tell her when she came back — or even *if* he'd tell her. To keep his options open, he'd cleaned up the plaster-dust footprints so there would be no physical evidence to explain.

Malcott — who was either the Devil or a con man/magician of devilish cunning — had told Smart he would be willing to make him "a very favorable offer." Smart had scoffed and ordered him out of his house, but Malcott had scoffed in return. "You summoned me by entering this room," he had said, "so you can't back out. There's no getting rid of me until we come to an agreement," he'd added, smiling his joyless smile. "And I can be a very persistent negotiator."

Smart had railed awhile, pacing in front of the desk as Malcott sat looking bored. His eyes were blank, almost as if the mind behind them had gone elsewhere. But Smart's own eyes were drawn to Malcott's cravat. It had seemed a nondescript business tie with a dot pattern, but now he noticed that the dots were actually faces — dozens of them. And as Smart stared, he saw that each was different — and that the features of each face were writhing in expressions of unutterable horror, as if attached to bodies that had been impaled like bugs in a child's collection box. He'd flinched at the sight of these tiny, tortured faces, and when he looked back at Malcott's face, the eyes were powerfully alive again.

"You can't simply dismiss me, Mr. Smart. As you know, you have a lot to atone for."

It had been Malcott's use of that word — atone — that had demoralized Smart. His past, in the form of the tenant of the Devil's room, had caught up with him. He'd run from it halfway across the world, only to find it in his new home.

Who had he been 20-30 years ago, during what he now thought of as his "dark ages"? Sometime academic, sexual swashbuckler and ravisher of coeds, heavy drinker, backdoor sneak and druggie: He'd been out of control for over a decade, and he'd left a lot of wounded in his wake. Two of them had been Perdita and her mother, the delicately lovely Serena Smale.

Serena had been little more than a child herself when he'd gotten her pregnant, and although she'd begged him to marry her, he'd had no intention of doing so — until, on a night when he was out screwing two other women, she'd borne him a gorgeous little girl — an infant so transcendently mild and helpless that his heart had been swept away in a sudden, inexplicable flood of love.

He and Serena made plans to marry, and he tried to clean up his act — going sober for weeks, attending AA meetings, buckling down to his duties as an assistant professor at Montana State, and glorying in his role in creating such a radiant little creature. But the night before the wedding he let some of his lowlife friends take him out.

His good resolve, a more fragile thing than he had realized, was no match for booze, and when someone gave him a snort of cocaine in the men's room he felt an overwhelming need to have a woman — right then and there. So he lurched around the bar, according to what he heard later — he couldn't remember anything from that night — and found a willing wench, driving to her apartment and sleeping through the appointed hour the next morning. Serena had screamed at him when he came crawling back a few days later. She even pummeled his chest with her tiny fists, and the baby had begun to wail.

He'd signed his paycheck over to her in an absurd act of contrition — as if that could pay for rending her soul — and placed it on the kitchen table, but she tore it up and threw it in his face. Then he ran away — just jumped in his car and stomped on the accelerator.

He'd thought of returning to Billings many times over the ensuing years, but the allure of the bawdy life had always proven too strong. He'd sent a postcard once at Christmas — something that played off the idea of the prodigal son's return — but she hadn't responded. Nor had she ever come after him for child support, probably out of pride. He had met Libby about 10 years after Lauretta's birth, but he didn't tell her much about his past. He hadn't wanted to scare her away, because he had realized from the first that she could save his life.

* * *

He wasn't sure how long he'd been in the Devil's room, but he noticed that it got warmer as they spoke. Did Satan bring a little hell with him wherever he went? Smart tried to open a window, but Malcott laughed. "It's been painted shut for ages, Mr. Smart."

"All right, let's end this farce. What do you want with me?"

"You're a writer, are you not? Use your imagination."

"Let's see — it must be my soul, right?"

"Oh, come on!" Malcott almost sneered. "You can do better than that. Besides, I've got too many souls now — particularly scribes. No, I'd prefer to have Libby." He paused a moment before looking Smart in the eyes. "In the flesh."

Smart stared at him, but Malcott cooly returned his gaze. "She's a very attractive woman, Mr. Smart. You've done well to keep her to yourself all this time. But now, after all, you don't seem much interested in her. Maybe that's because there are more important things for you — maybe you'd like to produce that blockbuster novel you've been working toward. The publisher will set you up with any number of attractive escorts for the promotional tour, as you know."

"And maybe" — here he'd given Smart a look that froze his soul — "you'd like to see Perdita and tell her you're sorry. There may still be time to help her find the right path at this difficult juncture. I can assist you with all that, Mr. Smart — if you'll deliver Libby. It would be a simple matter, really. I can look like anyone — even a skyscraping fellow like you. I could take your place. No one would know but us. Think about it, Mr. Smart."

With that, Malcott had risen from behind the desk and shown him the door. Smart, too stunned to resist, had followed meekly but turned back just as the door was closing behind him. "When will you return?" he asked. There was no answer, and when he tried the door, he found it locked.

A few moments later, as he was walking toward his office, he heard his fax machine start up inside. But as the paper issued forth, it turned brown and curled up, then burst into flame. Strangely, though, the flames didn't harm the machine's plastic shell. A minute or so later another fax came through — this one on stationery that bore the name E. Finister Malcott. It read:

DAMNED HEAT-SENSITIVE PAPER!

I'll be back soon, Mr. Smart. I want to get some use out of my room, now that I've gone to so much trouble with it.

Smart poured himself a drink and tried to sort it all out: He had to find Perdita, there was no doubt of that. From what Malcott had said, it sounded almost as if she'd joined a cult of some sort. And he certainly couldn't consign Libby, his true love and savior, to the tender embraces of the foul fiend. He looked for his image in a large mirror across the room but didn't see it. He knew it was only because he was sitting down and the angle wasn't right, but it was still disconcerting. Was it some kind of omen?

Just then the phone rang at his elbow, causing him to start violently and his drink to slosh onto his crotch. A horrifyingly familiar voice boomed in his ear:

"Hello, your lordship, it's Roland Scaiffey! Remember us, back in New York? How goes it in the Emerald Isle?"

Smart didn't answer for a moment. It was too much — first Beelzebub, now Scaiffey, Smart's tax attorney.

"Hello, Roland," Smart said in as bluff a voice as he could muster. "You caught me having a few yokels drawn and quartered just for the sheer amusement of it. Can you hear their groaning in the background? Big babies, these Irish."

"Yes, I believe I can hear it, Trel," Scaiffey said in huge good humor. "You've got to show them who's boss, I suppose."

"Absolutely. Now what caused you to call here so bright and early New York time?"

"Well, I wish I could say it was good news, but it isn't. The IRS has named you to a list of tax delinquents and put out what's basically a warrant for your arrest should you come back to the States."

"A warrant for my arrest? The bastards! You *are* kidding, aren't you?"

"Well, it's not exactly the kind of warrant used for robbers and murderers, but ... they can detain you if you come back until they've had a chance to present a demand for back taxes. And they can get a court order to keep you here until the demand is answered."

Smart couldn't believe it. Scaiffey was telling him that if he tried to find Perdita, he risked losing what remained of his money — not to mention his freedom.

"Trel?"

"Yes, I'm here. I'm just having a hard time absorbing this. What can we do about it?"

"The main thing is, stay away from the States. Of course they've filed a lien against your rental property, and we're trying to prevent seizure, but ... well, if they catch you here they can hold you until you've posted bond in the full amount they're seeking. Then they've got you, Trel, because this case is already lost."

"But I have important business in the States, Roland. Can I call you if I need bail?"

"You can always call on us, Trel. You know that. But it would be better if you could have us or someone else take care of the business for you."

"Thanks for the thought, but this is something I have to do myself."

"Well, at least try to wait a while if you can — it would be good to let the warrant grow cold."

"I don't think I can wait. But thanks for the advice. I'll call you if I need help."

"Good luck, your lordship."

"Thanks," Smart said, frowning slightly at Scaiffey's little barb. "It looks like I'll need it."

Smart hung up, shaking his head. What else could go wrong?

He heard a car pull up to the back of the house and went to the kitchen window. Libby was back from shopping. He winced involuntarily at the mountain of packages in the back seat, but gave her a big smile at the door, where she pecked his lips and handed him some boxes and a copy of *The Irish Times*. Before going out to the car for the rest of her load, she said: "Check out the front page. It's something about taxes."

Smart scanned the headline: "Writer's tax bye eyed as red ink rises."

Sixteen

Smart didn't tell Libby what had happened; he thought she might try to have him committed. And although he couldn't say for sure that he didn't belong in an asylum, he had no desire to be sidetracked now. Aside from that, there was something so shameful about the whole business with Malcott that he didn't want to tell anyone about it, least of all Libby.

After all, if he hadn't been such a jerk in his younger days, the fiend would have had nothing on him and no way to pressure him to do anything. He certainly didn't want to tell Libby that an atrocity he'd committed some 20 years ago had put her in jeopardy of a new atrocity — perhaps the ultimate one.

Of course, he had to tell her that he would soon have to return to the States, and he did so. But he left out quite a bit.

"I had a phone call from Roland Scaiffey while you were out yesterday," he told her the next morning over coffee. She was absorbed in the gardening section of the newspaper and didn't look up.

"Oh?"

"Yes. He says he thinks we may have a chance to save the rental property in Tuscarora if we cut a deal on the income tax demand."

She put down the paper and stared at him. *Why is it,* she wondered, *that when he talks about income, it's always 'I,' but when the subject is income tax, it's alway 'we?'* She saw no point in voicing her thoughts just then, but she stored the question in her mental arsenal for possible future use. She had always left the tax maneuverings to him, but she knew enough to recognize that this represented a significant new wrinkle.

"Save the house? What did he mean by that?"

"Well, if we sell it now, the IRS will seize its value toward what they say we owe in income taxes. But since it's worth less now than what we paid for it, Scaiffey thinks it would be better to sell the property unencumbered, if possible, and try to take a write-off of the capital loss against the income tax liability."

She glazed over about half way through this explanation, which he'd been counting on.

"Sounds complicated. Are they sure about this idea?"

"They say it's our best shot to get a deal. But I'll have to go back to Tuscarora for a while." She gave him her laser eyes.

"You're going back? For how long? And what about your book? I thought you were making progress on it."

"Well," he said uncomfortably, "I've hit a bit of a block, and I may need to rethink the premise. In any case, it might do me some good to get out of here for a while, re-establish contact with a few people at Wordsworth — you know, Van and a few others — and just get my head cleared of this place for a while. It's been a very hectic five months, as you know."

"How long is 'a while'?" she asked, looking him full in the eyes. He didn't allow his own gaze to waver as he improvised.

"I really don't know, but Scaiffey thought a deal could be finalized in a month or so. Maybe less, with any luck."

"A month? That's a long time to be away. And where will you stay?"

"As luck would have it, my love, the upstairs apartment is vacant now, so I thought I'd stay right in Tuscarora on the days when I'm not required in New York."

Libby's eyes clouded as she thought of the svelte coeds who lived in the downstairs apartment. It was too easy to go astray, if you were so inclined, in a college town. "Can't you handle it by phone and fax?"

Smart smiled. "Impractical, my dear. This will involve a lot of negotiation, and the phone charges probably would cost at least as much as the airfare, if not more. Besides, I have a feeling that this will have to be done eyeball-to-eyeball to get the best deal. That's what Roland suggested, too," he said, playing his ace.

Libby wasn't fully convinced, but she had no professional opinion to put up against Scaiffey's. She'd had to trust Smart on his own before, and it looked like this would be another of those times. Although she'd never caught him in a dalliance, he often made too free with his eyes, and she wasn't a hundred percent sure of his fidelity. But she, too, had another card to play.

"What about this fiscal crisis over here? I haven't read much about it, but Bess McCaughey says it could mean higher taxes for everyone — even writers."

She said this last pointedly, as if to let him know she was well aware that his main reason for uprooting them and moving them across the ocean now seemed to be in jeopardy. She didn't lower the boom on him, however, and he thought he knew why: She was, when all was said and done, quite happy in Ireland. She'd found the ideal life for herself — riding, remodeling a grand old manse, organizing social events and hobnobbing with the local gentry. In fact, she was even beginning to speak with the hint of a brogue. She wasn't prepared to flail him with their problems just yet, but her forbearance could vanish in a heartbeat, Smart knew.

"Well, I've spoken to Hickey about that several times. He says it's nothing but talk. They've made noises about removing the writer's exemption before, but according to him it's too much a part of the Irish psyche to do away with."

Libby said nothing but seemed skeptical.

"Still," Smart continued, "I think it probably makes sense to try to tie up loose ends and get our house in order, so to speak, over there — in case things take a turn for the worse here. I mean, I'd be more inclined to hang tough with the IRS if I felt our tax position here was absolutely secure, but we probably should at least recognize the possibility that the exemption might be compromised at some point, even if temporarily. I think it would be a good idea to have the other situation behind us if that happens."

Libby sighed. "Well, go if you think it makes sense. But try not to stay away so long — I'll miss you. And running this place is a big job."

"I won't, my lovely bride. You know I can't stand to be away from you for long anyway. You have the lock to my key."

She smiled and blushed faintly, but went back to reading her paper without replying.

Great! Smart thought. *I've got her permission to go. But what the hell will I do when I get there?*

The first thing to do, he decided, was to try to get in touch with Perdita. He retired to his office and began the tedious process of calling information in the States, beginning with Billings, Montana. There was a listing for Serena Smale, but not for Lauretta. He punched in the number, his heart in his mouth. A bored-sounding male voice answered: "Yeah?"

"Hello. Is Lauretta Smale there?"

"Who?"

"Lauretta Smale. At least I think that's her name. Serena Smale's daughter."

"I don't know who you're talkin' about, man. Bye."

"No, wait," he said quickly. "This is a long-distance call. It's very important that I speak to Lauretta Smale."

"If you're talkin' about the tall chick who used to live here with her mother, she moved. I think she went back East to go to college. Wordsworth, I think it was."

"Wordsworth College?" Smart asked, beside himself. "Are you sure?"

"I'm not sure, man, but I think that was it. OK?"

"Thanks!" Smart heard himself burbling. "You've really helped a lot."

"Later, man." Then the line went dead.

Over the next several hours a plan began to hatch in Smart's mind. It was predicated on the idea that he'd need a lot of help — preferably from God rather than His opposite number, E. Finister Malcott.

After lunch, Smart went to his office and studied the stationery Malcott had faxed him. Underneath the name, the header read: "Voice or Fax: Dial all sixes." Smart dialed 666/666/66666 and waited. After two rings, he got a recording: "To access your life account, press 6 now. To leave a message for Mr. Malcott, press 66 now. To send a fax, press 666 and start now." Smart pressed 66 and said:

"It's Trelawny Smart. I need to speak to you ASAP. And by the way, what's with all the sixes?"

A short while later a fax appeared on Smart's machine:

Terribly busy with inductions — the platform collapsed at a political gathering. But will visit briefly tomorrow afternoon. As for the sixes, I just like them — the Hebrews were right about that!

— EFM

Smart smiled in spite of himself. His situation was beyond absurd, but now his ego was engaged. Clearly, contending with Malcott would be the supreme challenge. He dashed to the calendar in the kitchen, looked at the date and let out a long sigh of relief. Tomorrow was Libby's dressage day, and she would be riding all afternoon with her club on the far side of the Slieve Bloom hills. A perfect time for Malcott's visit.

Smart spent the rest of the day thinking about Perdita. He noticed a curious thing as he schemed and plotted: He was getting ready to put his money and freedom in jeopardy with hardly a second thought. Why would he do this for someone he didn't know and who represented such a painful chapter in his own life that he was loath to contemplate it? The answer, he decided, was the image of the baby he'd carried in his mind all these years — a sweet, tender face smiling up at him with unseeing eyes, trusting that he would be there for her. He never had been, but he would be now.

He'd driven out of her life nearly 20 years ago. He didn't know what kind of trouble she was in — did Malcott know more than he was telling? — and she might not cooperate in her own rescue. She might not even believe he was her father, and if she did, she probably would be more angry than relieved. But anger, Smart knew, was a powerful tool if you could get it focused in the right direction. And she just might respond to his honest longing to be the father he'd never been before.

In any case, he would have to find her and perhaps get her to come back to Ireland with him, which meant he'd have a hell of a lot of explaining to do when he got home. Maybe he could get Malcott to help in some way, Smart mused. How much mileage could he get from his lust for Libby without giving the Devil his due?

Smart spent most of the day in his study, playing computer games intermittently to make Libby think he was working on *Pagan Prince* again. He didn't come out for supper, although he was grateful for the food she left by the door, and ventured forth only after he heard Libby go up to bed. He continued brooding with the aid of a scotch in the living room, but the more he thought of the enormity of his task, the more discouraged he felt. He needed help, that was clear, but he couldn't ask Libby and he didn't want to run up his tab with Malcott if he could possibly avoid it. He stretched out on the couch, intending to rest for only a few moments before heading up to bed himself, but he soon fell asleep.

A few hours later he awoke with a familiar floral scent in his nostrils, and its name popped into his head: hyacinth. It was faint, almost a hint rather than the thing itself, but it was real enough to him, and it made him think of Lady B. *She must be in the house,* he thought as he stirred awake. He looked around the room — the room in which they'd met in what now seemed increasingly like another lifetime — but saw no one. With the hyacinth leading him by the nose, he found himself mounting the stairs and following the second-floor hallway around a corner to the door that led to the attic. It was slightly ajar, and he could see a dim light at the top of the stairs. He also heard voices — quiet voices in murmured conversation rather than the angry, violent exchanges he'd heard before. The scent was stronger here, and he decided to go up.

The sound of talk from above ceased as the first step creaked from his weight, but he kept going — if Lady B. was in the house, he knew he had nothing to fear from her. As his head rose above the level of the third floor, he saw an antique table with an oil lamp on it. Seated at the table were a man and woman in Georgian attire — the man was bald on top but had longish, straggly hair and a pinched face. The woman was more substantially built and had a shawl on her shoulders and a slightly seedy flounce cap on her head. They were a picture of 18th-century gentry at home. Behind them, just out of the full glow of the light, stood Lady B.

Smart bumped his head on the low ceiling when he got to the top of the stairs, and Lady B. laughed.

"It seems we're doomed never to meet without your bumping your poor head, Mr. Smart!" She swept forward into the light, and held out her hand. She was wearing the same dress she'd worn when they met.

Smart smiled involuntarily and bent to kiss her hand, surprised at the fleshly feel of it. It wasn't warm, however, as it had been five months before.

"You're amazed to see me here, aren't you, Mr. Smart? Well, have no fear — I won't be expecting free room and board. I'm just back for a little visit."

"You can stay as long as you like," Smart said, as if bantering with a ghost were the most natural thing in the world. But her signature scent was real, as were the musical tones of her voice in his ears. And Lady B. looked every bit as alive as on that enchanted night they'd met. Now, after his encounter in the Devil's room, he was far less skeptical about things.

Lady B. smiled graciously, then indicated the seated lady and gentleman with a sweep of her arm. The man stood up.

"This is Randolph Atkinson, the first Lord Brimston, Mr. Smart, and his wife, Althea, the first Lady Brimston. They built Mordalee and lived here ... from 1783 through about 1826, wasn't it?" she said, turning to the dour Lord Brimston. He nodded brusquely. "Quite right. Very pleased to meet you, sir."

He extended a gnarled hand to Smart, who found himself bowing slightly as he shook it. "The pleasure is mine, my lord." Now his wife stood and extended her hand across the table.

"Very pleased, m'am," said Smart as he kissed her fleshy hand.

"Mr. Smart," she said as she smiled briefly and nodded her head.

"I suppose you're wondering what we're doing rattling about in your attic, Mr. Smart," said the last Lady B., smiling conspiratorially.

"Well, my attic is your attic," said Smart somewhat lamely, trying to gauge the mood of the two unsmiling apparitions who had sat down again at the table. "I'm glad to have any former Brimstons here in their ancestral home." He regretted saying "former" as soon as it was out of his mouth.

Lord Brimston cleared his throat as if to inform Smart that while his sentiments were appreciated, nothing further need be said. The senior Lady B. smiled at Smart quickly and nodded her head, then looked at the junior Lady B.

"We are much obliged indeed, Mr. Smart," she said, as if picking up a cue. "But we are gathered here with a specific purpose in mind and don't intend to tarry. You see ... we've got wind of your encounter with Mr. Malcott."

Here she paused as Lord Brimston scowled and a flash of anger seemed to leap the ether between his eyes and those of his wife. She cleared her throat in turn. Staring at her husband, whose eyes now were fixed on his hands, which he'd folded in front of him on the table, she said:

"We should like to help you if possible, Mr. Smart."

Seventeen

It was about 11:30 in the morning when Libby Smart left Mordalee, ostensibly to run some errands in Dergh. She did have a few groceries and other items on her list, but her main mission had to do with Fegan Fergus, and she thought she had a pretty good idea of where to find him. Her pupils widened as she went from the unusually bright sunshine outdoors into the dimness of The Drowning Man, but even before her eyes had fully adjusted, she spotted Fergus on a stool across the bar from Seamus Gall. He was just about to nip into his first Guinness of the day.

"Ah, Fegan," Libby said brightly as she settled in next to him. "Having a late breakfast, I see." Turning to the smiling but somewhat nonplussed barkeep, she added, "I'll have black coffee, Seamus, if you have such a thing at this hour. Or tea if you don't."

Gall said he could have coffee in a moment or two if she could wait, and at her nod he bustled off to the back room to set up the coffee maker. Libby turned to the gingerly sipping Fergus and fixed him with her most businesslike stare.

"Top of the morning to you, Mrs. Smart," he said.

"Fegan," she said, "I was hoping to have a word with you."

"Oh? What about?"

"Travel. Mr. Smart is going to New York soon, and I want you to go with him."

Fergus coughed a bit as his stout went down the wrong pipe.

When he had regained his composure, he said: "You want me to go with him, is it?"

"Yes. I'm worried about him."

"Well, then ... why don't you go with him, if I might ask?"

"I can't. I've got to stay and run Mordalee. And besides, I wasn't invited. It's supposed to be a business trip — taxes and real estate and so on. I have no intention of getting caught up in that ball of wax. But I think he may need someone to help him. Almost like a secret agent."

"Is he ... in some danger, then?"

"Not physical danger, I don't think. But he's been acting strangely lately, and I know there's something on his mind — something he can't or won't tell me about. I've got a feeling he'll need a helping hand while he's in New York, Fegan. And," she added slowly, "I ... feel I'd like to have some 'eyes and ears' over there."

It was Fegan's turn to be nonplussed. This secret agent business sounded a lot like garden-variety marital spying. "But — ."

"And I'm prepared to pay for your airfare and your time. This is important to me."

"I see," said Fergus, warming to the possibility. Since real-estate sales had dried up, his creditors were like a pack of hounds on his heels.

They paused for a moment as Gall brought the Bewley's dark roast, whose strong aroma had filled the place while they spoke. Fegan insisted on paying, and Libby complimented the barkeep on his coffee before he went off to pour a draught for another early bird.

"Business been a bit slow lately?" Libby asked.

"Dead is more like it. There's not a thing selling in this market. But ... what exactly do you think Mr. Smart will be encountering in the States? Should I plan on packing some heat?"

Libby had to suppress a guffaw at the thought of Fergus shadowing Smart with a revolver in his pocket. "Nothing like that!" she said. "And where would you get heat in the first place, if I might ask?"

"All things can be had at the right price, Mrs. Smart," Fergus said oracularly. "There's such a thing as the black market, you know."

"Well, I wouldn't want you consorting with crooks in Dub, Fegan. No, I don't think there'll be any need for a gun. I just have a feeling he may need help. Maybe only moral support. Someone to be on his side. God, I'm babbling. I don't know ... it may turn out to be nothing but an opportunity for you to do some sightseeing and make some money."

"And is he to know that I'll be, you know — guarding his back, then?"

"No — he'd never admit he needs help. We'll have to work it out so that he doesn't know you'll be there for that purpose."

"I still don't understand," Fegan said, wiping the clay-colored foam off his top lip. "What exactly is it you want me to do?"

"Just try to stick with him once you're both over there. And let me know if you think he's in any kind of trouble. In other words ... ."

"Spy on him for you?"

Libby blushed. "Not exactly. It's for his own good, Fegan. Something's wrong, there's no doubt in my mind. He's trying to handle something by himself, but he may need help. If I'm wrong, you get a paid vacation in the states. If I'm right, you let me know and I'll fly over, too, if need be. The important thing is to provide him with some back-up."

Fergus was quiet for a moment or two, digesting this strange offer from a woman he didn't know very well.

"Have you ever been to the States?" Libby asked.

"No, I haven't. But it's a grand country, and I've always wanted to go. I have a cousin near Albany in New York State, come to think of it."

"Do you really? Well, well. That's not far from Tuscarora Falls. A visit to your cousin might be the perfect cover."

Fergus looked thoughtful, and Libby bought him another round. They settled on his fee — 300 pounds a week for his time, plus round-trip airline tickets and 100 pounds expense money — and she left, swearing him to secrecy. She'd seen Gall looking at them with interest several times and knew that if Fergus breathed a word of their deal to him it would be all over town by the end of the day.

Fergus promised to say nothing of their bargain to Gall. "I'll put him off the trail with a story about you wanting to look at some pasture land," he said.

"Excellent. Actually, we could do some looking before you go to reinforce that story." Then she gave him a conspiratorial look and added: "But I won't be doing any buying until prices have come down more."

He winced, and they laughed.

Libby gave him a thankful look, patted his hand quickly but meaningfully and said she'd contact him soon with more details. "Goodbye, Seamus," she called as she left.

A moment later, Gall's large, ruddy face was no more than six inches from Fergus's. "So, you rotten dog, you're getting your leg over the lady of the manor, yeah? Don't deny it, now, the look of love was in her eye."

"Now Seamus, lad, I am the champion swordsman of these parts, as you know" — here Gall's brow clouded — "but in this case it's all as innocent as new lambs gamboling about the fields. A matter of fields exactly, in fact. She wants to look at some pasture land at the end of town, now."

"Pasture my arse! You're plowing a furrow, there's no doubt of it, and it's not in anyone's land."

Fergus and Gall went back and forth in this manner for some time, Fergus's face reddening in inverse proportion to his actual innocence. He couldn't give Gall or anyone else the real story; and it was flattering to be thought such a stud that as handsome a woman as Libby would succumb to his charms. What harm would there be if Gall got the wrong message, as long as he didn't tumble on the truth?

By the time Fergus left The Drowning Man a few hours later, an equivocal smile plastered on his face, he was being roundly toasted as the first Ballymorda man to bed the Yankee Duchess.

Eighteen

Ralph Karlin, a balding man who owned a real estate agency in Tuscarora Falls, was reluctant to let Lauretta Smale pose as a rental agent for the Smart property when she'd called him about it. So she decided to get in his face.

"Mr. Karlin," she said when they were seated in his cramped office, "we've had a tip that the owner of 114 Cattaraugus Street is coming back to the United States. We don't know why, but we want to find out. And this position would give me the perfect cover to make contact with him."

"But, Miss —" Karlin stammered.

"Mizz," Lauretta corrected. "Mizz Smale." Her gaze was steady, and her skirt was short and tight. She could see Karlin was having a hard time focusing.

"Yes, well, I'm not sure about this. I work for Mr. Smart, not for the IRS ... ."

"Mr. Karlin," Lauretta said, "we would very much appreciate your cooperation in this case. We're sure that you, as a law-abiding citizen whose tax records probably could withstand any level of scrutiny, wish along with us that all taxpayers would fulfill their obligations as you have. Don't you wish that, Mr. Karlin?"

She'd caught him eyeing her breasts, and he was clearly flustered as he looked up quickly to meet her gaze. Lauretta smiled. It was so simple to make boobs of men.

"Well, of course, whatever you say." His tone was resentful, but he'd gotten the message and didn't want his own books audited. "I suppose we could arrange for you to ... represent us to Mr. Smart."

"Good," Lauretta said, smiling. "Can you get me a blazer with your logo on it?" When she stood up and took off her own jacket, thrusting her shoulders back in the process, she caught Karlin checking her out again. But she didn't mind; she'd gotten what she wanted.

* * *

Later, as she lay in her hotel bed, she marveled at her new life. If someone had predicted a few months ago that she would become a special agent for the IRS lying in wait for her own father based on a tip from someone in Ireland, she would have said: *Give me a break!* But it was the fulfillment of a longtime ambition. She'd always wanted to nail Trelawny Smart.

Her mother had tried to suppress her own bitterness toward Smart, especially in front of her, but it would seep out in small, almost imperceptible ways at times, and the salt taste of it had flavored Lauretta's childhood. There was the time the repo man had come to drive away their car, when she was nine. The man's timing couldn't have been worse, from Lauretta's standpoint: She'd invited some friends over for a play tea party, and one of them, a doctor's little princess, simply couldn't understand how someone could just show up and drive off with the family car, perfectly legally.

"Aren't you going to call the police, Serena?" she kept asking as Lauretta kept her eyes on her mother and Serena tried to keep her composure. Middle-class moms, Serena knew, did not throw fits and fling housewares at tradesmen. She'd pounded her fist on the kitchen counter and said nothing but "Damn him!" Only Lauretta knew that she meant her own absent father, not the repo man.

Finally, to shush her friend and regain some semblance of control,

Lauretta had announced: "I'm sure it's all a big mistake. We'll get our car back tomorrow."

But they hadn't gotten the car back the next day or any day, and Serena had had to take cabs and cadge rides from friends when they needed to get somewhere they couldn't walk to. Her mother had done her best by her, Lauretta knew, but she hadn't finished college and simply didn't qualify for jobs much better than waitress and, later, clerk at the college — a big step up because of the benefits, which included free tuition for Lauretta when she came of age.

It wasn't exactly as if Smart had willfully denied them a car and a shot at a normal life — the one thing a child craves above all other things. Lauretta knew that Smart had tried to get in touch and that her mother had spurned him. She also came to realize, as she grew up, that Serena could have gone after her father for child support but chose not to — she would rot in hell, she said, before accepting a dime from him. So she knew it was at least partially Serena's fault that they were always living one step ahead of eviction notices and bill collectors. But it was hard to blame Serena; in all other ways, she'd been an excellent mother: patient and kind but also firm and dependable. And Smart had been the missing element from which all others seemed to flow. At the very least he'd cheated her out of having a dad, a loss she felt sorely many times, although she'd never confided that to anyone but her raggedy stuffed animals.

And in her gut she understood and completely agreed with Serena's soul-deep, smoldering hatred of Smart. He'd dishonored her, used her as a public convenience and turned her young life into ashes. He deserved to be punished.

Such thoughts brought on the familiar symptoms she'd felt for so many years: cold sweat forming on her neck and brow, clammy palms and a tightening in the pit of her stomach. It was coming again, right on schedule — the hazy but sharp-as-glass memory of the day

Serena had left her, at age 7, with the man who had become her steady boyfriend. He had a handsome, good-humored face, although Lauretta usually blotted it out in her memories. What she couldn't blot out, though, was the feel of his humid breath on her neck like a jungle breeze.

Serena had always regarded a man's conduct with her only precious child as a kind of acid test — if he was "good with kids," she'd consider having a relationship with him. If not, it was "hit the road."

This man had been good with Lauretta from the start. He had an easy smile and a generous, open-handed manner that had begun to make Serena think he might be a candidate not only to become Lauretta's stepdad but the father of more children as well. He had a steady job with the county and showed himself to be a kindly and responsible man for several months before the day when Serena, desperate for a babysitter, had asked him to watch Lauretta for an afternoon.

He'd played frisbee with her in the yard, then pushed her on the swing — higher and higher, his hands propelling her little rump upwards. It had been the first time he'd put his hands anywhere but on her shoulders, but Lauretta was enjoying this quality time with the man who seemed like the dad she'd never had, and she didn't take it amiss. When she jumped off the swing, he took her by the hand and led her inside the Smales' aging mobile home for Kool-Aid. But then things had started to get weird. The man's smile took on an increasingly fixed, glazed cast, and he fumbled with his zipper before insisting that she sit on his lap while he told her a story.

The story was about a jackrabbit named Peter who liked to pop up out of his burrow. "Go ahead," the man said, holding her tightly on his lap, "touch him. He won't bite. You can even kiss him."

Serena, acting on a premonition, had hurried home just in time to prevent contact. She hustled him out of the house — and out of her life

— immediately. She almost called the police, but felt too vulnerable to risk turning him into an enemy with a grudge. Lauretta had been left feeling like she needed a bath, but no matter how much scrubbing she did that night, she still felt the same way. Serena took her to a head doctor, a cold, businesslike woman who had asked her some questions and then told Serena that the girl appeared to be fine.

Serena always felt that it was her own inability to pay the going rate for therapy that had produced a clean bill of health so rapidly, but whether or not that was the case, she didn't notice Lauretta acting differently after her close encounter with adult lust. Serena gradually quit worrying about the incident amid the myriad daily crises that made up the fabric of their lives. But Lauretta had never forgotten. The waves of chills washing over her now, 13 years later, were a testament to how close she felt she'd come to being raped, sodomized or worse.

Serena had been much more leery of men after that, never letting anyone too close and dooming herself to an abstemious life. It had made her sad and unfulfilled and intensely lonely at times, but it was a sacrifice she was more than willing to make if it helped ensure that her daughter would never again face such a threat.

As for Lauretta, the incident had left her cold and skittish toward men, an attitude that was confirmed by the few encounters she'd had with horny but clumsy boys in high school and college. As far as she could tell, she was better off without men now. Let them pant after her; it made them easier to manipulate. As for the smiling man who'd tousled her hair and pushed her so high on the swing that long-ago afternoon, she didn't really blame him for what had happened, or for what he apparently was contemplating. She blamed her absent father.

Nineteen

"He's a cunning villain, Mr. Smart, and you would do well to remember that!"

The first Lord Brimston looked to his wife for support, but she looked away, as if to say: "And you were a fool to utter the oath that let him into our lives." As Smart and the three Brimstons conversed, Smart found out the answer to the question he'd wondered about ever since being awakened by the brawling in the attic: The first lord and lady had been arguing that night, as they had periodically for almost 200 years, over whose fault it was that Malcott had ever gotten the rights to the Devil's room.

The last Lady B., ever tactful, cleared her throat discreetly.

"We must remember, your lordship, that while he is undoubtedly a villain, Malcott is also a formidable adversary who has given us all scores to settle with him. As for my own," she said, "who but Malcott could have motivated my beloved Thomas to abandon me?"

Smart used this opening to bring up his own dilemma — how could he get Malcott's help with Lauretta without sacrificing Libby?

"I would never depend on help from Malcott, Mr. Smart," said the first Lady Brimston. "He might seem to offer assistance, but everything he does will have but one end: to catch you more firmly in his snares and make you more completely his slave."

"In order to get rid of him," Lord Brimston interjected, "I had to agree to hand him down generation to generation in my family like a curse. All from what seemed a harmless request of his: a clause in the deed ceding that small part of the room to him in perpetuity."

"Why didn't my lawyer notice that clause?" Smart asked.

"Only the owner of Mordalee can see it," Lord Brimston answered. "It's not visible to anyone else."

Here the last Lady B. looked fretful and apologetic. "I was quite ignorant of it, Mr. Smart, since I inherited the property and never looked over the deed. I feel so awful when I think that I led you into this trap!"

Before Smart could utter the forgiveness that was on the tip of his tongue — it was he, after all, who'd torn down the door — Lord Brimston cleared his throat significantly.

"There is a sort of 'escape clause' in the perpetual lease with Malcott, Mr. Smart," he intoned. "If you can trick him into going back whence he came directly from that room, he can't come back to Mordalee, and the lease is null and void."

"But how can he go back directly?" Smart asked. "There's only one door, and it leads to the bedroom."

"When next you're in that room, Mr. Smart, observe carefully. You'll find that there are always at least two exits wherever he is, although one may not be immediately apparent. Get him to use that second door, and he can't come back. Or so I am told."

Brimston didn't seem inclined to reveal his source, and Smart didn't press him. An escape hatch — it made sense that the conniving Malcott would always have one.

"Above all, Mr. Smart," said the senior Lady B., "recall that in spite of his awesome powers, Malcott also has grave weaknesses. He is by nature a common liar and a scoundrel, for all his learned airs, and although he is a master at controlling people through their baser impulses, he, too, can be manipulated."

"What do you mean?" asked Smart, sitting forward in his seat and fixing the apparition with a keen stare. Averting her eyes and shifting uncomfortably, she admitted that she didn't know exactly how to pull Malcott's strings. "But look at what he's asked of you, Mr. Smart. He's a slave to his lusts, which is why he was cast down in the first place. You must consider how to use his brutish nature to your own ends."

"And I think, too," the junior Lady B. added, "that he perhaps looks more formidable than he actually is."

Smart looked at her quizzically. "Formidable? I'd say so. Aside from being able to create something out of nothing, he seems to know everything."

"Exactly," said Lady B. "*Seems* to know. I believe he is a master of appearing to hold all the cards. But does he really? Or isn't that a way of gaining an advantage over his victims?"

"You mean you doubt his powers?" said Smart.

"I doubt they are quite what they appear. His greatest power is that of deception, of creating what seem to be inevitabilities. In the end, though, he must have your acquiescence. You must agree to do what he seeks. He can't make you do it. You can, in fact, put him behind you. But to the extent that you don't believe you can do that, you won't try. And then he's won."

"He's ... what? A manipulator, then? A charlatan and confidence man?"

"A con artist of the very highest order, Mr. Smart," Lady B. sighed. "The original of that ilk. He's a genius at reading people, and at directing them — setting the stage so that the script he gives them seems the only possible course. But you have a choice. You don't have to do whatever he says. You can, as Lady Brimston said, turn the tables on him."

Smart closed his eyes for a moment and sat back to mull these startling ideas. He opened them after what seemed like only a few seconds, but he felt he must have fallen asleep again, because the scene had changed. The first light of dawn was glimmering tentatively through the attic window, the lamp was out and the three spirits were gone. Had he dreamed them all? *No*, he thought, sniffing the air and smiling. The scent of hyacinths had not faded entirely. Looking down at the table in front of him, he saw a note on a small piece of old, peach-colored bond. He held it up to the weak light and squinted as he read: "You have a devilish side — we all do. Beat him at his own game!"

He gingerly made his way downstairs, exhausted but hopeful.

Twenty

Smart paced, cursed quietly and checked his watch, afraid he'd made a terrible mistake in depending on Fergus for a ride to the airport. But there was no good train connection from Ballymorda to Shannon, and he hadn't wanted to bother Libby with driving him back and forth, so Fergus had seemed the logical choice. The estate agent had cheerfully assented, surprising him with plans of his own to visit a long-lost cousin in New York's Capital region. In fact, Smart was doubly amazed to find out that they had booked seats on the same flight over. But now, in the brittle light of early morning, he was sure they both would be late.

Just as he was about to go back in the house and call the pub, Fergus's black Rover came tearing up the drive in a cloud of dust and gravel. Smart put his bags in the back seat, climbed in and was about to growl something when he noticed the self-satisfied grin on Fergus's face. He thought: *Why bother?* Being late was just Fergus's way of relating to the world, and besides, he was doing Smart a big favor — assuming they got to the airport on time. Still, his companion's carelessness — as evidenced by the big bandage on his left little finger — made Smart uneasy.

His fears proved groundless, however. Traffic was relatively light on the N7 in Roscrea, Nenagh and even Limerick that morning, and Fergus displayed a knack for getting them out of incipient jams, skillfully passing tinker caravans, tanker trucks and livestock wagons and making excellent use of short cuts. They had time to spare when they got to Shannon, and Smart was in a much better mood.

After they had checked their luggage and gotten their boarding passes, they walked over to the lounge, whose styling, like that of the whole building, was straight from the late '50s. With summer tourist season still some weeks off, the lounge and the airport were largely empty, and the staff went about their business with an unhurried air.

The two hadn't talked much in the car — Smart had found Fergus's driving unnerving, if effective, and he'd been preoccupied anyway with his half-baked plans for finding Perdita. Now, however, he felt the need to mellow out. The die was cast, he'd do what he could when he got to Tuscarora and there was a bit of time to kill. Who better to kill time with than Fergus?

"This cousin of yours," Smart said as they settled into their seats with their drinks, "have you ever met him? Do you correspond?"

"He's not exactly a cousin, Mr. Smart. More like a once- or twice-removed relation on my mother's side. We've never met, but I've spoken to him a few times when his family called at Christmas time. It's always been a matter of a great many longings to visit being expressed and invitations being extended and promises being made, but ... well, you know how it is, Mr. Smart: easier to promise than to do. In any case, he once urged me personally to come over and visit him, and I said I would. He lives in a place called CO-hoes, I believe. Odd-sounding name," the man from Ballymorda added with no trace of irony.

"Oh, you mean Co-HOES," Smart laughed. "Just north of Albany. Dutch, like many names in that area."

"Dutch, is it? And why would there be Dutch names there, now?"

"They were the first European settlers in that area, following the lead of Henry Hudson himself in the *Half Moon*. In fact, that's the name of another town near Albany ... ."

The Knickerbocker history lesson went on for a while, until Fergus excused himself in favor of the men's room. While Smart was sitting alone, he heard a loud impact and a sharp cry of pain from the general vicinity of the lavatories. Then he saw what seemed to be a related commotion, as security personnel and paramedics scrambled through the lobby toward the restrooms.

* * *

Malcott had been watching Smart and Fergus from a dim corner of the bar, and when he saw Fergus get up, he followed him after a few moments. Inside the men's room, Malcott did nothing but comb his hair and wash his hands as Fergus stood at a urinal. If anyone else had come in, he might have noticed two odd things: The man washing in front of the mirror looked exactly like the man at the urinal; and he cast no reflection in the mirror. But no one else entered. While Fergus was still zippering his fly, Malcott dried his hands quickly and walked out, waiting just beyond the heavy wooden door. When he heard Fergus's footsteps approaching from the other side, he pushed the door inward with perfect timing and stunning force, catching the estate agent on the forehead and knocking him out. When Malcott joined Smart a few moments later, he regarded him intently, seemingly more interested in Smart's reaction to himself than to the incident playing itself out near the men's room. His eyes — light blue, like Fergus's, but different somehow — searched Smart's.

"What's all that commotion about, Fegan?" Smart asked him.

"Freak accident, I think, Mr. Smart. Someone apparently hit his head on the door on the way out of the men's. The medics and Gardai are attending to him now."

Smart looked over toward the men's room door, some 20 yards away, and then scrutinized Fergus closely. "He must have been right behind you, eh?"

"It would appear so. There was one other man at a stall while I was in there; it must have been him. But I finished before him, and my back was turned when it happened."

Odd, thought Smart. *Fergus doesn't seem quite himself somehow.* But he couldn't specify the difference, if in fact there was any, and he chalked it up to the effect of his companion's somewhat unnerving experience.

They both looked toward the men's room, where a man was being carried away on a stretcher. From that distance, and with all the police and medics surrounding him, they couldn't make out his features. But he appeared to be tall, thin and red-haired. *Not unlike Fergus himself,* Smart noted mentally.

Nor could they hear the Garda sergeant as he used his walkie-talkie to report to the stationhouse in Limerick that they were assisting a man who seemed to have given himself a nasty bump on the head and would be taking him to the emergency room at the hospital. The victim wasn't able to speak, the Garda said, but the papers in his wallet identified him as one Fegan Fergus, estate agent of Ballymorda, County Dergh.

* * *

Later that day, while Smart was still suspended somewhere out over the Atlantic, Libby picked up the phone and dialed The Drowning Man. She'd been thinking about making this call ever since she'd gotten up, long after Smart had gone.

"Pub," a man's voice growled into her ear after several rings.

"Seamus Gall?"

"The same. And who would this be, now?"

"Libby Smart. I know you're probably busy setting up for dinner, but could you spare a minute to talk?"

"Of course, of course, Mrs. Smart," Gall boomed. "I'd always have a minute and more for you. What can I do for you, then?"

"Well, I'd like to get some work done on Mordalee. Mr. Smart will be away for awhile, and I was hoping to be able to surprise him with a finished job when he gets back."

"What kind of job, Missus?"

"Do you remember that funny little room on the second floor? The one that's called the Devil's room? I want to take that silly wall down and remodel it."

There was silence on the line. Then Libby continued: "Mr. Smart told me all about how you and Mr. Shaughnessy gave him such a hard time about doing the job last week, and I assumed you were putting him on. You *were* putting him on, weren't you, Seamus?"

Here, Gall knew, was his defining moment: stud or coward? The Yankee Duchess was giving him an entree to her home while her husband was away, but the price of admission was steep: a possible meeting with the lord of the underworld. Steep, that is, unless it could be finessed. Gall had no desire to tear down the legendary wall — like all the locals, its tale had been a staple of his childhood, and old women had made the sign of the cross or muttered over their rosaries at its every mention — but he had a strong desire to get intimate with the smashing Mrs. Smart. And if Fergus could have his way with her, as the publican believed he had, why shouldn't the great Seamus Gall?

"Oh, he didn't take that seriously, did he, Missus? Of course we were having a bit of sport with him that day, no offense intended. I'd be glad to come out to Mordalee today and take a look at it, if you'd like."

"So soon? That would be very good of you, Seamus," said Libby. "What time shall I expect you?"

"I'll get someone to watch the till for me and be out almost directly, if that will do."

Twenty-one

Lauretta Smale sat in her rented, cherry-red Taurus at a light on Broad Street in Tuscarora Falls, and looked up to see, once again, the grinning visage of Gloryanna Green, self-proclaimed real-estate diva of the Racing City. This time it was on a passing truck, but it didn't seem to matter where you looked in this little burg, you couldn't get away from Gloryanna. Lauretta frowned slightly and goosed the accelerator when the light changed a moment later. Then she looked down at her fawn-and-maroon Karlin Realty jacket and had to smile in spite of herself. Absurd as it was, Old Glory, as she was sarcastically known among local realtors, was pissing her off.

Gloryanna claimed to be the most successful real-estate agent in town, if not in the universe, and her ads implied that sellers of property in Tuscarora Falls had to be fools to waste their time listing with anyone else. Lauretta, whose socially and financially tenuous childhood had reacted with her proud nature to make her fiercely competitive, would have loved to move a property or two while she wore Karlin's colors just to stuff it in Gloryanna's face. And Karlin had told her that she could represent his agency as a salesperson during her "temporary assignment," even though she didn't have a broker's license and wouldn't be entitled to a full commission. "If you help us sell something," he'd laughed with enough condescension to make Lauretta want to stuff him, too, "we'll work out some way to supplement your government pay." A savvy businessman, he knew that the sight of Lauretta around town in a Karlin jacket would have a tonic effect on his trade all by itself.

Just then her cell phone rang. She quickly pulled off the congested street and found a spot in the tiny municipal lot next to Diamond Jim's restaurant, a favorite with the racing crowd when the horses were running. "Hello," she said after throwing the gear lever into park.

"Ms. Smale?"

That voice; odd, flat somehow, with the trace of a generically British accent. It was her informant, the man who'd told her he was calling from Ireland and that Smart would be returning to the States, probably to Tuscarora Falls.

"Lauretta Smale here. Where the devil are you?" She heard a dry chuckle.

"On our way, your package and me. I'll make the delivery soon."

"But ... ."

"I'll call you when we're in your neighborhood, Ms. Smale. Have no fear; he's here. And he'll soon be there. But I'll have to be a bit sparing with information until I've obtained my ... commission." He laughed without mirth. "Just a precaution, of course. I hope you understand."

"You'll get your reward, Mr. Malcott. When will I hear from you again?"

"Soon, Ms. Smale, soon. Don't worry."

The line went dead. Her expensive, government-issue phone had a caller ID feature, but it seemed to have gone on the fritz: The return number on the screen was 666/666/6666. She frowned, pressed the dial-back button but got a recorded message to the effect that there was no such number or area code. Frustrated and even slightly flustered for some reason she couldn't quite pinpoint, she checked her rear-view mirror before backing out of her parking spot. There, directly behind her and framed in miniature, was a poster with a smirking face over a picture of a playing card levitating out of a deck and a message in large block letters: "Need an Ace? Put Glory on the Case!"

* * *

Seamus Gall, eyes out for Libby, pulled up to Mordalee at about 8 p.m. in his old but reasonably respectable Citroen half-van. It was a very useful vehicle, with its spacious cab and short pickup bed in the back, but it wasn't quite the thing for grand arrivals, and he'd briefly considered borrowing or renting something a bit more showy. But since the mistress of the manor was nowhere to be seen as he got out, he was just as glad he hadn't gone to the expense. Besides, it had taken some doing to arrange for help at The Drowning Man on such short notice. But he'd managed it, and he had a strong feeling his efforts would be well rewarded.

Libby had been roosting among the armadillos, about thirty yards away, when he pulled into the wide courtyard, and now she popped up in their pen and hailed him: "Just go in, Seamus. You know where it is, don't you?"

"Yes indeed," he called in response, swinging toward the front door. "I'll just have a look at it, then."

She thought it a bit odd that he would be willing to work so late in the day, but since the long spring days of Ireland provided plentiful light until 10 or even 10:30 — and since Gall was known to be extremely enterprising — she assumed he was just trying to make hay while the sun shone. Still, there was a missing element.

"Where are your tools?" she called, seeing him empty-handed.

"Oh, I always carry me power tool, don't you worry," he yelled in return, pausing in the doorway to grin at her. She shook her head and grinned quizzically, but he didn't repeat his answer. If she had been a bit closer, she might well have wondered about that ardent, somewhat lewd smile, and about the lavish application of gold chain on the publican's neck, chain which, he thought, set off to perfection

·147·

the thick, manly expanse of rusty chest hair that spilled from the open top of his pearlescent rayon disco shirt.

"I'll be with you in a few minutes — I'm just going to hop in the shower first," Libby called, well aware that she needed some freshening after consorting with her somewhat fragrant pets. She'd gotten used to their sharp scent long ago, but she knew that most people — particularly Irish people — considered them hard-shelled skunks.

"Take your time, Missus," Gall called expansively, "take your time!" He smiled and waved like a teen heartthrob before disappearing into the house. The thought of Libby taking a shower — peeling the blouse off her magnificent torso, smoothly dropping her slacks and panties before stepping out of them, laving her long limbs and full breasts, suds collecting in the profundity of her cleavage, the pert and delectable nipples at full attention — all these images and more worked powerfully on his imagination and caused a pleasurable stirring in his pants. They also helped confirm, in his mind, that she was available. Why else would she tell him that she would soon be naked and wet and in his general proximity?

He practically gloated as he climbed the stairs, like a miser who'd just found an abandoned cache of gold. Would she come out of the bathroom in a sheer silk robe that clung to her moist skin, fresh and smoldering and ready to get all sweaty again? He could almost feel those long legs tightening around his back and had to stop for a moment to keep himself from rushing to her directly. There was supposed to be some thrill in the chase, but, like most men, he was more than ready to cut to the kill.

"Steady, lad, steady," he said softly to himself.

Twenty-two

Smart tapped on the glass of the phone booth, pointing to his watch. Fergus nodded, spoke for another moment or two, and then hung up. It was the second call Fergus had made, and Smart was anxious to get back on the road.

"Me cousin, Mr. Smart," he said as they walked toward their rental car, which was parked at a rest stop on the Massachusetts Turnpike. "We got cut off the first time, so I had to call back. He's called Roddy Fakem. He's a singer, or so he claims, and he's performing tonight at a place named The Iron Horse over in Northhampton, which is on our way, more or less. Do you fancy stopping to hear him?"

"Well, no, not really," Smart muttered. He wanted to get to Tuscarora Falls as soon as possible. But he also felt a countervailing sense that it might not be a bad idea to proceed cautiously, or perhaps circuitously. They'd had what had seemed a close call coming through Customs, and he wasn't sure it would be wise to follow a predictable travel pattern or mount a direct frontal assault.

"We'll need to stop for supper anyway, and according to this map," Fergus said, waving the one he'd gotten from the rental agency and had been referring to in the phone booth, "we should be arriving at Northhampton around supper time. Roddy said we could get a bite to eat there, and that they wouldn't charge us admission because he would tell them we're coming as his guests."

"Oh?" said Smart. "That was very considerate of him. What kind of stuff does he sing?"

"Irish music, he says."

"Do you like Irish music, Fegan?"

"Well, I wouldn't know, Mr. Smart." Fergus grinned as they got into the car they'd rented in his name, but which Smart was driving. "I only listen to jazz and Delta blues, myself. Robert Johnson — he's my main man."

As they motored west through the midsection of Massachusetts, Smart pondered his almost surreptitious return to the land of his birth. He didn't feel like an Irishman in America, that was for sure. Yet he didn't feel totally like a returning native, either. His identity, he realized, was stuck somewhere between Boston and Limerick.

He also regarded Fergus furtively whenever he had a chance. And he had many chances, because his companion seemed to be on autopilot for much of the trip. He wasn't asleep, but he sat so still and stared so fixedly in front of him that Smart had the impression he wasn't really there at all.

It was but another part of a strange pattern. There was something different in his voice, his bearing — even his looks, which seemed to have undergone a subtle upgrade. His hair appeared thicker and more lustrous, his chin ineffably firmer, the cut of his jaw somehow sharper — he was still demonstrably Fegan Fergus, but it was as if he'd undergone jiffy plastic surgery rather than taken a trip to the men's room at Shannon. The transformation was bugging Smart, and the explanation for it seemed to be hovering just under his radar screen. But try as he might, he still couldn't quite put his finger on it. And then there had been that curious encounter at customs.

Smart had been feeling guilty and nervous as he waited on line at Logan, and when he had gotten to the agent's station he'd actually broken out in a sweat. The agent had cast a professional eye over him, checked his passport mechanically, then fixed him with a brief but telling look before picking up a clipboard with a sheaf of papers on it. Smart could make out the word "Wanted" in bold type at the top of the first sheet, and he noticed a tightening of the agent's jaw muscles. The suspense, coupled with his strong anticipation of being led away in handcuffs, was almost unbearable, and as the agent began to scan the list, Smart's passport in hand, he wavered for a moment between quietly turning himself in or bolting off through the airport in a desperate bid for freedom. But then an inexplicable thing had happened.

Fergus had been standing directly behind him in line, but he suddenly stepped forward, next to Smart, and coughed discreetly — just loudly enough to draw the agent's attention. The agent looked up sharply at Fergus, and their eyes locked. The agent's face relaxed, and he assumed an almost beatific expression. He put down the "Wanted" list and gave Smart his passport back. "Next, please," he said. Fergus's passage through the customs station was routine.

Smart had attempted to make eye contact with Fergus afterwards, but the estate agent had deftly avoided his gaze without seeming to do so. And they'd had a lot to do, between renting a car at the hectic and crowded airport and then getting their combined luggage into it. So it had been easy to let the whole incident pass without comment. But Smart had seen the customs agent's expression change just before he put the list down, and he had a sense that Fergus had intervened in some way to save him. But how could he have done so with just a cough and a glance? And what could Fergus know about Smart's situation? Was he some kind of double agent for the IRS or another government agency?

Both were preoccupied with their own thoughts as they drove, and Smart found the atmosphere in the car slightly oppressive. Maybe a touch of "diddly music," as he thought of it, wouldn't be such a bad thing after their mostly silent ride. After taking the cutoff north onto Rt. 91 and arriving in Northhampton, a picturesque New England mill and college town, they inquired at a gas station about The Iron Horse Café and found it at about 4:30 p.m. A poster in the window showed a large, balding and earnest-looking man singing and playing a folk guitar, along with the words: "Catch the Celtic magic of Roddy Fakem — tonight! Two shows."

* * *

Libby dressed quickly after her brief but refreshing shower, during which she'd been fantasizing eagerly about what she would do with the new space that formerly had been consigned to the Devil. The room would be much larger and brighter now, and she had been looking for something she could use as an office. A nice big 18th-century desk that she'd seen at an antiques store in Dergh Town would be just right for it, and she planned to test several ideas for window treatments, from elaborate to elegantly simple. Trel would be amazed at the transformation when he got back!

She put on a pair of clean but well-worn jeans and a sweatshirt and some old sneakers. Then she took a quick detour to the potting shed and grabbed a pair of cotton work gloves, thinking Gall might need a bit of help with moving the door frame and the larger chunks of plaster. As she left the shed, tucking the gloves into her back pocket, she felt a rising sense of exhilaration — she hadn't realized just how much that silly old room had been bothering her. She wondered excitedly whether Gall would already have the wall down by the time she got upstairs. But then a thought furrowed her brow: *Why hadn't he taken any tools with him? Well,* she answered herself, *he must have left them in the truck and gone back for the right ones after he scoped out the job.*

Odd, she thought as she mounted the back stairs, *he's being incredibly quiet for someone taking down a wall.* She stopped in the doorway of the outer room in some confusion — there was no sign of Gall, and no work had been done. *What's going on?* she asked herself.

She walked to the end of the corridor, which overlooked the courtyard where Gall had parked his truck. There it was, which presumably meant that Gall was still on the premises. But where?

"Seamus?" she called out tentatively. "Where did you go?"

"Down here ... Libby!" Gall's husky voice was coming from the bottom of the main stairway.

Libby? thought Libby. Tradespeople called you by your first name all the time in America, but almost no one had addressed her familiarly here. Most of the townspeople seemed to treat them as if she and Smart had bought the Brimstons' title and lineage along with their ancestral manse.

She walked to the top of the stairs and looked down to see an astonishing sight. There stood Gall, one foot planted on the third step as if he were modeling for a statue of Adonis. His shiny shirt hardly seemed appropriate garb for remodeling work, Libby thought, and it was open half-way down his hirsute chest. And, she noticed disapprovingly, he seemed to be wearing five gold chains around his neck, each with a tiny totem of some sort attached to it. This would never do — the chains presented a clear choking hazard in the workplace. Then she looked at his face, which wore an expression that reminded her of Valentino in the old silent movies — a parody of smoky masculine come-hither. And in his hand, which he was proffering to her as if in salute, was a piece of crystal stemware that appeared to be filled with a bubbly substance — possibly champagne. What could it all mean? She turned involuntarily to see if someone else was standing behind her. But there was no one. She turned back toward him in disbelief.

"Seamus! What are you ... ? I thought you were going to take that wall down."

The sight of the Yankee Duchess standing above him and looking down in what could almost be interpreted as awe nearly overwhelmed Gall, who contemplated rushing up the stairs and sweeping Libby off her feet and into one of the many bedrooms on the second floor. Not the one next to the Devil's room, though — you didn't want that kind of distraction at such a time.

But something in her demeanor gave him pause, so he stayed where he was and allowed his eyes to devour her. She was a proud beauty and a fine figure of a woman, no doubt of that, her sensuous mouth open in a suggestive little oval and her eyes wide as she stared at him, Seamus Gall — a classic hunk of a working man and not some attenuated ex-academic and scribbler. He noticed that she was not, to be sure, dressed for amour, but he knew that most women approached the making of the two-headed beast differently than men. She might have chosen plain clothes for their tryst because that was just the fashion in New York or L.A., but it didn't necessarily signify anything; she might still be an absolute tigress in bed. He could easily imagine her long nails, glimpsed as they hung over the bannister, etching red furrows of passion into his broad back.

"Supper," he said huskily. "It's time to dine. Won't you join me?"

Twenty-three

Smart and Fergus found a table near the stage, ordered something to eat and then went downstairs to the men's room.

"When will your cousin be getting here?" Smart inquired as they stood at adjacent urinals.

"Oh, any minute now, I imagine. He said he'd come over early to have supper with us. He'll be an hour or so before he has to get ready for his first show. He says he's a fan of yours, by the way, Mr. Smart. He's read all your books."

"Oh?" said Smart, subconsciously ratcheting Roddy up several notches in his estimation. "How nice of him to say so. I don't think we can stay for the whole show, though, Fegan. If he's singing till 9 or 10, we won't get to Tuscarora before 11 or 12. And I wanted to get an early start there tomorrow, if possible."

"I doubt he expects us to stay late, Mr. Smart. I told him you were planning to be in Tuscarora tonight, and what I may do is to go back with him to his place tonight. Or, maybe I'll leave at intermission with you, if I find his Celtic magic not quite to me tastes."

Smart smiled as he zipped up; knowing Fergus as he did, he doubted he would stay for the whole show. Folk music just didn't seem right for this thoroughly modern young Irishman. *On the other hand,* he said to himself as they moved over to the washstand, *how well do I really know him at all?*

Such thoughts had troubled him ever since Fergus had returned from the lavatory in Shannon, which already seemed like ages ago, and he felt no closer to solving the mystery now than he had been then. Lost in these unproductive speculations, he happened to glance down at Fergus's hands as the estate agent pumped the soap dispenser and thought: *Why can't I put my finger on it?* He found himself looking at Fergus's left hand — at the little finger, to be exact — and his mind suddenly snapped to attention. *That's it!* he nearly blurted out. *His finger! It was still bandaged when he picked me up at Mordalee and when he went to the men's room at Shannon. And now the bandage is gone, and there's no trace of a wound!*

He looked at Fergus involuntarily, as if to see whether he had tipped to Smart's revelation, but the estate agent seemed to be preoccupied with his own concerns and didn't notice his glance. Actually, he was anxious to get away from the mirror in front of them before Smart saw that he cast no reflection.

"Fegan," Smart said, paying no attention to the mirror and trying with only limited success to keep the sound of "eureka" out of his voice, "what happened to that bandage that was on your finger?"

"Bandage?" Fergus looked at him blankly. "Which bandage was that, Mr. Smart?"

"You know — the one you had on your little finger, the finger you smashed in your car door last week. A nasty wound — you couldn't have forgotten it so soon." He looked keenly into Fergus's pale blue eyes.

Fergus appeared nonplussed and stared blankly at his hands. Then he smiled and returned Smart's almost triumphal gaze. "Oh, yes. The bandage that was on me little digit. Well, it was falling off like when I went to the men's at Shannon, so I decided to have a peek under it while I was in there. And it seemed to be all healed, so I just took it off. That's the whole story, I'm afraid." He met Smart's eyes with a good-humored challenge.

"Remarkable!" Smart said, pulling on his chin. "It was such an ugly wound to have healed so quickly. Let me see."

Fergus gamely held up his left hand for Smart's inspection, and Smart took the little finger and regarded it closely, like a jeweler checking a loose setting. *No sign of that nasty, jagged hole,* Smart thought. *Impossible!*

"Amazing, Fegan," he said out loud. "It seems to be as good as new. How did you manage this miraculous recuperation? Did you drink from the sacred springs at the shrine of Our Lady of Ballymorda, or was it the salubrious draughts of Seamus the shaman Gall?"

"Clean living, Mr. Smart," Fergus said in mock earnestness. "I recommend it highly."

Smart laughed as he dropped Fergus's hand. But he wasn't fooled for an instant. The wound could not have healed so quickly, which meant that he was traveling not with Fergus but with an extraordinary facsimile, perhaps a twin brother, who didn't want to reveal himself. But how, and why?

* * *

Lauretta Smale did a slow burn as she stared at the note on the door of 114 Cattaraugus St. in Tuscarora Falls. Actually, there were two notes. She had left the bottom one herself earlier that day. It read:

Mr. Smart — Please contact us immediately regarding this property.
Thanks,
Lauretta Smale

She had included a phone number with a special feature that rang not only her private phone in Karlin's office but her car phone. If neither phone was picked up, the office phone would record a message.

Stuck on top of her note with breathtaking, in-your-face insouciance was another note with a competing message:

Mr. Smart — Don't waste your time trying to sell or rent this house with anyone else but me! I'll do it for you sooner and better!

Best regards,

Gloryanna

The Insufferable One, who must have come snooping around after seeing the "Karlin Realty" sign on the lawn, had added her own number, along with a scrawled encouragement to "Call me anytime — 24 hours a day, seven days a week!"

I'm going to strangle this bitch if I ever meet her, Lauretta decided, tearing Gloryanna's note into tiny pieces and strewing them over the lawn as she stalked from the door to the curb. She sat in her Taurus, thinking evil thoughts at first but then coming grudgingly to admire Glory's gall. *She really must be one hell of a salesman,* Lauretta thought. Then she smiled a wicked little smile. *But I wonder if she's declaring all of that commission income she's been raking in?*

She put her car in gear and drove off.

Twenty-four

With all the impact of a falling brick to the head, it suddenly dawned on Libby that she was at the center of an elaborate seduction being orchestrated by none other than Seamus Gall, tradesman, publican and Don Juan of Ballymorda.

She was not entirely unaware of her impact on the male species in general — she'd seen heads swivel and heard a few heartfelt expressions of admiration as she walked the streets of Dergh and Dublin, both with Smart and without him — but she was now in her mid-40s and had become accustomed to thinking of herself as just an old married hen. It had never even occurred to her that one of the village buckos might be scheming to get in her pants. She didn't know whether to laugh or cry, so she just sat down at the top of the stairs in mute wonder.

Even Gall could see by this point that he may have miscalculated slightly. But, as many of the locals said of him, he was not called Gall for nothing, and he was not much daunted.

"It's suppertime, ma'm," he said with an engaging smile and more matter-of-factness and less huskiness in his voice than before. He would leave himself an out, if he needed it. "I've brought a few items from the pub, and I'd be pleased to have you share them, so."

Just then the phone rang. *Saved by the bell,* thought Libby, although the phone really sounded more like a spring peeper.

"I'll just grab that up here, Seamus," she said. "Then I'll be down to join you for a few moments before you start work." She didn't want to encourage him in any way, but she also didn't want to insult him or hurt his pride, which could have all kinds of unintended consequences in a wee fishbowl like Ballymorda. Besides, it was kind of fun, in a way, to realize that she was the object of so much unanticipated ardor. It certainly had been a long time since she'd felt anything like ardor from Smart. That thought brought a twinge: Did he have someone in Tuscarora that he'd been pining for? Was that why he hadn't been taking much interest in her? She tried to put it out of her mind: He wouldn't have moved to Ireland if he had a lover in Tuscarora, would he?

She refocused on Gall and caught the somewhat crestfallen but far from defeated look on his face before hurrying down the corridor to pick up the phone in the master bedroom. She carefully closed the door behind her but didn't bother to lock it. She was at least as tall as Gall and had taken karate classes in college, and although she was a bit rusty now, she had no doubt that she could take the wind out of Gall's sails, if need be, with a well-placed kick or chop.

"Hello? Libby Smart here."

"Libby, it's Bess. I hope you're well."

"Yes, Bess, I'm well ... more or less." But she didn't elaborate; there was a note of urgency in Bess's voice that made Libby want to hear her news. "What's up?"

"Have you not heard about Fegan Fergus, then?"

"No, what about him?"

"He's been hurt in some kind of an accident at Shannon Airport — a blow to the head, apparently. He's laid up right now at the hospital in Limerick, groggy and not quite himself."

Libby didn't answer immediately. If Fergus hadn't gotten on the plane with Smart, as he was supposed to do, why hadn't Smart gotten in touch? *Well,* she thought, *maybe he just didn't have time before boarding.*

"Libby?" said Bess, somewhat alarmed. "Are you all right, dear?"

"Yes, of course, but I'm just a bit shocked. Fegan was supposed to be going to America with Trel."

"Ah, I thought you had told me that. Well, apparently he never made it onto the plane. His sister, Moira, told me just a while ago that she spoke to him briefly in Limerick. He doesn't know what hit him, she says, but the Gardai told the hospital people that it looked as if he'd given himself a great thump on the head with the men's room door at Shannon."

When Libby put the phone down a few moments later, she was feeling almost disoriented. First Gall as hairy-chested Lothario, now Fergus as bog-bound invalid instead of companion and helper, if need be, for Smart in the States.

There was a tentative knock at the door, then a familiar voice:

"Pardon, ma'm, but would you have a bit of Grey Poupon in your pantry now?"

* * *

Roddy Fakem was not your man for tender ballads of love, Smart decided after listening to him hold forth at their table for a while. He was a decent enough person, and surely must have talent in order to have made a career of interpreting Irish music, but his somewhat prating, stentorian voice made Smart wince.

He noticed Roddy was having a similar effect on Fergus, who seemed vaguely uncomfortable with their conversation, particularly when Roddy inquired of various members of Fergus's family. Fergus either couldn't or wouldn't give the folk singer much in the way of specifics, and Smart had even found himself helping Fergus with a few facts about his sister, Moira, for instance, and her daughter, Siobhan, whom Lady B sadly had never had the chance to tutor. *Strange,* Smart thought. *It's almost as if I know more of Fegan's family than he does himself.*

He again contemplated the possibility that Fegan wasn't Fegan at all, but some kind of weird clone. But how could that be? He shook his head and listened to Fakem rattle on. Then he remembered, with a start, that he'd promised to call Libby upon arrival at Logan. It was now more than two hours after their arrival, but better late than never. He excused himself, then ventured down to the pay phones in the basement, where it was quieter, and punched in his phone card number.

"Hello?" Libby sounded dazed as well as distant, as if she'd just been hit with some astonishing news.

"It is your anointed, my love. You sound … a bit out of it. Are you all right?"

"Oh, fine, Trel," said Libby, feeling a strong urge to burst out laughing. "Considering that I just heard from Bess McCaughey that you're over there by yourself because poor Fergus never made it onto the plane, and that I am even now fending off the amorous advances of none other than Seamus Gall, who I made the mistake of asking to take down the wall of the Devil's room."

Libby expected a torrent of reaction from Smart, but the line was silent.

"Trel? Are you there? Did you hear me? What happened to Fegan?"

Smart reeled back against the wall close behind him in order to keep from sagging to the floor and dropping the phone. But the sudden, forceful movement pulled the phone out of his hand anyway. He began to massage his temples as he heard his wife's distant-sounding voice issue form the handset dangling beneath him:

"Trel? What's going on? Are you still there?"

He reached down and picked up the phone, but it was another moment or two before he could summon up words.

"Don't hang up," he said finally. "I'm still here. Just trying to come to grips with … the situation. It's quite a shock."

"What do you mean? You must have known about Fegan. He never made it onto the plane with you — something about a bang on the head. He's at the hospital in Limerick now, still groggy."

He was silent again, and Libby was getting alarmed.

"Trel — what is it?"

"And you say," Smart said weakly, trying to change the subject for a moment until he'd had a chance to absorb all the implications of the news about Fergus, "you say Gall is trying to seduce you? Are you sure?"

"Oh, Christ, Trel, I guess I know when a man's got the hots for me. Although it *has* been a while … ." Smart winced.

"But, you … you hired him to take down the wall? And instead he's trying to get his leg over?"

"You writers have such sweetly poetic ways of putting things. But yes, that's the general picture."

She expected a stream of invective and a demand to put Gall on the phone. Instead, Smart said: "Don't let him touch the wall. Do you hear me? Don't let him touch the wall! I'll call you back later."

He was about to hang up, but Libby was too quick for him: "Trel! What the hell is wrong over there? Are you in some kind of trouble? I was hoping Fegan would be able to lend a hand if you needed it, but now … ."

"Oh, he's lending a hand all right," Smart said.

"Honestly, I'm beginning to think you dropped your mind somewhere out over the Atlantic. How can he lend a hand when he's in a hospital in Limerick?"

"Because he's not," Smart said. "He's right here with me in the good old U.S. of A. Or at least, someone is."

Twenty-five

Lauretta Smale sat at her temporary desk at the real estate agency and scrutinized some documents she'd been faxed from the IRS processing center in Andover, Mass. She figured that as long as she would have to wait for Malcott and Smart to arrive, she might as well put the time to good use by subjecting her esteemed rival to a little game of truth or consequences. The forms were a mass of lines, numbers and the Service's inimitably obtuse prose, but they told an interesting tale nevertheless: Gloryanna Green either wasn't selling nearly as much property as she claimed to be selling, or she wasn't reporting a good deal of her income.

But how, Lauretta thought, tapping a pencil absently on the desk, *can she be selling property without reporting income?* She didn't know a lot about the real-estate business, but she knew that property deals typically weren't cash transactions, and that agencies nearly always got their money in the form of a separate check at closing. She went back over the forms, this time focusing on the itemized expenses, and realized the sad truth about real estate: You have to sell a great deal of it to register any real income. Gloryanna had, for instance, sold about $2 million in property the prior year. But the agency's 7% commission came to only $140,000, and she had gotten to keep roughly half of that amount. Once promotional expenses were subtracted — and these were high, in keeping with Gloryanna's campaign to dominate the market — she was left with an income of less than $50,000.

"So the empress has no clothes," Lauretta said out loud.

Karlin, who'd been ogling Lauretta from the side for several minutes and imagining her in exactly the same state of dress, said: "What was that, Ms. Smale? Who has no clothes?"

She laughed. "Oh, no one in particular. I was just contemplating the gap between image and reality in the business world." She was tempted to tell Karlin, in strict confidence, that Gloryanna's bottom line was, as the Texans said, "all hat and no cattle." She knew Karlin couldn't stand Old Glory; she had quickly found that everyone else in Tuscarora real estate — even Gloryanna's boss, or so the rumor went — felt the same way. But although she was well within her rights as an IRS agent to check on Gloryanna's returns, she knew she could face not only dismissal but even prosecution if Karlin ever told anyone she'd divulged information from them to him or anyone else. Discretion, in this case, was definitely the better part of valor. She put the faxes in her briefcase but mentally filed the information they contained for future use. Then the phone at her elbow rang.

"Karlin Realty, Lauretta Smale speaking. How may we help you today?"

"Help me? Hah!" a brassy voice snorted in her ear. "Judging by that pathetic note you left at 114 Cattaraugus, you couldn't help me if your life depended on it! Why don't you help yourself by finding another career?" There was a loud click as her caller hung up. She hadn't identified herself, but Lauretta had no doubt who it was.

"My God," she said wonderingly to Karlin, "Gloryanna really is a jerk, isn't she?"

He laughed. "Did she just give you the treatment? Don't take it personally — that's her calling card to all new agents in town. Kind of like a wolf marking its turf by pissing on rocks and logs. She's a sweetheart, all right." Then he shook his head ruefully. "But as much as I hate to admit it, she's killing me. Her husband's rich, so she can just throw money into advertising like there's no tomorrow. And it's working: Everyone wants to list with her now because she's drummed it into their heads that she's the best."

"Why don't you just crank up your ad budget to match?" Lauretta asked, amazed at his defeatism.

"Unlike Old Glory," Karlin sighed, "I have to turn a profit."

* * *

"Sweet Jaysus, what hit me, now?" Fegan Fergus fairly bellowed. "Nurse, darlin', can you just tell me that?"

The nurse, a middle-aged and somewhat plump lady who had been wrapped up in her own thoughts as she puttered about the small divided room getting its empty half ready for potential use, was a bit startled by Fergus's sudden loud return to consciousness.

She didn't answer, for in truth she had no idea who or what had hit him, but urged him to "lie back, now" and checked his pulse, which was regaining strength and regularity. She made a note or two on his chart, then asked him if he needed anything.

"Something to drink, if you please, for the love of God and all his angels. Guinness might be best."

"We have none of that, Mr. Fergus, but we do have the finest Limerick water." She passed him a glass filled with that very liquid, and he drained it off gingerly, as if it was a colorless and odorless form of poison, then slumped back on his pillow. "Oh, me poor head," he said. "It feels like I got hit by the Cork Express."

"Sure, it was a very nasty blow, Mr. Fergus. Have you no idea how you came by it?"

"None, save that I was walking out of the men's, and as I reached for the handle to open the door, the next thing I knew ... it was stars, planets and little colored floaty things in the air. And here I was." He began to shake his head in wonder, but the motion brought swift retribution. "Oh fooking hell!" he howled. "The pain is beyond belief!"

The nurse looked concerned and put a hand on his shoulder until he quieted down. "Where's me sister, by the way?" he said with a start, remembering dimly that Moira had come, as if in a dream, to visit him.

"She was here a while, but went out for a bite. She'll be back later, she said to tell you."

He fingered the bandage on his left pinky and remembered that he was supposed to be chaperoning Trelawny Smart in America, and had accepted Libby's money for that purpose.

"Shite!" he exclaimed. The nurse looked at him with narrowed eyes. "Now what is it?" she said.

"I've got to call someone right away. It's me head now, but it'll be me arse if I don't!" He made a tentative motion as if to get out of bed.

"Now, Mr. Fergus, calm yourself," she said, firmly pushing him back. "I'll bring a wheelchair in here directly the doctor has taken a look at you, and then you can use the phone."

* * *

Libby wasn't quite sure how to proceed and was wondering if the entire male race had lost its collective mind. Smart seemed to have gone mad the moment he touched down in the States, and Gall apparently had gotten hold of Love Potion Number Nine or watched one too many German porn epics off the satellite.

She ignored his question about mustard, which was still hanging in the air, and went over the conversation with Smart in her mind: Fergus — or someone who apparently looked a lot like him — was there, in America, with him. Yet she had it on good authority that he was in Limerick, stretched out on a hospital bed with a huge bump on his head. She was not to allow Gall to touch the Devil's room; Smart had stressed that quite forcefully. But he'd said nothing about what to do if the publican put moves on her or how she was to deal with him. She didn't want to jump to conclusions, but this failure of the dog to bark was certainly suspicious. What *was* he really doing over there?

"Miss Libby?" The door opened slightly. *So it's 'Miss Libby,' now, eh?* she thought warily. *He may be getting his courage up. Or something else.*

"Seamus," she said firmly, "you'll find whatever condiments we have in the refrigerator, not the pantry."

"Oh, so that's where you keep that yoke, eh?" He peeked around the edge of the door, a jaunty grin on his ruddy face, which was not without a certain rough allure. Not a movie star's face by any stretch, but you could imagine it opening village boudoirs without too much strain. "No wonder I couldn't locate it — folks here generally leave their mustard and such out. If you don't mind, then, I'll just help meself. Will you be down for some of the glorious ham and cheddar I brought? It's the best," he said with evident pride, "fresh from Cashell this morning."

She had to smile in spite of herself. *Someone must have told him that the way into my knickers is through my stomach,* she thought. But there was a certain charm in his oafish advances. As long as he didn't get carried away, she could imagine herself enjoying this.

Twenty-six

Smart leaned back against the wall next to the phone, his long legs bent slightly at the knee and his feet out at an angle just sufficient to prop him up. He let out a long, heartfelt sigh and smiled a tentative smile, as if he'd barely passed a difficult test.

It's him, he thought. *Fergus is Malcott. How could I have been so stupid?*

Then Malcott's own words at Mordalee came back to him: "I can look like anyone — even a skyscraping fellow like you." He'd actually been worried that Malcott would appear to Libby as him while he was gone, inveigling himself into her arms with a story about not being able to stay away and coming home early to surprise her ... he inwardly pummeled himself again for being so blind. But he'd been too wrapped up in his own obsession with Perdita to evaluate the clues. His expression darkened as he thought of Malcott's arrogance.

He told me exactly how he would fool me, but he assumed I'd be too dumb, or too dazzled, to glom onto it anyway. Or maybe, he thought with a grudging smile, *he was trying to give me a sporting chance.* He thought of the advice he'd gotten from Lady B. in the attic:

"He's a con artist of the very highest order ... a genius at reading people, and at directing them — setting the stage so that the script he gives them seems the only possible course." She'd nailed Malcott dead to rights, Smart thought admiringly. And she had added a hopeful coda: "You have a choice. You don't have to do what he wants ... you can turn the tables on him."

It was ironic, he thought, that the benevolent apparitions in his attic had warned him that Malcott might try to manipulate him through his baser impulses, when in fact Malcott had used his better nature — the profound regret of a parent who wanted to compensate a daughter for a lifetime of neglect — to maneuver him into such a dangerous venture.

One thing seems clear, Smart said to himself. *Libby probably isn't his target. Otherwise, he wouldn't have come this far with me.* Who, then, was Malcott's real prey?

Suddenly he found himself face to face with the false Fergus, who had come downstairs and was now eyeing him curiously.

"Mr. Smart," he said, "Roddy is about to play. Shall we stay or go?"

* * *

Lauretta was still waiting by the phone at closing time, like a lovesick girl with no date for the prom, but she hadn't heard back from the mysterious Mr. Malcott. She realized, with a sudden feeling of something akin to desperation, that although she knew nothing about him, she had come to pin a lot of her hopes on him. The hopes of a lifetime, in fact, because she'd wanted to punish her arrant father since she'd been old enough to know what the word "punish" meant. Now here she was, powerless — while Malcott seemed to hold all the cards.

She couldn't bust him until she had him in her sights, and she was apparently dependent on this Malcott character to deliver him. "The package," he'd called Smart. But when and where was she supposed to sign for him?

She cast a sidelong glance at Karlin, who was hunched over some paperwork at his desk, alternately scribbling on a pad and punching numbers into a financial calculator. From her 20-year-old vantage, life seemed to be about procuring — Malcott procuring a tax cheat who happened to be her natural (strange term for Smart!) father; Karlin and Gloryanna and others in a ceaseless struggle to procure buyers for sellers, financing for buyers so that sales could be consummated, new listings so that sellers' happiness could be procured, along with their own livelihoods ... .

She glanced at Karlin again to find him staring at her. He quickly looked away and went back to his work, but she knew what that look meant. He wanted her. If she were to suggest to him that they go back to her place for a drink, he'd probably have the "Closed" sign out in a flash. Yet he was more than twice her age — about the same age as her father, she estimated. She'd heard he was divorced, had two kids in high school ... and she assumed he had a love interest (or at least an available squeeze) somewhere in his life, given that he was a reasonably big fish in a small pond and not impossibly hard to look at.

She found tears issuing suddenly from her eyes and running down her cheeks, a soft rain that had come with no warning. *Maybe,* she thought, *I'm just not right for the role of avenging angel.* She wasn't the hysterical type, thankfully — she could control this lapse relatively easily, she told herself, and Karlin need never be the wiser.

As she discreetly cleared her throat, blew her nose and dabbed at her cheeks and the corners of her eyes, however, Karlin knew exactly what was happening. His own daughter, who was only five years younger than Lauretta Smale, sometimes wept this way and tried to hide it. Women were cursed or blessed, depending on how you looked at it, with the ability to liquidate their emotional burdens by turning them into tears. During the long and torturous months of *Karlin v. Karlin,* he had done most of the paying while his wife had done nearly all of the crying. But he felt that she had somehow cleared her account this way, while he still had a great deal of clearing to do.

Karlin studiously avoided letting on that he'd seen and understood what had happened, and Lauretta was grateful for that, because she didn't feel like trying to explain things to him. At a few minutes after

5 o'clock, he made a show of putting away his work and getting ready to go, and as she stood and turned to say good night, he gave her a somewhat tentative smile.

"It's been a long day, eh? Why don't you and I get something to eat up the street at Diamond Jim's?"

He knew that her first instinct would be to refuse, so he quickly added: "No big deal. I'm just tired of eating alone, that's all. No expectations, eh?"

She looked at him skeptically, but then her gaze softened; he passed the test. She'd seen lust in his eyes more than once during their brief acquaintance, but now what she mostly saw was fatigue. He probably was what he looked like at that moment: a lonely and somewhat vulnerable man whose hair was thinning, receding and graying and whose brow was permanently furrowed. She sympathized; she was feeling more than a little isolated and besieged herself.

"OK," she said, surprising both of them. Karlin made small talk as they walked to the restaurant, and Lauretta smiled and let down her guard somewhat, although she didn't respond. She was thinking that getting to know Karlin better might help her understand the man she soon hoped to arrest.

Twenty-seven

Libby had been grazing all day but hadn't had a solid meal, and the prospect of a hearty supper had strong appeal. But she walked toward the familiar precincts of her own kitchen with some trepidation. Would Gall read her presence as a tacit sign of encouragement or surrender? She was prepared to call the Gardai if he tried to force himself upon her, although there was only one officer stationed in the vicinity of Ballymorda, which meant that response time could be leisurely. But she doubted such a call would be necessary, because she sensed that while Gall was up for an affair or a notch for his belt, he wouldn't risk a stay at Dergh gaol.

She entered the kitchen in full "repel-boarders" mode, but quickly saw that Gall had shifted gears. Gone was the strutting, preening personification of machismo, although his chest hair still stuck out comically from his absurd shirt. In his place, and lacking only a chef's hat and white smock to make the transformation complete, was Monsieur Gall, gourmet and impresario of country dining *Irlandois*.

At one end of the long table sat an empty picnic hamper. Its contents, along with a few things he'd found in her cupboards and fridge, had turned the table into a veritable groaning board of gastronomic delights. There was an open bottle of champagne in a handsome pewter ice bucket; four kinds of cheeses, including the prized Cashell cheddar, arranged with some flair; a varied selection of stouts and lagers in bottles; a luscious-looking ham, fresh salmon from

Lough Ree and a pile of cold sausages on separate platters; a fresh loaf of dark soda bread; and dishes of flavored yogurts along with Bewley's dark chocolate and several kinds of nuts and fruit for dessert.

"Including," he said, when he saw her gaze light at last on the fruit plate, "apples from New York State. Very hard to come by in these parts." He practically glowed with self-satisfaction, and she couldn't help but return his smile. She had always loved the combination of apples and chocolate.

Her smile, always a glorious sight, gave Gall new courage, although he had realized by now that a romp with the Her Ladyship might be a long shot. But you never could tell about such things; he'd known the salivary glands to set other juices flowing, and he had detected a certain longing in her — he couldn't define it exactly, but something was lacking in her life. Maybe she missed her husband, even though he'd only left that morning. But he guessed she might have reacted the same way if Smart had only gone to Dublin for the day instead of the States. She was starving at some level, and he might actually touch that need through his artful display of edibles.

"Seamus, you've worked wonders here. I'm very impressed. So few men know their way around food ... ."

"Now, Missus ... er, Miss — oh, shite, what should I call you?" His discomfiture was genuine and appealing. *Thus to all Valentinos*, she thought. *They're so much more believable as teddy bears."*

"Libby will do, Seamus. Now that you've got my mouth watering, why don't you pass me some of that ham and bread and excellent Cashell cheese? And since the bottle's open, you might as well pour me a glass of champagne, too."

* * *

Smart stared at the counterfeit Fergus for a split-second but pulled himself together quickly. There was no sense letting Malcott know that he was on to his game until he figured out exactly what that game was.

"I'm sorry, Fegan. I was preoccupied. What was that you asked me?"

"Should we stay or go, Mr. Smart?"

"Oh, right. I saw we go, Fegan. Roddy's a charming man, but we've still got a long way to drive. What do you think?"

"I'm of exactly the same mind, Mr. Smart," Malcott said, regarding him with narrowed eyes. Then he switched the subject: "Were you … is something the matter?"

"No, I was just taken aback by something Libby said, that's all." Malcott looked interested, so Smart pressed on. He, too, could play this misdirection game. "She said she was having Gall take down the wall to open up the Devil's room." He checked Malcott's reaction, but Fergus's features hardly moved. *He's playing it cool,* Smart thought.

"I'm surprised to hear it myself, Mr. Smart," Malcott said. "Why would she want to do that?" Aware he'd stepped slightly out of character as Fergus, he hastily added: "If you don't mind my asking, of course."

"No, not at all. Well, she's thinking of using that space for an office, but I asked her to have Gall hold off until I get home. No sense having all hell break loose while I'm away, eh?" Smart laughed and slapped Malcott on the shoulder, and Malcott smiled as well, seemingly reassured that his disguise was still intact.

"No need of that at any time," he said, his smile broadening. "Shall we go and take our leave of Roddy now?

Fakem was disappointed — perhaps because attendance was somewhat sparse and he felt the need of moral support — but understanding, letting them go with a hearty handshake for each after extracting a promise that they would call from Tuscarora Falls so the three could plan another get-together before they headed home to Ireland. As they were about to leave, Malcott said he needed to visit the men's room once more and went downstairs for a few moments. Smart suspected he was going to use the phone instead, but said nothing. *Who would he be calling?* he wondered. He thought again of the customs agent and wondered if Malcott was in league with him somehow. *Did he save me at Logan to set me up elsewhere?*

By the time he got back, Roddy had launched into his first song, a rollicking ballad about bad faith, betrayal, agony and death. Related subjects were on Smart's mind as they drove south on Rt. 91 and then west toward Albany on the turnpike.

So, he thought, *Malcott's here with me after maneuvering poor Fergus into the hospital.* Knowing that his traveling companion wasn't above a little physical violence to gain his ends made Smart even more apprehensive. And what were his ends? Smart had a strong hunch that they were linked in some way to Malcott's upgrading of Fergus's appearance. But how? Maybe he was just being vain. No, it had to be more than that. *Well, whatever he's planning,* Smart thought to himself, *he doesn't seem to have caught on that I've caught on to him. At least, not yet.*

* * *

Lauretta enjoyed a convivial meal with Karlin, who proved to be excellent company once he'd put aside the hope of landing her in the sack. As for him, the very act of being seen with Lauretta in a setting that could easily be mistaken for a tryst was almost as much of a tonic as the real thing. People would marvel at his romantic prowess, but he wouldn't have to deal with the usual messy details — the easily dashed expectations, the proliferating misunderstandings, the vicious arguments, the killing indifference. He caught several glances from acquaintances and business associates, the men looking at him with ill-disguised envy and the women with new respect.

"So," he said to Lauretta as they drank their coffee after dessert, "have you heard anything from Mr. Smart yet?"

"No," she said in mock seriousness. "Maybe he's avoiding me."

Karlin widened his eyes and shook his head theatrically. "I can't imagine any man wanting to avoid you, Lauretta. I really can't."

It was the first time he had called her by her first name, and she wasn't quite sure how she felt about it. It implied that they were friends, which would be going too far. She was still a revenue agent on an official case, after all, and she had had to use intense persuasion — bordering on coercion, she acknowledged to herself — to get him to cooperate.

She cleared her throat, shifted in her seat, and got more businesslike. "Well, I'm pretty sure he'll be in touch either tonight or tomorrow. And then I should be able to wrap this case up quickly."

Karlin nodded, but he didn't answer immediately. He'd noticed her suddenly cooler mood, and he knew that their relationship had begun problematically and could easily slip back in that direction. But he wasn't willing to let the delightful new Lauretta vanish so soon. He grinned and said: "Well, if things don't work out, you can always come to work for me. I need a real tough, smart woman to save me from Gloryanna."

She flashed a quick, noncommittal smile, then signaled the waiter to bring her the check.

"No way," Karlin protested. "I invited you. Come on, now," he added, reaching for his wallet. "Let me pay."

She held up her American Express card like a talisman, gave him an enigmatic look and practically grabbed the check out of the startled waiter's hand. "Expense account. You're cooperating with a government investigation, so dinner's on Uncle Sam. How's that for a return on your tax dollars?"

Karlin didn't answer, and his smile faded. She had reasserted control over the situation and reminded him who was really boss. Worse, she'd deftly punctured his lothario scenario by making a public show of paying. He wanted to take the initiative in some way and briefly considered repeating his offer of employment. But he thought the better of it: There was a good chance she would laugh it off. And it might be worse if she didn't, because hiring Lauretta Smale to combat Glory Green might be a bit like bulldozing your house to save it from a fire.

They parted amicably enough outside Diamond Jim's. "See you tomorrow," Karlin said. But he noticed a further cooling in Lauretta's demeanor.

"Right," she answered somewhat distantly.

As she walked away, he couldn't help but follow her high, firm and shapely derriere with his eyes. Then he let out a low whistle that was part admiration, part exhaustion. But the sound didn't reach Lauretta, who was hurrying toward her car. She had left the windows partly open, and she could hear the cell phone ringing inside.

Twenty-eight

Libby was having perhaps the most entertaining meal she'd ever had with anyone on either side of the Atlantic. Gall, it turned out, was a man of many parts — charming raconteur, amateur gourmet and chef, local factotum, entrepreneur and Renaissance man. He'd been married once, "a foolish matter of feckless youth," as he put it, and he had a son growing up far away in Killarney whom he saw rarely and missed sorely.

"Well, she's got someone new," he said, referring to his former wife, "and she doesn't want me bollixing her life if she can help it. So she sends young Keiron over to me for a few weeks a year, and we go fishing and shite, but the truth is, he hardly has any use for his old dad."

Gall didn't encourage and wouldn't allow commiseration, though. He took full responsibility for his life, the successes and "near successes," as he characterized his worst disasters, and he didn't see the point of pity or regrets.

He kept the food and drink coming as steadily as the patter, and Libby found herself fascinated by this Irish type: a satisfied bachelor who lived in the day and for the day, and who answered to no one, it seemed, but his conscience and his customers.

"So you wouldn't want to remarry, then?" Libby asked him.

"Oh, no! I've learned my lesson, haven't I? I'm not the man for marriage. It's not in my repertoire, so to speak. No, I'm the roaming kind, and I don't mind being alone, if it comes to that. But there's usually some coll willing to share my company and keep me from hoarding my many charms, if you take my meaning." He said this with a bald leer, and Libby took his point perfectly: Gall was a back-door man, a rambler who wouldn't try to put hooks in a woman and didn't want any in return, thank you. The kind of man, he seemed to imply, that you could just have a damn good time with, never mind the ties that bind and all the expectations that went with them.

"And you don't fall in love with any of these compassionate women of yours, eh Seamus?" Libby teased.

"Fall in love? I'm not sure what that means, to be honest with you. I live to enjoy myself in this gorgeous atrocious old world and give enjoyment in turn, if I can. Love's like any other commodity — here today, gone tomorrow. It disappears, and no one knows where it goes. I've heard that said many a time over the bar at the Drowning Man. No one knows where the hell it goes, would you listen? Why put so much stock in it, then?"

Libby said nothing, but Gall's words were having a subtle effect, as perhaps he'd intended all along. What was love, after all? She had thought she knew the answer to that question when she and Smart had settled down together, and when they'd moved to Tuscarora Falls and when they'd moved again to this strange old house in this curious little country. But now Smart was gone, and Gall was near, and she felt strangely free, as if released from a spell or a sentence. It wasn't that life with Smart was bad, or that she didn't have deep feelings for him. But were the two of them necessarily to be the only ones for each other for the rest of their lives? Was there to be no intermission from each other, no chance to see how things might go with someone else? Such thoughts were dangerous for a married woman, Libby knew, but they refused to go away.

The champagne seemed to be bubbling right behind her eyes, and

Gall could see he'd hit home in some way. But he wisely refrained from pressing. Smart was far away and would be gone for more than a day, and her silence told him that he might profit more by pushing less. He passed her a piece of Cashell cheddar and an apple.

"Try that combination, Your Grace." She smiled, and he knew he'd found the correct form of address. "They were made for each other, so."

She met his gaze as she tasted the cheese, then bit into an apple. They were indeed made for each other, so.

* * *

"Ms. Smale? Malcott here. I'll be at the coffee shop at the Armada Magnificence hotel in Tuscarora Falls tomorrow at 11 a.m. Don't worry about recognizing me; I know what you look like, and I'll seek you out. But make sure you're alone, or there'll be no deal." The phone went dead.

"Damn him!" Lauretta fumed. Once again, she was powerless; her caller-ID screen showed another useless batch of sixes. She threw the expensive phone down on the plush seat next to her and watched it bounce into the padded armrest.

She noticed Karlin looking at her quizzically from in front of Diamond Jim's and cursed again. She didn't want him or anyone else asking questions. She turned the ignition, threw the car into gear, forced herself to smile and wave jauntily to Karlin as she pulled out of her parking space, and sped off toward Cattaraugus Street. She didn't know what she would do at Smart's house, but going there felt like doing something, which was better than doing nothing.

What did he mean, "I know what you look like?" she thought as she drove. *I've never met anyone named Malcott. So where does he know me from?* She liked to think of herself as a pretty tough cookie who'd seen it all despite her tender years, but she had to admit that something about this Malcott character was freaking her out.

Twenty-nine

The drive from Northampton to Tuscarora Falls took about two hours, but this time Smart let the succubus — if that's what the Malcottized Fergus was — do the driving. He was bone-tired, whereas the Devil presumably could call upon limitless stores of demonic energy, and he figured that if Malcott was occupied with driving, he couldn't zone out, as he had on the first leg of their journey, to wreak who knew what havoc in other people's lives.

Watching Malcott out of the corner of his eye — he had to keep reminding himself that the doppelganger was, indeed, Malcott rather than Fergus — gave him a wry thought: *Maybe I'll get a gold star in heaven for keeping Beelzebub tied up like this.* Then again, maybe not. He wasn't at all sure he believed in heaven, although now that he'd had dealings with hell's proprietor, he had to admit that the case for heaven looked much stronger. *If there is a God,* he thought to himself, *I hope He'll lend me a hand.* Then he imagined himself as the figure of Adam on the Sistine Chapel ceiling — reaching out to touch the divine finger, but not quite connecting. Maybe he would have to stretch more.

Malcott's driving offered further confirmation that Smart was traveling with the Devil and not the estate agent. Fergus would have been flying through the darkness, heedless of deer or any other possible obstruction, glorying in the sheer openness of American highways as opposed to the narrow concrete roads of Ireland. But his companion's style was anything but hell-for-leather. The irony of it appealed to

Smart. Malcott drove like a middle-aged professional, like someone who was concerned about his insurance rates and should have been taking a minivan full of kids to soccer practice. *Like a life accountant,* he thought, *whatever that is.*

They hardly spoke during the trip, and Smart caught himself beginning to nod off a few times. He jerked himself awake, not wanting to give Malcott an opportunity to shanghai him. He began to reconsider, as they neared Tuscarora, the idea of staying at his own rental property. True, it contained an empty apartment, and he had the key. They could just open the door and walk in, and he kept some bedding, a hot plate, dishes and other useful items in the attic. But what if they were walking into a trap? He had a strong suspicion that Malcott must have set something in motion on this side of the Atlantic if he'd gone to all the trouble of disposing of Fergus and coming with him on this trip. But what could it possibly be? Smart drew a blank, but he decided that a little razzle-dazzle of his own might not be a bad idea.

"When we get to Tuscarora Falls," he said to Fergus when they were about 10 miles from town, "we'll go straight to the Armada hotel downtown. Don't worry about the expense — I have a credit card that gives me a substantial discount off their regular rates. Assuming they have two empty rooms, of course." He didn't think finding two rooms in the big hotel at this time of the year would be a problem, though.

"The Armada?" Malcott echoed. "I thought we'd be staying at your rental house."

"Well, I forgot one little detail in the hurly-burly of setting up this trip, talking to my lawyers, and all that. The apartment is empty, but it's also unfurnished. If we want to stay there for any length of time, I've got to arrange to rent some furniture."

"Oh," said Malcott. "I see what you mean." But he seemed unconvinced.

"It's no problem getting temporary stuff in a town like Tuscarora — with students and professors coming and going at the college and transients in town for the summer racing season, there's a whole instant-living establishment there. But I'm not sure it's worth it, because I don't know how long my business will take." He hadn't told Fergus what that business was while Fergus was still himself or after Malcott's hostile takeover, and he didn't elaborate now.

"Well, whatever you say, Mr. Smart," Malcott answered. "I had expected to pay my share of expenses either way, naturally."

"I'll just rent us separate rooms with my card, and then you can pay me for yours either now or later, when we're back in Ireland. I'll leave that to the exigencies of your cash situation."

"You'd better take payment now," Malcott smiled, "while I'm flush with cash. After a few days in the States, who knows?"

Spoken like the true Fegan Fergus, Smart thought. *Malcott must have done a fair amount of researching him at The Drowning Man.*

* * *

Lauretta parked in front of 120 Cattaraugus Street, a few houses down from Smart's property, but she left the motor idling. *Why,* she asked herself after a few minutes, *did I leave the engine on?* Was her subconscious telling her she wouldn't be able to face the moment of truth once the Bogey Man of her life arrived? She mentally kicked herself, then shut off the ignition. Now, at least, she felt less conspicuous as she sat there. But staking out a house was weird, no matter how you sliced it. Crime dramas made it seem routine in big cities, but here in little ol' Tuscarora Falls she felt like the proverbial sore thumb, even though she wasn't directly aware of anyone looking at her.

She sat there for maybe 20 minutes, willing herself and her car to just blend into the streetscape, and she avoided eye contact with the few pedestrians and motorists who did make their way down the street. *What am I really waiting for?* she asked herself. This time, however, she was ready for the tears before they came, and she suppressed them with a ruthless effort of the will. *No! I will not cry about this man! He's a jerk and a tax cheat and he wrecked my mother's life.* It was comforting to mentally rehearse the scenario she'd imagined so many times — how she'd coolly take revenge, strictly business, get another deadbeat dad and tax cheat off the streets, another minor menace to society disposed of. Maybe it wouldn't be the same thing as nailing Al Capone, but then you had to start somewhere.

Except that she knew there was more to her feelings than that. And she knew that stifling them was not the same thing as dealing with them. At some very deep level she wanted to throw her arms around this man and cry on his shoulder. She wanted to tell him of all the love she might have felt for him if he hadn't run out on her, she wanted to commiserate with him about her mother's death. *What would Mom say now?* she thought to herself.

Arrest the bastard! came the answer in her head like a voice from beyond. *Make him pay for what he did to us!* Serena had never cut him any slack, and wasn't she her mother's daughter? She wrenched herself back to the present and focused on 114 Cattaraugus, her eyes sharp again.

And soon, although the light was fading, there was something to see: a large sedan coming slowly down the street and pausing in front of Smart's house. Her pulse began to race: would this be it, after so many years? No — she couldn't make out the driver's face clearly in her rear-view mirror, but she could see that it was a woman. The car paused for a moment or two, then suddenly sped off, past Lauretta. Just before it came even with her, Lauretta saw a gratingly familiar slogan emblazoned on its side: "Why waste time? Let Gloryanna sell it for you!"

She caught a fleeting look at the bitch goddess of Tuscarora real estate as she flew by, although she didn't think Gloryanna, no doubt focused like a laser on her next sale, had noticed her. She was apparently a big woman, from what Lauretta could see, but no beauty. She remembered Karlin's comment at dinner about their budding sales rivalry: "It's ironic," he'd digressed, as if savoring one of life's bittersweet little appetizers, "that you two could be mistaken for each other from behind, or from a distance. She's about your height, and has the same hair color and ... proportions. But her face would stop a clock. Hard eyes, mean mouth. Not very appealing from the neck up."

So that was Old Glory, eh? thought Lauretta. She started her engine and drove pensively toward her hotel, having given up on seeing Smart until tomorrow in the cold light of day. She'd waited 20 years, so one more night wouldn't hurt too much. But what was Gloryanna doing nosing around? The answer was obvious: She was hoping to pick up Smart, too — but as a client. She smiled. Denying Glory a sale was just one more good reason to hustle her father off to jail.

Thirty

Fegan Fergus was dreaming of America. He was riding shotgun on a stagecoach, inside of which were Smart and Libby — he dressed in fancy clothes with an elaborate bow tie, the picture of a banker from back East, and she, in a hoop skirt and bonnet, his refined and beautiful lady. But the driver, who looked like Gall and was incongruously holding a pint of stout in one hand as he drove and, worse, refusing to share it with Fergus, looked anxious as they came to a narrow pass between boulders that loomed over them.

"Injuns!" he suddenly cried, whipping the horses and spilling his beer. Fergus cocked his carbine, but before he could squeeze off a shot, a fierce-looking redskin hurled a huge, jagged rock down at him. "Duck, you eedjit!" the driver called. But he wasn't fast enough, and the rock hit his head a glancing blow. His skull rang with the impact, and he reeled nearly off his seat, his rifle gone, his mind paralyzed. Oddly, though, the pain seemed to sweep over him in the form of waves of sharp, high-pitched sound, ringing and ringing and ringing ... .

"Mr. Fergus' room." He heard the nurse's voice as he struggled toward consciousness. The ringing had thankfully stopped.

"Well, he was asleep, but now he looks like he's coming around. I'll see if he feels well enough to speak to you."

"Who is it?" Fergus asked, rooting the sleep out of his eyes with his knuckles.

"Seamus Gall of Ballymorda. A friend of yours, so he says."

"Seamus?" Fergus mumbled. "Why would he be calling, now?"

The nurse smiled. "Maybe because he's heard you're here, so."

Fergus finally snapped to. "Of course, of course. It's a wee small place, Ballymorda. The news must have spread by now. I'll take the call, nurse, if you please."

She handed him the phone and left the room.

"Seamus, it's Fegan. I'm in a terrible way, I'm afraid. My head feels like the anvil chorus was played upon it."

"We heard about it, so. You got knocked on your pate coming out of the men's at Shannon, eh? But how could that happen, would you please tell me that?"

"Fook me if I know, Seamus. I was just walking out, you know, not a care in the world. I reached for the door when it suddenly swung in, hard. Then it was the big bang, and no theory about it! Knocked me clean out, and when I woke up I was here at the hospital in Limerick."

"You were banjaxed, now, Fegan, weren't you? How else could you nail yourself with a latrine door?"

"No, I swear it, Seamus, I was sober as a nun on Sunday morning. I'd had maybe one or two drinks with Mr. Smart in the lounge, then went in to tap a kidney, and the next thing I know, I'm seeing stars. And I didn't hit myself. Whoever was coming in hit me. But I never saw him."

"Did you tell the Gardai that someone hit you?"

"No. They haven't talked to me yet. I've been out for hours."

"Have you heard from Mr. Smart yet?"

"No. I have no idea what happened with him, although I assume he got on the plane without me."

"He did, so. And he wishes you a speedy recovery, no doubt. But we're going to drive over now to see how you're doing and bring you some clothes and food and sundries to make your stay more comfortable."

"We? Who's we?"

"Libby Smart and yours truly. See you in a bit, Fegan."

* * *

Smart directed Malcott to the Armada hotel, an angular brick building whose architectural highlights, like those of virtually all newer buildings in Tuscarora Falls, were said to "refer" to the classic old clubhouse at the track, as if buildings could make adoring or snide comments about each other. He noticed, however, that Malcott didn't really seem to need directions. *Interesting,* thought Smart. *Apparently he's done some reconnoitering here, too.* He felt even better about his decision to stay at the hotel tonight, which almost certainly hadn't figured in Malcott's plans.

There were two single rooms available, but not next to each other. *Just as well,* thought Smart, who wasn't keen on sleeping next to another Devil's room. It would be good to put some distance between himself and the scheming impostor; and maybe it would allow him to lose Malcott for a while, or at least make him wonder what he, Smart, was up to.

They got their bags out of the car and split up at the elevator. Malcott's room was on the first floor, and Smart's was on the third. Just before the elevator doors closed, Malcott stepped a bit out of character and reminded Smart of their planned rendezvous. "Remember — 11 sharp at the coffee shop." Then he laughed awkwardly to cover himself, as if to say "I'm so tired I don't know what I'm saying." But Smart felt he knew very well what Malcott was saying — the trap would be sprung on the morrow. But not if he could help it.

It was about 8:30 when he got to his room — too early to turn in, although he'd been feeling quite tired on the drive over from Northampton. But now a second wind was beginning to kick in, and he decided that a stroll about the old town would be just what he needed. He might meet someone who could help him or at least jog a positive thought or two loose from his cluttered brain. And besides, he felt a strong need to put some distance between himself and Malcott. After showering and changing into fresh clothes, he left the hotel at about 9:15 and headed for Diamond Jim's. The music wouldn't be too loud there, and he was hungry again after having such an early supper.

He knew the bar at Diamond Jim's like the back of his hand. It was a place in which he'd spent many an hour on the verge of inebriation — sometimes far over the verge — although now it seemed alien somehow, as if he'd only read about his times there in a novel. His "home bar" was The Drowning Man now, wasn't it? He thought of that cozy little nook with its peat fire, the dartboard on one wall and bags of pork rinds hanging from a display, the Guinness and Harp taps prominent behind the dark polished bar, and Seamus Gall working wonders in foam behind it … . *Seamus Gall! My God, I've got to call Libby right away,* he thought.

But it was too late to call, since it would be the wee hours of the morning in Ireland. Frustrated, he imagined the phone ringing on the night table in their bedroom at Mordalee, Libby languidly pulling the pillow over her head as Gall moved a hairy paw to silence it. It was a thought that should have brought his blood to a quick boil, but somehow it didn't. In fact, he felt more demoralized and depressed than anything else. How had he and Libby allowed things to come to such a sorry pass? Shaking his head at the sadness of it, he looked up to see Gloryanna Green bursting through the door. He recognized her immediately; she'd tried to land the listing for his house, and she'd given him the impression more than once that she had the hots not only for his listings, but for him, too. He was about to turn away, but it was too late — she'd seen him.

"Trelawny Smart!" she whooped, practically hauling him up off his barstool and throwing her arms around him. She gave him a huge smile, then a lusty, lubricious kiss on the lips. Before he knew it, her tongue was probing down his throat, her full breasts were pushing against his chest and her hands clasped his butt, pulling him firmly forward. He had never been particularly attracted to her, but clearly the feeling wasn't mutual.

"Gloryanna, you sweet thing!" he said, disengaging himself somewhat from her ardent grasp and grinning. "I didn't think you'd still remember me." Her husband traveled frequently on business, she had told him once, adding that they'd agreed to let each other satisfy their carnal desires in each other's absence. He'd found that hard to believe, but since he wasn't interested in her anyway, he'd never pursued it.

"Remember you? Hell, how could I forget? The tallest man in town with the biggest ... literary talent! You know I've been having wet dreams about you for ages!"

She laughed, a loud, brazen sound, and sat down next to him. He ordered another drink, then smiled tentatively at her. Her face hadn't gotten any more attractive, but she was a fairly impressive specimen from the neck down, and her animal spirits were infectious.

"Of course," she said conspiratorially, "I'm assuming you're alone. Am I right?"

"You might have had quite a scene on your hands if you weren't. But you are. Libby's minding the store in Ireland. And how is ... ?" He couldn't think of her husband's name offhand.

"Oh, never mind Jake. He's gone, as usual, but you're back. Live for today, baby, that's my motto!"

She took a deep pull of her drink, then smiled lasciviously and moved closer to him, so that his left knee was between her knees. Her skirt was about half way up her thighs, as Smart couldn't help but notice. He felt a pleasant scrotal warmth as Sir Smartie began to stir. Gloryanna might not be a prize in the looks department, but she was willing and she was there, next to him, radiating heat. And who knew, at this point, what might have passed between Libby and Gall? It wouldn't be all that difficult to rationalize having a go with Gloryanna, given Libby's great distance and the fact that the real-estate queen would never be more than a one- or two-night stand.

But, he thought to himself as she prattled on about what a desperately bereft place Tuscarora Falls had become in his absence, *I didn't come here to get it on with Gloryanna. I came to find Perdita.* He slid almost imperceptibly back on his seat, away from her. She noticed, but she was used to having men play hard to get, and she didn't let it bother her. She'd set her sights on him and was determined to close the deal that night.

* * *

Lauretta Smale lay on the bed in her room, her shoes off and her Karlin jacket draped carelessly over a chair. She wouldn't need the jacket much longer. The charade, after all, was about to end, and she was thinking about how she would handle Malcott and his "package" the next morning in the coffee shop. This would be the defining moment of her young life, and after she had dealt with her father, she had no idea what she would do with the rest of it. Tax law was for geeks — she'd only forced herself to master it to the degree necessary because it seemed to be her most effective weapon against Smart. After he was behind bars or ruined by Uncle Sam's vengeful judgment, she would have to take some time off and plot a new course. Given how much her "commission" for nailing him was likely to be, she'd have the resources to explore various possibilities — Paris? Rio? — at her leisure.

The phone rang, jarring her from her pleasant reverie. She had a strong intuition of who it was, and she didn't really want to talk to him, not now. But there was business to conduct. She picked up the phone.

"Ms. Smale?"

That unmistakable voice. Hollow, somehow. As she'd expected, it was Malcott.

Thirty-one

This could wreck my life, thought Libby with an inward groan as Gall careened around a hairpin turn on their way to Limerick. The sun had set long ago, yet they had at least another hour to drive. What had possessed her to go along with his crackpot plan?

"Oh, don't worry yourself, Your Grace," he'd said in that rich, confident brogue of his, "we'll not take no for an answer if they try to keep us from seeing Fegan. We'll tell them you're a long-lost relative from the States, and they won't have the heart to tell us to come back in the morning."

It had seemed such a bold, funny, engaging thing to say at the time, and she'd gotten swept up in the spirit of mad adventure. Now, with her stomach lurching each time Gall heaved the wheel over, she realized she'd drunk more champagne — and perhaps imbibed more of Gall's blarney — than she'd intended. This had been a damned silly idea, especially since he was sure to suggest, after the hospital turned them away, that they go and find "someplace to sleep, so." Only sleeping would be the last thing on his mind, and she had no intention of spending the night with him. How could she have let herself get into such a stupid situation?

"Seamus," she began through clenched teeth.

"Yes, Your Grace. I know exactly what you're going to say, so don't bother to utter the words. You've decided that this was a daft idea, and you want me to turn us around and head back to Ballymorda. Isn't that right?" He looked at her with raised eyebrows.

"Well …" she said, slightly taken aback by this sudden onset of reasonableness, "it is awfully late. I would have liked to see Fegan, but there's no reason why it has to be tonight. We could go tomorrow instead. And besides, he'll be out like a stone when we get there, even if they would let us in, which I doubt — relative from the States or no."

Gall had been slowing the Citroen as Libby spoke, and now he pulled a deft U-turn on the empty road and reversed course without a word. Then he said: "It's funny, isn't it, how it seemed like a good idea at the time … going off at dusk to see Fegan, I mean. I guess we got a bit carried away."

She looked at him, expecting to see disappointment, perhaps anger. Instead, his smile was almost beatific. He looked like a man who was full of secret knowledge, perhaps a fond remembrance of some wild tryst of his youth. Just who was this improbable character she'd almost eloped with, anyway?

His hand was on the gearshift knob between them, and when he looked at her, still beaming, she smiled back and put her hand on his for the briefest moment. She didn't look directly at him for the whole way home, but she sensed that the grin never left his face.

* * *

"Yes, Mr. Malcott. This is Lauretta Smale. Is everything ready for tomorrow morning?"

Malcott stood in front of the mirror in his room, leering, with Fergus's angelic face, at the very prominent bulge in his pants. He was ready for Perdita right now. He had told her he expected to receive his commission before the hand-over of Smart, and he was taking no chances that she would nab him on her own — especially now that all three of them were in the same hotel. He spoke into the phone again.

"Everything is ready. Except the small matter of my well-earned reward."

"Mr. Malcott, the United States government is fully prepared to reward you once the full extent of Mr. Smart's tax liability has been determined. I'll fill out a claim form for you tomorrow, after he's been served with the warrant, and you can ... ."

"Ms. Smale," said Malcott, a strange, powerfully husky tone surging through his voice, "I'm not interested in government claim forms. I have no desire for money. I desire something else. Something only you can give. Do you understand me, Ms. Smale?"

Lauretta sat up in bed. She couldn't believe what she'd just heard. A blind dread began to take control of her, making it difficult to breathe, much less speak. Where was it coming from? It seemed to have flowed directly out of the phone line and into the most secret recesses of her soul.

"Mr. Malcott," she stammered, "what are you saying ... ?"

"You know what I'm saying, all right. I want you. I want you now, tonight. You can't imagine how much I want you, and what that desire will feel like inside you, burning hot as a torch in your very core."

She was silent, stunned.

He went on: "I'm planning to make unforgettable love to you, Ms. Smale. An experience to wash away that nasty business with your mother's boyfriend and any other so-called sex you may have had. I know all about that childhood encounter, and how you never really recovered from it. But I'll heal you as no doctor ever could and give you something you'll treasure for the rest of your life. In fact, you'll beg me for more, and I'll give you more and more and more. My fires are inexhaustible. Don't think of refusing, because if I don't get what I want, you won't get what you want. You can be sure of that. I'd kill Smart before I turned him over to you without my reward. Or if you tried to arrest him yourself. I'm in room 166, Ms. Smale. The lights are low, everything's ready. Don't keep me waiting long."

The line went dead, and Lauretta felt herself falling into an abyss of horror and despair. Who was this man who knew about her deepest secret and promised her a new life even while he threatened Smart's? She sensed she would have to give him what he wanted, she could feel the strong pull of it — even the fierce attraction of it. Whoever this Malcott was, he was a man of extraordinary power. The force of his will had transcended his words and come through his voice, and now she felt like someone who has been gripped by an irresistible compulsion. He was in room 166, right now, and he was waiting for her with a leer of lust on his face. But what did his face look like? She'd never even seen the man.

She felt faint, staring at the phone as if it were the head of a poisonous snake that might strike at any moment. She edged away from it, then summoned up her faltering will and jumped up and grabbed her jacket and shoes. She had to get away from this dreadful man, leave this room, maybe even leave town. Would he really kill Smart if she didn't yield to him? She hated her father, but she had never wanted him dead — especially now that her mother was gone. If only she could contact Serena now!

She hobbled down the hall, slipping on her shoes as she went, then hurried through the lobby to the bustling street, where she took a deep breath as she leaned against a light stanchion. The room, the hotel, her whole world had come down to an infinitesimal point at the bottom of a whirling maelstrom of fear, and she had found herself almost suffocating with it.

After a few moments, she started somewhat unsteadily toward the shops and restaurants of Main Street. Should she get her IRS supervisor involved? The police? She wasn't sure of what to do or where she was going, but she knew she had to get away from that awful voice, whose echoes in her mind were like quicksand pulling her down, down, down.

Thirty-two

As Gall drove up the long, dark drive to Mordalee, Libby was awash in contradictory emotions. On the one hand, she had come to know this bluff Irishman in a way she suspected few others did, and she had, to a greater extent than she cared to acknowledge, come to admire him. Maybe, she admitted to herself, more than admire. On the other hand, it wasn't the kind of feeling you consummated between the sheets. It was a gentler, almost sisterly kind of attachment for a man who seemed to be a kindred spirit, in many ways, and much more complex than the comic-book stud he liked to project. She was glad they'd laughed together and shared this very strange tryst. In a way, she felt Gall had not only given her a key to him, but to her adopted country as well. But she already had a lover, and she was prepared to wait for his return.

For his part, Gall had no regrets. He hadn't gotten his leg over and didn't expect to, true, but he'd spent a whirlwind evening with the Yankee Duchess nevertheless, and they'd laughed and bared their souls to each other just a bit, if not their bodies as well, and sometimes what you got was better than what you'd wanted in the first place, and that was the way of it. She was a fine, handsome woman, but she had put him unaccountably in mind of another fine, handsome woman — his estranged wife. And he felt oddly grateful for that.

He'd also come to understand, during their long conversations, that he had misinterpreted Libby's meeting with Fegan at The

Drowning Man, and he was determined, now that Libby had shown him a better version of himself, not to let any such misunderstandings crop up about their own time together.

The huge, dark shape of the house loomed up before them, and Libby was thankful that Pike had as yet failed to return from visiting his relatives. The sight of herself disembarking from Gall's van late at night was one she was glad he would not witness.

Gall coasted the Citroen to a quiet halt, and he and Libby got out. There was a hamper in the back that they'd prepared for Fergus, and he fetched it and joined Libby at the back door, where she paused after turning the exterior light on.

"Seamus," she said, giving him a bittersweet smile.

"Yes, Your Grace. I know. I fear I've made a bollocks of it all. Still, you enjoyed yourself this evening, as I did. But it's not that way between you and me, not the way of lovers. I understand. You're a fine lady indeed, and Mr. Smart is more than lucky to have you to himself. I'll be going now, and nothing will be said to anyone on my part."

He put the hamper down just inside the door, then turned to leave.

"Wait," Libby said, staying him with a hand on his arm.

She kissed him, deliberately but without ardor, once on the mouth. Then she gave him a quick hug. "You've helped open a new world to me, Seamus, and I thank you for it. And I think you're a fine man, too."

He smiled, then turned and headed back to his van. *It's passing strange*, he thought, *that a woman like her could kiss me and leave me feeling more like a blushing schoolboy than a man in his prime.* What would his buddies at the pub think if they knew? But although he did feel a faint frisson in his nether regions, he was prepared to let it die out of its own accord and keep what was left: the afterglow of a very memorable night. And he would have a chat with Fegan, perhaps tomorrow morning, to make sure that he understood and would respect what had and had not passed between Libby and himself.

Libby watched him go, then made her way upstairs to the bedroom. On her way she passed the Devil's room, its door and wall still untouched. *Just as well,* she thought. That was something to tackle in concert with Trel, or not at all. As she was beginning to understand, there was no telling what kinds of strangeness might be unleashed by the taking down of such a wall in such an odd old house. You might own a place like Mordalee, but you had to acknowledge that it owned you, too, to a certain extent. It had its own imperatives, and they demanded respect.

It had been a long day, and she was bone tired. But sleep eluded her for twenty minutes or so as she lay in bed, naked except for a thin cotton shift between the burgundy satin sheets, thinking of Smart and Seamus Gall and the empty place next to her where neither one was. She fell asleep after making up her mind to discuss the whole Seamus business with Smart as soon as he got back. She knew it would be risky, but she also felt that it might lead them toward the discussion they'd been needing to have for so long but had avoided: the discussion about them.

* * *

Sergeant O'Boyle of the Limerick Gardai was peering at Fergus with ill-concealed skepticism.

"Now let me get this straight, Mr. Fergus. You say you were heading out the door when it just swung inward with great force, striking you on the head? I've never heard of that kind of an accident before."

"It was no fooking accident!" said Fergus heatedly. "Someone purposely bashed me with that door, although the why and who of it I'll be damned if I know."

"Well, if there's no likely suspect and no likely motive, sir, then accident is the more likely theory, wouldn't you say?"

"I wouldn't say that at all. I don't know who it was, but someone apparently wanted me out of commission. It couldn't have been an accident, not with the speed and force of it. I had no time to react, sergeant — would you listen? None!"

O'Boyle scribbled in his notepad, but he kept what he was thinking to himself: that Fergus must have been in the horrors to have had his head at the forward pitch and angle it had taken to make contact with the door. He must have been damn near staggering drunk, but the emergency personnel and the airport security officers on the scene hadn't noted anything about alcohol or drugs in their report. And since it hadn't been a vehicular incident and had looked like an accident rather than a crime, no one had bothered to do a blood or breath test. Still, he was of half a mind to charge Fergus with public drunkenness just to see how he would react. He cleared his throat as Fergus blazed up again:

"What about Mr. Smart? Have you tried to contact him in America? I was traveling with him, the famous writer and owner of the Mordalee estate in Ballymorda, and he might have had some sight of who did this to me."

"Well if he did, he didn't file a report or step forward to talk to the airport people after you went down. Strange, that, eh? And he hasn't called from the States, so far as I know." The sergeant studied Fergus's reaction, which was of repressed consternation, and decided to let him go without a charge. Maybe there was something to his story of being whacked after all. And maybe Smart himself had done it. He'd seen cases like this before: In all probability, Fergus had been fooling around with Smart's wife or girlfriend or daughter, and Smart had chosen his moment to punish him. Well, hopefully he'd learned his lesson.

"I know Mr. Smart had important business in the States, officer," said a somewhat subdued Fergus, "but I don't know the exact nature of it. You could perhaps find that out from his wife, though, who's in Ballymorda now, as far as I know."

O'Boyle nodded noncommittally. "We'll keep the case open for now. Keep in touch with us from Ballymorda if you find out anything else, and we'll do the same."

With that, the garda turned on his heel and left, and Fergus was fairly certain that that would be the last of it as far as the police were concerned. They had no witnesses, no suspects, no motives ... not a hell of a lot to go on, he had to admit, except his own suspicions. Why hadn't Smart called? That was strange, indeed. And why had Gall called last night to say he'd be visiting with Libby Smart? Or had he dreamed that?

Never mind, he thought to himself. *I'll be out of here in less than an hour anyway, and then I'll find Gall myself and get to the bottom of it all.*

Thirty-three

An hour after walking into Diamond Jim's, Smart had forgotten about eluding Malcott's toils and fallen into Gloryanna's instead. He certainly wasn't overcome with lust for her, but he was tired, confused and apprehensive, which made him vulnerable to her gung-ho approach. At one point she used her lips in some very intriguing ways on a pretzel stick while he was talking, and noted with a wicked smile that she had an "oral fixation" that found its ultimate expression in the practice of fellatio. This information, and its arresting presentation, made a big impression on the wavering Smart. Besides, he didn't have a clue about how he was going to combat Malcott except to stay away from him.

Borne along like a cork on the raging torrent of Gloryanna's desire, he found himself agreeing to a romp at "his place," since she didn't want the busybodies in her neighborhood thinking they had something on her. "Which they wouldn't anyway," she told Smart. "I'll tell Jake myself when he gets home. But I wouldn't give those assholes the satisfaction of feeling smug!"

At this point, with the hour getting late and several scotches under his belt, Smart was beginning to acknowledge a certain inevitability — if not desirability — about Gloryanna. He hadn't experienced the joys of the flesh in several weeks, and he felt he needed something to kick-start his libido. And it seemed that if anyone could provide a kick-start, it would be Old Glory.

Just before she left the bar she said she'd meet him at his room in an hour or so, after picking up a few pieces of "inspirational" lingerie at home and returning a few calls. "I've got to take care of business, you know," she said. "And it's business before pleasure. But then I'm going to pleasure you like you've never been done. Got that, Mr. Big Man?" She addressed his crotch as she said this and winked lewdly at him. Then, with several flamboyant strides, she swept out of the bar.

A few minutes later, he paid the tab and headed out into the cool night air. He still had no idea what he'd do about Malcott, except that he had no intention of joining him at the appointed hour. In fact, he had decided to start the next day at the Wordsworth campus looking for Perdita.

Lost in his own thoughts, he didn't notice the tall, strikingly attractive young woman coming out of the coffee shop several doors up from Diamond Jim's until he had nearly bumped into her. His first thought was that she was one of the most beautiful creatures he had ever seen, although she seemed distant or troubled somehow. Still, his mind began to fill with an instantaneous fog of lust. God, he'd like to … . Then he looked her straight in the eyes — Serena Smale's eyes. His rakish smile faded as he stopped about a foot from her and stared. Two teenage boys walking behind him nearly piled into them, but they split up and surged around them and smirked to each other when they saw what had caused him to stop so suddenly. What an incredible babe the old man had spotted!

Lauretta looked up at the man in front of her and instantly became oblivious, as he had, to the busy street scene that surrounded them. She knew him at once — her father, the man she'd loved to hate for so many years, the man she'd hoped to bring low if she possibly could. But he was also her only remaining parent, and she felt sorely in need of a parent — of someone, at least, who was wholeheartedly on her side — after talking to the evil man who was waiting for her and who had even threatened to kill Smart. That is, to kill her father.

Smart's reflexive desire changed into astonishment as he studied her face, which was like a genetic link to a lost love: Serena's lustrous, thick hair, wide eyes and lush mouth, his own strong nose and firm chin. But the features had been shaped as if by a master sculptor into a near-perfect blend that far transcended the two parents. Smart was reasonably good-looking and Serena had been very pretty, but Perdita was breathtaking. Yet she was deeply troubled somehow — he could sense that, even through her obvious shock at encountering him. He couldn't help but smile a tentative, wondering smile that didn't quite mask the terror he was feeling: the terror that she would reject him, thrust him away with a crushing rebuke, hurt him more than he would be able to bear.

"Lauretta," he said, reaching out to touch her arm as if she were a long-sought, legendary treasure, "my own dear child. I'm so sorry. Please forgive me. Please ... ."

She was paralyzed for an instant. He'd merely confirmed what she had known the moment she saw him, but this was nothing like the scathingly satisfying scenes she'd imagined. Here he was, a melancholy and somewhat tentative man with a graying mustache who looked much older in person than the pictures on his book jackets made him look. They didn't capture the deepening fissures that began at the corners of his mouth, or the furrow over his brow. He may have been a very flawed person in his younger days — must have been, to do what he'd done — but he also didn't look the part of the heartless bastard she'd so often vanquished in her fantasies. They both trembled as she looked into his eyes and saw waiting in them what she needed most: unreserved love.

Then he put out his arms, but instead of falling into them she gathered herself up to her full height and slapped him across the face as hard as she could.

"That's for Serena, you bastard! And ... for me."

The blow, which had caught him full on his left cheek, whipped his face sideways, but he made no move to defend himself or stop her from hitting him again. He slowly turned his aching face back to her, keeping his arms out, and she suddenly found herself crying. Spent and confused to her core, she threw her arms around this hated stranger who had suddenly and quite unexpectedly been reincarnated as her loving father. The boys who'd been following Smart had stepped back a pace, shocked, when she had slapped him. Now they smirked and high-fived each other as they saw Lauretta bury her face in his chest. They didn't see the tears slipping and then rushing out of the corners of his eyes or hear what he was whispering, his face in her hair: "Oh, Perdita, my Perdita ... thank God my dear little lost girl is found at last."

* * *

Gloryanna was in the midst of trying to choose between a red peek-a-boo bustier and a black lace teddy when the phone rang at her house about 40 minutes later. She threw both into her overnight bag, along with some edible panties, and grabbed it. She assumed the caller was Smart wanting to know what was taking her so long.

"Patience, dear," she said into the phone. "I want to bring a nice selection, the better to trigger your massive erection."

Smart laughed and complimented her carnal doggerel, then said there'd been a slight change in their plans.

"What's up? Besides you, that is."

"Nothing, really. The hotel just moved me to a different room. You know how they get in a bind sometimes when they're crowded and need to put several rooms together? Anyway, they had a group booking and needed my room. I raised a bit of a stink, of course, but they ended up giving me a better room — with a king-size bed to play on — and a complimentary bucket of champagne. I figured that couldn't hurt, eh?"

Gloryanna laughed, a harsh grating noise. How had he managed to ignore that sound at Diamond Jim's? "Oh, you're so right, big boy! A little champagne makes me even naughtier than I am normally."

"That would seem almost impossible," said Smart.

"Oh, you ain't seen nothing yet," said Gloryanna, zipping up her monogrammed bag. "Or tasted it, either. You ever had panties sauteed in Glory sauce?" She didn't wait for his reply. "Anyway, I'm almost ready to come. Go, I mean. So what room is it?"

"One-sixty-six" said Smart. "Bring your horns."

Thirty-four

Later, when he was at leisure to think about it on the long flight home, Smart almost felt sorry for Malcott. At thirty-five thousand feet it was possible to get a broader view of things, and he wasn't quite sure if Malcott's crimes had been deserving of such drastic punishment. Yes, he'd bashed Fergus and scared the hell out of Lauretta, but did he really deserve a night with Old Glory? He shrugged inwardly. Maybe there had been no punishment after all. Maybe they had been meant for each other. He chuckled, then thought once again of his miraculous child.

He had been surprised — almost shocked — at the surge of paternal emotions his meeting with her had unleashed. Women were always said to have such strong motherly feelings, but he suspected that fathers felt paternal bonds at least equally, although they were not so good as women at showing how they felt. Now, though, it was as if a stifled, atrophied part of him, something that had been buried so far down in his psyche that he'd lost track of it, had burst out and flowered. He was a father; he had a daughter. He felt an indescribable fulfillment.

Of course, it hadn't looked like anything would flower when she'd slapped him. The blow had been the unreserved product of almost twenty years of anger, and it had hurt — but only in retrospect. Just after it landed, in the moments just before and during their embrace, he hadn't felt the pain at all, although its force had rung his skull, and his cheek even now had a bit of bruise from it under the airline ice he was using to bring down the swelling. What had stanched the pain on Tuscarora's bustling main street? He'd come to believe it was the power of miracles, which could smother hurt with a countervailing love that had been as long suppressed as the anger that had produced the blow.

After holding each other for a while on the street, he and Lauretta had found a quiet corner in the coffee shop where they had quickly unburdened themselves. Smart grasped the full dimensions of Malcott's perfidy almost immediately — he'd always been after Perdita, not Libby, and he'd come damn near to manipulating her rightful rage into the ruination of both father and daughter. But as soon as he grasped Malcott's plan — and Lauretta understood that Gloryanna had set up a romp with Smart — their mutual way out had presented itself. If Malcott and the bitch goddess of Tuscarora real estate were so damned hot to trot, let them go at each other.

He didn't try to explain to Lauretta who Malcott really was; he saw no point in straining his own fragile credibility with her. Rather, he told her that Malcott was a dangerous con man who had somehow gotten wind of his difficulties and followed him from Ireland to take advantage of them. She had begun to ask more questions there in the coffee shop, but he answered most of them when he told her that Malcott was the most diabolical person he had ever met. That seemed to sum up and confirm Lauretta's own feelings.

They agreed that Smart would head back to Ireland immediately, before the IRS hierarchy even knew he'd come to the States. Lauretta would follow as soon as she could — she already had a passport because of a semester-abroad program at school the year before — after first attempting to clear up his problem with the IRS or at least seeing if she could get him a better deal.

It was funny, he thought as he looked out the airliner's window into a nothingness so profound that it might as well have been the bottom of the ocean as the night sky: Now that he had his daughter back, the money he was contesting with the IRS seemed far less important. He could always earn more, once he'd gotten his other problems straightened out. And he felt that finding Perdita had been a major step on that road. There had been a gaping hole in his soul, he realized, and even his own dear Libby hadn't been able to fill it completely. Hence the drinking, the periodic upending of his own life, the compulsive searching for the missing part, the nagging lack. But that was all behind him. He'd clean up his act, make amends with Libby and rid Mordalee of Malcott once and for all, if he could. In fact, a plan for that was beginning to form in the back of his brain. He knew it was an ambitious agenda, but he felt he could do almost anything now. The fog over his life had lifted; he was no longer flying blind.

They both had checked out of the Armada that same night, Lauretta passing Gloryanna as the latter made her way to Malcott's room and ignoring the ugly sneer she'd aimed at her. Then they'd driven down to the Albany airport to drop off her rental car, continuing from there to Boston in Smart's car. They were emotionally exhilarated but physically exhausted, so they stopped every so often for coffee and took turns driving, building a stronger and deeper bond with each mile. She told him early on that she had never been a true believer in the government's tax case; she had just wanted to use it to get even. These words had made Smart flinch, and it took him a while to respond. But when he did, he made a persuasive case that he'd paid a very high price in self-respect for his debacle with Serena and Lauretta. "If you have a soul, you can't just walk away from something like that and pretend everything's OK," Smart said. "I damn near killed myself with drinking and coke and craziness after that, just trying to forget."

She didn't attempt to free him of guilt; no one could do that, and he knew he would always bear some measure of it until he died. But she brought up the subject of Serena's obstinacy and said she thought it had been at least partly to blame for their woes. It was a halting step toward some shred of absolution for Smart, and he was profoundly grateful.

"I do think things could have been very different if your mother had been able to extend me some small measure of forgiveness," Smart told her. "Of course, I'd done her and you a terrible, terrible wrong, so her rage was completely justified. But if she could have seen fit to relent just enough to let me tell her in person how sorry I was ... ."

"Dad, do you think you could have gotten back together with Mom and me?" It was the first time she'd called him "Dad" — a moment he would cherish until his dying day.

"I don't know, honey. I can't say for sure if that would have worked. Though much chastened after my experience with her, I was still a lot younger and wilder back then. But I would have jumped at the chance to try. Maybe we could have made a go of it. We'll never know for certain. But you and I have gotten together at last, and this time we're going to make sure we don't lose each other, right?"

She had smiled at him, a little girl beaming out from behind the dazzling facade of a gorgeous and sophisticated young woman. And then she had taken his free hand in hers. It had made him realize how much love he'd missed out on for the past 20 years, and that realization hurt like a knife plunged into his heart. But he fought back the tears; he had found his sweet Perdita at last, and he would keep her as close as he could.

They'd rolled into Boston at about 2:30 in the morning and found two adjacent rooms at the airport Hilton. Smart would have preferred a suite with two bedrooms, but he didn't feel ready to suggest that. She was his little girl, but they didn't share the same last name, and they would look like that tawdriest of spectacles, the rich old lecher and the trophy mistress. Lauretta felt the same kinds of conflicts. Now that she'd found her long-lost parent, she would have preferred to keep him as close as possible. But having a father was a new and unfamiliar experience, and she wasn't quite ready for all its logical implications. Appearances were appearances, and after all, they didn't know each other very well.

She didn't sleep soundly after they'd said goodnight and retired to their own rooms, however. She kept waking up with the horrible feeling that her father had been a mirage and that she'd been left parentless once again. Haggard as she felt, she still fairly glowed at breakfast. But Smart didn't realize, sitting across from her and beaming as he poured her coffee and buttered her toast, that a major part of that radiance, which he ascribed to youth, was in fact due to relief.

Since Smart couldn't get a flight out earlier than 8:15 that evening, they had a whole day to explore not only Boston but each other's lives, and so they did. By the time he'd gotten on the plane, the love he'd felt for her there on Main Street in Tuscarora had broadened and deepened until he thought he would never comprehend the sheer joy of it.

* * *

Libby, looking troubled, was waiting for him when he got off the plane at Shannon. *Just Libby*, he thought. *No Gall. Thank God!* He had half feared that they would meet him jointly to deliver some intolerably bad news.

She looked at him searchingly, then threw her arms around him without a word and hugged him like someone grasping a life buoy. Then, uncharacteristically for her, she dissolved into tears. He took her chin between his fingertips and kissed her all around her face, and then on the lips. Then he said, "My love, whatever it is you have to tell me, let me say this first: You can't imagine how good it is to see you."

Then he wiped her eyes, and she wiped his, and they walked off hand in hand to get his bags. With all that had happened jumbled kaleidoscopically in his head, he could scarcely believe he'd left her at Mordalee only a little over two days before.

Once they were in the car, they both said "Well," at the same time, then laughed. "You first," said Smart.

"Trel ... there's something very strange about that house you bought. Especially about that little room, you know the one ... ?"

"Yes, I know the one." He sighed. "And you're right. There's definitely something strange about it. In fact, you won't believe just how strange. But I hope to get rid of it before too long."

"It? What do you mean?"

He told her everything — how he'd attempted to take down the door and wall himself, his first meeting with Malcott, Malcott's machinations regarding Libby and Perdita, his encounter with Lady B. and the long-departed Brimstons. She wanted to stop him for a full account of the long-lost daughter she'd never heard about — what other revelations might lurk in Smart's past? — but he hurried on, elements of the fantastic tale spilling out in a torrent. She listened with a growing sense of unreality, waiting for the punch line that never came. Finally she stopped him with a hand in the air.

"Wait a minute, Trel. You mean we're not only damned but haunted as well?"

"Um, well, yes. I suppose you could say that. But the haunting is relatively benign, and I suspect that once the source of damnation is removed, the haunting will cease as well. They're all bound up together, you see."

She looked at him as if she couldn't quite believe what she was hearing, but he returned her gaze unflinchingly. Finally, she said:

"You really believe in all this stuff, don't you?"

"I wouldn't have believed in it a couple of weeks ago, of course. Just like you, I would have assumed it was all so much Irish folderol. But I've seen what I've seen ... and then there's poor Fegan Fergus."

"Fegan! I forgot all about him. He's in the hospital right near here, Trel, as far as I know. Let's stop in and see how he is."

But Fergus, the hospital clerk told them a bit later, had already checked out.

"Anyway," said Smart when they were back in their car, "Fergus was here because Malcott needed to impersonate him in the States for his own vile purposes. I can tell you one thing for sure: I didn't bash him with the door. I didn't even know he'd been knocked out, which is why I was so shocked when you told me. As far as I knew, Fergus had been with me all the while."

Libby looked thoughtful. "Well," she said, "we should be able to get to the bottom of that particular story pretty soon, since he's probably on his way back to Ballymorda. We both know where to find him ... ."

They looked at each other, then Smart looked away. His face assumed a pained expression. Libby took his hand, sighed and said, "Trel, I'm still yours. But I'm not quite ready to talk about that yet. Give me a chance to catch my breath, and then I'll tell you about my ... close encounter of the Seamus kind."

Thirty-five

Roland Scaiffey was deeply engrossed in doping out the fifth race at Aqueduct when the buzzer on his desk jolted him. Vaguely annoyed, he punched a button and said "Yes?"

"Mr. Scaiffey, it's a Ms. Smale from the IRS, regarding Mr. Smart's case. Can you talk to her now?"

"I'll take the call," he said, hastily throwing the Racing Form onto a nearby mahogany credenza and rooting in a drawer for Smart's file.

A moment or two later, he heard a youthful-sounding but very smooth and businesslike voice: "Mr. Scaiffey? Lauretta Smale here. I'm the special agent in charge of Mr. Smart's file."

"What can we do for you, Ms. Smale?" Scaiffey asked cautiously. He was looking over the last notes he'd made, which were now several months old, and hoping that this Ms. Smale was not about to tell him that she had taken Smart into custody.

"We're interested in clearing up Mr. Smart's case if possible. Do you think you'd be able to meet with me this afternoon to discuss terms?"

Scaiffey could hardly believe his ears. What could have caused this kind of turnaround? "You mean ... you want us to consider an offer to settle?"

"I'll have details when I see you, Mr. Scaiffey. But I think you'll find what I have to say well worth hearing. Today at 1:30 at your office?"

"Absolutely, Ms. Smale. See you then."

Pleased but somewhat flummoxed, Scaiffey began poring over Smart's file again as soon as she had hung up. "They must have noticed a big hole in their case somewhere," Scaiffey mused to himself. "So why didn't we notice it?"

* * *

The armadillos ignored him, for the most part, as Peter Pike stared down at them in their pen. Noxious little creatures, he thought, yet not without a certain fascination. If they ever escaped and colonized the countryside, he supposed he would become known as the anti-Patty, the man who gave Ireland its first serious nuisance animal since the snakes had been driven out. But the pen had a concrete floor and walls of strong wire mesh; he didn't think the little buggers would be able to spring themselves. At least, not on his watch.

He'd arrived early that morning, but not early enough to catch Libby at home. The postman had told him he thought the mistress of the manor had gone to pick up the master at Shannon, and would be back before lunch, if they were reasonably lucky with the traffic around Limerick. Pike didn't bother to inquire how the postman could offer these theories with such confidence; postmen had their sources, after all.

He had left his flock in charge of a local lad during his absence, but the boy had been somewhat truant as a shepherd or perhaps not truant enough at school, because several sheep seemed to be missing from the nearby meadow, including a prize ewe who was due to drop a lamb or two any day now. "I'll have 'em back soon enough," he muttered to himself. The armadillos paused for a moment or two in their rooting and nuzzling to look at him, then resumed their business as if he was beneath further consideration.

"Weird little beasties," Pike said as he took up his crook and shuffled off toward the headache stone and the fields and woods behind it. "I wonder what kind of a stew they'd make?"

* * *

"You're serious, now?" said Fegan Fergus, looking at Seamus Gall with wide eyes. He quickly narrowed them a bit; having them open so much hurt his head.

"Yes," said Gall decisively. "I need to get away and attend to things with ... my family. If I can still call it that."

Fergus shook his head, wondering if this conversation was yet another of the hallucinations and odd dreams he'd had since getting his pate bashed.

"And you want me to run The Drowning Man for you?"

"Yes, that's it. You can run it for wages if you like or lease it from me by the month and make the most you can out of it. Murphy, my accountant over in Birr, could probably advise you on your best course. He says the pub could be run a lot better, so. And he's probably right; my mind hasn't been on it of late. I've been distracted, like. And I've been looking for love in all the wrong places, as the song says."

Fergus shook his head again; was this really Gall talking, or a weird clone? "You don't sound like yourself, Seamus," Fergus said. "I thought you were happy with the pub and with your contracting and ... laying pipe hither and yon."

"But that's just it, Fegan. I've been putting up a front to disguise what I really am, which is an unhappy man. I have a son; I had a wife. We were a family there for awhile, and I'd like to find out if it would be possible to put us together again."

"Have you heard from Shailagh, then?" said Fergus, referring to Gall's wife.

"No, and that's part of what's getting to me. I used to hear from her regularly with news of Keiron, her job, her mother and all. Now she's gone silent. I may be too late, of course — she may have found another man and a bishop who'll pull strings to give them a church wedding — but I've got to find out, and not just over the phone. I'm going to Killarney, perhaps for good. In which case, by the way, I'll be looking to sell out. So, do you want to take over The Drowning Man or not?"

Fergus looked about him; it was a good pub with a thriving business. But how had they gotten to this topic from what they'd started talking about maybe an hour before: Gall's strange, platonic fling with Libby Smart? The publican had taken pains to make Fergus understand that while they'd spent five or six hours together, and while he'd gone out to Mordalee expecting to be able to put another notch in his belt, something very different had come of it. He'd shared his soul with her, and she with him, and they'd found that experience much more meaningful than thrashing about between the sheets. Fergus had no more expected to hear Gall say any such thing than to hear the Pope advocate dancing naked in the streets.

But he could see that Gall was onto something here, something important to him, and if it meant that he, Fergus, could step into the breach and help himself while helping Gall fulfill his destiny as a family man, then why not? It wasn't as if the real estate business was any great shakes now, anyway.

"Let me think about it, Seamus. This is all so sudden, and I've just had my brains scrambled in my skull, so I'm not so quick as usual."

"Think, sure, but I want to be gone soon." He paced a bit as Fergus sat. Then he stopped. "It's a good offer, Fegan, you must know that."

Fergus nodded.

"Then what's troubling you about it?"

"Well," Fergus began, eyeing the gleaming brass tip of the Guinness tap, "to tell you the truth, I'm afraid I might ... ."

"Drink up all the profits, is it? And you might indeed if you don't follow this simple tip: Never drink at work. That is, never drink anything at all alcoholic while you're on the job. As much as you pour for others, never touch a drop of it yourself. Stick to the club soda or orangeade or whatever you like, but no stout or booze. Have you ever seen me drinking anything hard behind this bar in all the time you've been coming here?"

Fergus realized he never had. Whenever he'd seen Gall pour himself a drink, it had been from the soda tap. He shook his head.

"There, that's the whole yoke. You can do it, Fegan, if I can."

Thirty-six

"Why didn't you tell me?" Libby stared a challenge at Smart across the kitchen table.

Smart fidgeted. Then he sighed. He started to speak, then stopped. He had thought they were going to discuss the Seamus Gall situation once they'd settled in at home, but somehow Libby had turned the tables on him. Of course, she'd had almost a full day to think about things while he caught up on the sleep he hadn't been able to catch on the plane. Deep down, however, he knew that she had put things in the proper priority. He had left her, emotionally and then physically, and not the other way around. She had every right to ask why he hadn't told her about the Devil's room after his first encounter with Malcott.

"Don't you love me, Trel?"

It was a potentially devastating question, but Smart had the best possible answer. He went round the kitchen table, picked Libby up out of her seat and and kissed her passionately. Then he looked her directly in the eyes and said, "Yes. You are my life, and I love you with all my heart. But ... I got off the track somehow. I don't know what happened, really. I was focused on the wrong things, as people so frequently are. I thought I needed to get away from something, which is how we ended up here in Ireland, but in fact I needed to find something or reconnect with something. Someone, rather. I wasn't whole, my love, and you bore the brunt of it. I'm sorry. But you're the most precious thing in the world to me, and I do love you very much." He kissed her again, and this time, she kissed back.

They hugged and stroked each other for awhile, and then Libby took a step back. "I have a confession to make," she said. Smart's heart sank; he didn't want to hear that she and Gall had made love, even if it had been only a one-night stand or a bid to pay him back for his own inattention. He looked away, but she took his chin between her fingers and brought his face back into alignment with hers.

"I spent a wild evening with Seamus. And with the way I felt ... something might well have happened between us. He clearly had come out here to seduce me in your absence, there's no doubt of that. I don't know why he thought he could, because I'd given him no encouragement. But he did. And it almost happened."

"Almost?" Smart said hopefully. "You mean ... ?"

"We kept it platonic. We shared our feelings, which was something we both really needed to do, I guess. But that's as far as it went. I was tempted, especially after drinking champagne with him. He's ... an intelligent and charming man, Trel."

Smart turned away again, but she brought his face around once more and looked him in the eyes. "And because I didn't know what you were up to ... I suspected the worst, I guess."

Smart cringed inwardly; if he hadn't stumbled onto Lauretta there on Main Street, he might well have betrayed Libby with Gloryanna. But he had, and so he hadn't. Lauretta had been his guardian angel, helping to keep him from doing something he would have regretted tremendously at this precise moment.

"Anyway," Libby said, stepping forward and putting her arms around him again, "I want you to know that it's you I love, not Seamus Gall. And ... it's you I want."

She kissed him urgently and placed his hands on her swelling breasts. He felt an immediate jolt of desire. He began to kiss her neck and grind his hips softly against her. Just then the phone rang.

"Hold that thought," said Smart, as he disengaged. Libby gave him a comically smoldering look, and he was heartened. Most of their best lovemaking seemed to begin with a laugh.

"Hello?"

"Trel? Roland Scaiffey here. Hope I didn't catch you at a bad time?"

"A bad time? Oh, no, Roland," Smart said, grinning at Libby. "There's no bad time for you. What's up?"

"The most amazing thing," said Scaiffey. "I can hardly believe it myself. The government — in the form of a young special agent named Lauretta Smale — a real knockout, by the way — seems to have thrown in the towel on you."

"Is that so?" said Smart. "The IRS settled," he said in an aside to Libby.

"Yes. I must say, though, you don't sound very surprised."

"Let's just say I had a hunch they would come to their senses. After all, I had the best tax attorney on the planet working for me, didn't I? I figured they'd eventually see the error of their ways."

Scaiffey laughed, although he sounded a bit uncomfortable. "Well, up until today it didn't seem that our brilliance had swayed anyone in the agency or in the courts. But this Ms. Smale offered a very attractive deal, and we took it on your behalf."

"How attractive?" asked Smart, blowing a kiss at Libby.

"They offered to settle all claims and fines for ten cents on the dollar, Trel," Scaiffey said with a kind of astonished pride.

"Ten cents on the dollar? And you took it? My God, I can't believe you'd be so swayed by a pretty young thing. I wanted every last, red, fucking cent!" Smart was enjoying himself hugely. There was no answer for a moment or two.

"But Trel, I ... ." Scaiffey finally stammered.

"Just kidding, Roland. Can't you take a joke?"

Scaiffey got off a hearty laugh, but Smart knew he'd had him going. "It's unbelievably good news, and of course I'm one hundred percent okay with it."

"Well, I thought you would be, Trel. We've never seen anything like this kind of turnabout. And her supervisor signed off on it, too. So we've given them a check and gotten a receipt, and as of now, at least, your troubles with Uncle Sam are over."

"Thank heaven!" said Smart. He saw no need to fill Scaiffey in on the family connection.

"Speaking of that," said Scaiffey conspiratorially, "this Agent Smale had the most heavenly face and figure I've ever seen. Sensational! Made me wish I was a younger man, if you know what I mean."

"Tut, tut, Roland," said Smart. "I'm surprised — a respectable married man like you."

"You had to see her, though, Trel. Tall, long legs ... ."

"I get the picture, Roland. The stuff that middle-aged male fantasies are made of. And I'm sure you were a terror when you were younger, but those days are long gone. It's best to forget the occasional dreamboat when you see one and count your blessings, otherwise they can make you crazy."

Libby was looking at him quizzically. He'd told her about finding Lauretta and had mentioned that she was a looker, but he hadn't gone into detail. He hoped she wouldn't feel overshadowed when the bombshell arrived at Mordalee.

"Well, I guess you're right about that, Trel." But there was still a trace of longing in Scaiffey's voice. As Smart knew all too well, it was a hard lesson for any man to learn.

"Anything else?"

"Oh, yes; I also got a call from a real estate agent up in Tuscarora: Gloryanna Green. Strange name — Gloryanna. Anyway, she says she's sold your house at the asking price. And she insisted that I give you a personal message."

"Oh?"

"Yes. Is there ... anyone else on the line?"

"No."

"Now these are her words, not mine: 'Tell Mr. No-Show he missed a hell of a good time.'"

"I see," said Smart. Gloryanna apparently had enjoyed herself. What about Malcott? He was yet to be heard from. "Well, that's another piece of great news. Please forward the funds to me as soon as possible, Roland."

Scaiffey was a bit disappointed that Smart hadn't told him anything about his dealings with the real estate agent, but he was pretty sure he knew why not.

"Will do. Well, that's it for now. I'll send you the net proceeds and all the paper work as soon as we get it done. Please give my regards to Libby, too, will you?"

"She's right here," Smart said, confirming Scaiffey's guess. "Roland says hello," he said to Libby. "She sends her best, Roland. Goodbye, and thanks for everything."

He hung up the phone, then turned to find her staring at the red welt on his cheek. "This daughter of yours," said Libby. "She must be something else, eh?"

Thirty-seven

Smart felt some trepidation as he set out for The Drowning Man the next morning. He was looking for Fergus and figured he was more likely to find him at the pub than at his real estate office in Birr, but he wasn't particularly keen on seeing Gall. No words — and certainly no blows — needed to be exchanged on the matter of Libby, but such an encounter would be damned awkward anyway, given the circumstances. Upon entering the pub, he was therefore delighted if somewhat surprised to find Fergus, not Gall, behind the bar.

"Mr. Smart!" Fegan cried, putting down a towel and stepping out to shake his hand. "It's good to see you back."

"Good to be back, Fegan," Smart said, pumping his hand enthusiastically and making a mental note of the bandage still on his finger. "I didn't realize it would be possible to miss Ballymorda so much after only two days away from it."

"Two days, was it only that? Yet it seemed so much longer."

"Yes it did. Strange thing, eh?"

They both fell silent, neither one knowing quite how to broach the bizarre incident at Shannon. Smart had already decided he wouldn't tell Fergus the whole truth about Malcott if he could avoid it. He had no desire to set off another round of legends about Mordalee and its occupants, tales that might well last for several more generations. He had wanted a house in Ireland, but he had never wanted to become part of Irish folklore into the bargain.

"Well," Smart began, "what are you doing behind the bar? Is Seamus laying ... I mean, has he got a contracting job today?"

"The fact is, Mr. Smart, I've taken over the pub from Gall, more or less."

"Taken it over?"

"I'm leasing it from him, while he's down south in Killarney on ... family matters. He may not come back, in which case I'll probably buy it."

Smart sat down at the bar to let this sink in. After a moment, he said: "What amazing news. Well, congratulations, Fegan."

"Can I pour you a pint, then, Mr. Smart?"

"No, thanks. I'm cutting back on the stout and on drinking in general. I'm sorry to have to tell you that just as you're starting your reign behind the bar, but that's the way it is. Just a cup of coffee for me, if you please."

Stirring some sugar into the black, aromatic brew in front of him a few moments later, Smart said: "Fegan, about that business at the airport ... ."

"It was none of your fault, Mr. Smart, so I hope you haven't been feeling badly about it. I've spoken to the Gardai over there, and they're going to keep looking for whichever fooker it was who did that to me."

"But I ... ."

"I know it must have been awkward for you, to get on the plane without me after we'd planned to go together, but after all you had important business to conduct, and you couldn't wait for me to get out of hospital. No, Mr. Smart, I would have done the same in your shoes — gotten on the plane, that is, and hoped for the best. You couldn't have seen it coming, as I didn't, and you couldn't have been expected to postpone your own plans on my behalf. So don't worry about it. I just hope they catch the bastard who nailed me, is all."

"I do, too, Fergus. I really do."

Smart drank his coffee in silence while Fergus bustled about his set-up work behind the bar. He had been prepared to give Fergus as much of the story as he thought he'd be able to accept without going into the whole Devil's room angle, but he realized now that he would be better off taking the dispensation Fergus had offered him. How could you explain what had happened without coming clean about who Malcott really was? It was virtually impossible, and since Fergus seemed to be trying to spare Smart's feelings rather than looking for an account of his conduct, he decided to let the matter lie where Fergus had left it.

"So you're going to try your hand at being a publican, eh?"

"I thought: Why not? After all, the real-estate game is dead these days, and good pubs like this don't exactly grow on trees. So I figured I'd give it a go."

"Tough to run a place like this on your own, though, don't you think?"

"Well, I won't be alone, exactly. Gall's part-timers will work for me as they did for him, filling in and giving me a rest now and then, so I should be all right. Besides, the activity will be good after the months of having nothing much going on. And I can always dabble in real estate on the side once that yoke picks up again."

"Well, good luck with it. And don't worry yourself about a fall-off in sales; I haven't given up on the Guinness entirely."

Fergus smiled, but Smart had noticed that he, too, seemed to be cutting back now that he'd assumed the mantle of proprietor. "To tell you the truth," Fergus said, "the margin's as good on coffee as it is on stout, if not better." They both laughed.

"I've got some happy news, by the way," Smart said. "My daughter, Lauretta Smale, will be visiting soon. In fact, I hope it will turn into more than a visit and that I can get her to stay with us permanently.

Although," he added with a shake of the head, "I'm not sure Ballymorda is ready for her."

"That's great news, Mr. Smart! I had no idea you had a child. When will she be arriving, then?"

"It could be as early as tomorrow morning. We're waiting for her to call and tell us when and where to pick her up. She's just clearing up a few loose ends in the States, then she should be on her way."

"Is she grown, then? I mean, is she an adult?"

"Oh, yes. She's ... fully grown, although still quite young — twenty years old. She'd be a great catch for some lucky man, by the way. A real looker, if I do say it, but not full of herself in the way of some beauties."

"But what was it you said ... something about Ballymorda not being ready for her?"

"Oh, that was just a proud father's vanity, Fegan. You'll understand that someday, if you have kids. Anyway, I'll bring her down here one night after she's settled in. I'm sure you two will hit it off."

"Great! I'll look forward to it" Fergus responded as his mind filled with images of gorgeous Hollywood starlets.

A few moments later, Smart left The Drowning Man and stood blinking outside for a moment as his eyes adjusted to the daylight. What would he do if, by some chance, his daughter and Fegan Fergus fell for each other? *Well, why not?* he thought. Fergus was basically an intelligent and goodhearted man — not bad at all for son-in-law material. And he almost felt like family already. His problem was that he just needed a little steadying from time to time. And who didn't?

Thirty-eight

When Smart's office fax machine rang the next afternoon for the second time, he just eyed it warily. He'd already had a piece of excellent news from it earlier in the day, and now he wasn't at all surprised, given the way the yin of life inevitably seemed to follow and confound the yang, to see what appeared to be bad news coming through. It was a brief message, but it was smoking as the machine spewed it out; a message from Malcott, as Smart could see at a glance. And His Malevolence almost certainly wasn't happy.

Time to face the music, Smart thought. But maybe he would be able to call the tune and make the Devil dance to it. Up till this moment, at least, it had been a very promising day.

Smart and Libby had driven to Shannon early that morning to pick up Lauretta, who had been too full of anticipation to sleep on the plane but who still looked radiant when she ventured, with a slight and touching hesitancy, into the airport's waiting room. Libby had insisted on going, and she had given Lauretta a joyous greeting. Inwardly, Smart surmised, the long-reigning diva of his life had been a bit shocked at the sight of his daughter, or perhaps taken aback at the prospect of being permanently upstaged in the looks department, but Lauretta had quickly put her at ease with a warm smile and an attentiveness that was almost daughterly.

She'd given Smart a rapturous welcome, throwing her arms around him and laughing and crying almost simultaneously, and Smart, who had seen out of the corner of his eye that Libby was very affected by it all, had been deeply moved. It confirmed his sense that he had now, at long last, found a kind of wholeness that had always eluded him. In any case, first impressions seemed to have gone extremely well between the two female pillars of his new life, and he hoped the warmth of their encounter boded well for the future.

They talked excitedly all the way home from the airport, Smart gradually receding from the conversation to better monitor its pleasing tenor — and the lovely, easy flow of words and looks between Libby and Lauretta. By the time they reached Ballymorda, which Lauretta found charming, she seemed almost giddy with the changes that had overtaken her: old job and life jettisoned; new family, country and destiny to discover ... all on top of exhaustion and a bad case of jet lag.

As soon as they had gotten home, Libby had made her a cup of herbal tea and put her to bed. He and Libby had talked for a while, and she had confirmed his sense that the two women had taken an instant liking to each other. Deeply satisfied with the way things were turning out, Smart had gone to his office with thoughts of restarting his long-neglected novel. That's when the first fax — the one from his agent, Sam "Sugar Daddy" Shuggerman — had come through.

Trel, it read, GOOD NEWS! *Hulkenberger has settled with the studio, and filming on Nagap the Warrior should get under way soon. Be on the lookout for a "down payment" of about $50k. I'm sure there'll be a lot more when the movie hits big!*

All best,

Sam

The news was excellent, but that closing — All best — always made Smart's flesh crawl. Everyone in New York's lit biz — editors, publishers, agents — seemed to use it: All best, all best. *All best WHAT, for Christ's sake?* Smart considered it meaningless, a faux courtesy, but in this context — with a much-needed $50K sweetener — he thought he could stand it. Writing was a very strange, stressful way to make a living, but one of its rewards was that it offered the possibility of an occasional jackpot.

He'd shown the fax to Libby, who immediately suggested that they take Lauretta to a fine restaurant in Dergh Town that night to celebrate — specifically, the one run by Dermot St. Clair, third son of the Earl of Dergh. The lad was a sort of patrician ne'er-do-well who had finally flowered as a chef and restaurateur, and Smart thought Libby might be getting ideas about pairing him off with Lauretta. Which would be OK with him; Dermot seemed to have a good head for food and business and was likable enough. But there was no need for Lauretta, just exiting girlhood, to be rushing into anything.

First, however, he'd have to deal with the still-smoking fax on the machine. Tearing it off, he read:

To: Trelawny Smart
From: E. Finister Malcott
URGENT

You, sir, are a scoundrel! Despite what you may have heard, I'm usually not the vindictive type. But I simply cannot allow your meddling and discourtesy to go unanswered. In fact, your Life Account is in even worse arrears now than it was before. I'm afraid I will have to spend much more time rectifying things at Mordalee and will see you soon.

So, thought Smart, *it wasn't as good for him as it was for Gloryanna.* He'd been hoping the Earth had moved for both, so that they could keep each other occupied, perhaps for all eternity. Now, however, it seemed he would have an angry fiend on his hands — one to whom a room in his house had been let in perpetuity. But Smart, a much wiser man than the one who'd set out for Shannon with Fergus just a few days ago, wasn't about to take Malcott's message completely at face value. And he thought he just might be able, if he played his cards right, to find a silver lining in this dark cloud yet.

An hour or so later, Lauretta was up and feeling much refreshed after her nap. Libby was out running a few errands, and Smart had just finished frothing some cappuccino for his darling daughter when they heard a door slam upstairs.

"What's that?" Lauretta said, looking toward the source of the noise. "I thought Libby was out."

"It's probably Peter Pike, love. The man I told you about on the way here, who runs the farming operation and is sort of our rustic major domo. He has a room in the west wing of the house. Come to think of it, I need to have a word with him about a few things. So why don't you finish your coffee while I talk with him; then I'll meet you out behind the house, near the spreading birch tree, in 10 minutes or so. It's a beautiful, sunny day for a walk — something this part of Ireland doesn't get nearly as much as we'd like — and I want to capitalize on it by showing you around."

"OK, Dad," she said, sipping from her cup. She was dressed in corduroy pants, a long-sleeved wool shirt and a sweater. "But give me a few minutes to put on some lighter clothes. I thought it was going to be cooler here, so far north."

"Good idea!" said Smart. "I'll meet you after you've changed."

His great height aside, he felt like David facing Goliath as he slowly mounted the steps toward the Devil's room. He would know within a few minutes whether his little scheme would work. If it did, he and Libby would be sole proprietors of Mordalee once again. If not ... well, he didn't want to dwell on the consequences of failure. He had no desire to witness Malcott's full wrath.

He reached the top of the stairs, then walked softly to the door, where he paused. The planet seemed to halt in its orbit at that moment, and the noisy old house became still as a tomb. Not a breeze stirred in the long and normally drafty hallway; nothing moved or made any sound. It was as if all creation was holding its breath along with him. Smart knocked once.

"You know it's open," a voice growled from within. "Stop wasting our time."

He entered, then turned to close the door behind him. When his eyes had adjusted to the brightness of the room, which faced directly into the brilliant late-morning sun, he noticed the somewhat hunched figure of Malcott standing about ten feet away in front of the far window and near the fireplace, with his back to Smart. *Good!* thought Smart. *Exactly where I wanted him.* From the rear, he looked like his old self — as opposed to Fergus — but he didn't bother to turn around. This was fine with Smart, who was wary of those dangerous eyes.

"Smart," he said to the window, "how could you?"

"Oh, come now, Malcott. Was it really all that bad? She seemed quite willing, and although she's not exactly a raving beauty, she had everything required for a good time. I thought you two would be a match made in ... an excellent match."

Malcott turned around and regarded him as if he were a noxious insect. His eyes were hooded with sullen anger, and his scowl — the blackest Smart had ever seen — threatened to blot out the strong sunlight that framed him. "You *owe* me, Smart."

Smart looked down, leery of the power of those bottomless, reptilian eyes. He needed some time for his plan to work, and above all he didn't want to fall under Malcott's spell, as the customs agent had. He shifted his feet somewhat guiltily, playing the part of the contrite prankster, then looked toward Malcott but without meeting his gaze directly.

"I didn't want her, and Lauretta didn't want ... well, let's say she wasn't in the mood. And I really did think you and Gloryanna might make a good pair."

He braced himself for the storm with averted eyes, but it never came. Malcott was silent for a while; then he moved a few steps toward the fireplace. Smart had a strong suspicion about that fireplace, since there was no corresponding chimney outside. But he didn't dwell on it, because he'd noticed something even more fascinating: Malcott was walking with a slight limp.

"Mr. Smart," he began, his return to the honorific making Smart hope he might be relenting just a bit, "I thought I, of all beings, knew what hell was. Then I met Gloryanna."

Smart couldn't resist looking directly at Malcott, and he was amazed to see Malcott's eyes closed. He seemed to be contemplating the unfathomable cruelties of life. There was a long silence as Smart waited for Malcott to finish his thought.

"She was ... insatiable. *Insatiable,* do you hear me?"

Malcott's eyes blazed at him, and he quickly looked away, letting his gaze wander toward the window and the sun-dappled greenery that surrounded Mordalee. Just as in the tourist brochures, the glorious emerald landscape seemed to sparkle. *An enchanted isle*, he repeated to himself like a mantra to ward off Malcott's anger. *An enchanted isle*, indeed. Finally, he answered.

"You mean ... ?"

"You know exactly what I mean — impossible to satisfy, even for me! You knew — that's why you sent her to me. I've never met a woman like that before. She used me up, turned me into a husk, then wanted more and still more. By morning I could hardly move!"

Smart made a supreme effort to keep a straight face. He felt the mounting hilarity invading his every cell like an irresistible virus, but the stakes were far too high to indulge in the belly laugh he desperately needed. He finally even managed to look sympathetic, and edged a bit closer to the downcast Malcott. The latter was now standing directly before the fireplace with his hand on the mantel, as if he needed its support.

"I'm sorry, old man," said Smart. "I really had no idea, since I've never slept with her, and I wasn't looking to save myself by foisting her on you." Of course he had meant to foist Gloryanna on Malcott, but in a lying contest with the Great Deceiver one might as well lay it on thick, because it would be a case of devil take the hindmost. He darted a glance at the downcast Malcott, then shifted his gaze out the window again.

There, finally, was the sight he'd been waiting for: his stunning daughter, smiling into the glorious Irish day as she walked toward the shade of the spreading copper birch. Dressed in brief shorts and a sheer, sleeveless top, legs long and shapely and with her thick, lustrous hair streaming out behind her, she looked like a sylph come out to frolic among the sun's rampant rays. She was a nubile wonder of nature, and he knew the sight of her would have filled him instantly with desire had he not been her father. He also knew Malcott possessed no such immunity.

"It's Lauretta," he said, smiling. Then his face clouded a bit. "But I'm afraid that outfit is much too skimpy for these parts!"

Malcott turned, caught sight of Lauretta and moved eagerly toward the window, his achy groin forgotten. But as he reached mid-stride Smart gave him a sharp push toward the fireplace. Caught off balance, Malcott fell heavily toward the brick aperture, his face registering shock, betrayal and then a terrible, malignant anger.

But he couldn't stop his fall, and Smart had been careful to step back after shoving him so he couldn't grab him for support or take him down with him. Malcott's upper back hit the mantel, then he collapsed heavily into the fireplace, knocking over the handsome bronze andirons and raising a small cloud of dust and soot. As he glared up at Smart, the flames of hell seemed to blaze up behind his eyes, and Smart despaired for an awful moment that he'd been wrong about the fireplace after all. Malcott's unspeakably spiteful face changed into something bestial, and his mouth opened to reveal horribly large, sharp teeth. A terrifying, gutteral voice — the sound of pure evil — issued forth in what Smart knew was the beginning of a dreadful curse. The unintelligible words flayed his soul and turned his knees to jelly.

Then the fireplace seemed to unravel like a rip in the fabric of reality and swallowed Malcott whole. Smart felt heat on his face and smelled pitch and sulfur as he caught a glimpse of an awful, yawning abyss behind Malcott, whose eyes transfixed him with impotent hatred as he disappeared. Smart quailed, shutting his eyes tightly and turning away, but when he reopened them the Devil's room had reverted to the tiny space that the ancestral Brimstons had cordoned off to preserve themselves from evil. The dead air in the little sunlit garret made it stuffy, hot, suffocating.

Lord Brimston had been right: Malcott always kept an escape hatch, and you could get rid of him if you could just get him to use it. His unwanted tenant was gone.

"Dad!" he heard Lauretta's muffled voice as if in a dream. "Where are you? I'm ready for our walk!"

Thirty-nine

Lauretta thought Smart seemed strangely preoccupied and almost dazed when he came unsteadily down the stairs to meet her, but he told her it was just a whopper of a headache that had come roaring up without warning. She wondered if it might have had something to do with his meeting with Pike. But he didn't say anything about Pike, whom Lauretta had hoped to meet, and she didn't press. But she was concerned.

"We could postpone our walk if you want to rest, Dad," she said. He was still shaken from seeing the very face of evil, but he demurred with a wan smile: "Actually, a stroll might do me some good."

As soon as they were out of the yard, though, he sat down heavily on a low retaining wall that separated Libby's newly planted packasandras and hostas from the drive and closed his eyes, massaging his temples with his fingers. She had a feeling that he didn't have a headache and that he was trying to hide what was really bothering him, but she chose not to pry. Instead, she threw an arm around his shoulders and smiled when he turned to her, and gradually he seemed to breathe more easily, putting his arm around her in return and suggesting that they continue on.

By the time they actually did meet Pike, who was in a far meadow with the sheep, she was glad to see that there was much more spring in his step. She surmised he couldn't have seen Pike in the house after he'd left her in the kitchen, given how far away from the house he was, but she decided to let him tell her what had really happened in his own good time.

He seemed even happier — almost ecstatic, in fact — when Pike told him that he'd finally recaptured the missing black sheep whose heedless ramblings had, among other problems, caused Fegan Fergus to swerve his car into the ditch some months back. Smart had mentioned Fergus to Lauretta, and she said she was looking forward to meeting him.

"Strange t'ing," Pike said of the ram, "he seems to have reverted to his former self now. He's old, you know, and he's become meek as a lamb again. All the vinegar seems to have gone out of him for some reason."

"Peter," said Smart, "let's see how much like a lamb he really is. Let's roast him up."

Pike protested that he might still have some limited use as a stud and noted that in any event he would be much too tough and gamy for eating. "Besides," he said, "there aren't enough of you to make much of a dent in him in one sitting, if you take my meaning, so you'd end up having to freeze most of him, which would make him even tougher."

"Get him over to McGurn's," said Smart, referring to the local slaughterhouse. "I know an old recipe for a marinade powerful enough to tenderize a tough old sheep from my younger days in Greece and Turkey. I'll make a big batch of it, and we'll soak the mutton in that for the rest of the day. I'll invite the whole village to come down tonight, and we'll have one of those ... what do you call it? Rhymes with bailey. An Irish hootenanny."

Pike looked at him with just a trace of alarm. Then he perked up. "Oh, you mean a cielidh? With music and dancing and all?"

"Exactly!" said Smart. "And don't worry about the meat being tough — those Greeks had marinades that could soften granite. I'll call Fergus and get him to bring out a keg of Guinness and some other refreshments, then you ... ."

As Smart gave Pike instructions, Lauretta found herself staring at this man she already felt she loved, despite how brief a time she'd known him. Who was this fascinating stranger who wrote best-selling books about a neolithic superman and whose wild youth had encompassed heartbreak and despair and adventures with Greek peasants? She didn't know, but she was eager to find out.

* * *

Much of Ballymorda and a good deal of Dergh, too, flooded onto the Mordalee grounds at about 8 p.m. for the festivities. Doc Gilchrist and his wife, Maeve, came, as did Bess McCaughey and her husband the vet, who happily wasn't on call that night. Fergus put a hand-lettered sign saying "Adjourned to Mordalee" on the door of The Drowning Man, and most of his usual clientele simply relocated to the manor house, glad of a chance to see the American proprietors on their own turf and to appraise what they'd done with the old Brimston wreck.

Smart's only regret was that Lady B. couldn't be there, at least in the flesh, but he led a toast in her honor before the dancing, and many villagers raised their glasses to her with fond thoughts and wistful eyes. Smart felt her presence strongly, and at one point, as he was passing through the front door to return to the party, he could have sworn he smelled the very faint scent of hyacinth, although there were none in Libby's garden.

The cielidh roared on into the wee hours, as Irish parties will, and no one seemed to care at all that the morrow would dawn on a workday. "The business of Ireland is not only business," Fergus reminded Smart at one point, having donated a keg to the general welfare (while staying sober, however, to dole it out). "It's monkey business!" a regular from the pub called out in response, a laughing village lass on his lap.

Fergus, though busy and sociable as ever, had somehow found

time to make conversation with Lauretta, who looked like a dream despite the fact that she had dressed for comfort and simplicity rather than for effect. But her many glories were much noted anyway, and she found herself surrounded by young men — and a few older ones, whose wives were either absent or gallivanting themselves — for the whole evening.

But Libby was the real heart of the party, spreading the merry-making spirit wherever she went and even dragging Smart to his feet for a jig, which he managed to turn into a hilarious Zorba O'Reilly cross-cultural dance experience. He drank but did not get drunk, which Libby noted with great relief and satisfaction. At one point she raised her own glass to him, eyes flashing, and proposed a wry Irish toast: "May you be in heaven for two hours before the devil knows you're gone!" and gave him a significant look. Returning it, he took a gulp of stout and smiled. *This IS heaven*, he thought. *Malcott's been gone for more than two hours, and hopefully for good!*

By the time the last celebrants had gone and Lauretta had retired to her room, dazzled by the sheer fun of her first night in Ireland, it was past 2:30 a.m. Smart and Libby both should have been exhausted. But on this early summer's eve a strange exhilaration seemed to have seized them. Or perhaps it was just a case of getting a second wind. In any case, they were lying in bed together and the lights were out, but neither was ready to sleep. Smart propped himself up on one elbow and faced toward Libby. He had so much to say, yet all that came out was a chuckle and a commonplace: "Life is rich, eh?"

"Very. And strange. For instance, who would have suspected your powers as an exorcist?"

Smart had told her about his ousting of Malcott, and he smiled. But then he thought of that last, horrific look on Malcott's face. It had shaken him to his core, and he flinched involuntarily. Libby, attuned to him as ever, felt the tremor and put a hand on his shoulder. "But you did it, Trel! You got rid of him for once and for all, and you've lifted a great burden from this house. You've given us all new lives."

Smart knew exactly what she meant. The last six months had been extraordinarily frustrating. Nothing had seemed to work out, and their difficulties had only seemed to compound. He had begun to think that their lives would devolve into a miserable parody in which they would ultimately stand revealed as the opposite of the happy, wealthy and enviable couple they seemed. But Malcott's vile manipulations had backfired, and they were rid of him and his baleful influence. Beyond that, Smart had found himself at last after locating the missing link to his own unhappy past. Malcott had indeed, if mostly inadvertently, played the role of "life accountant" and impelled Smart to deal with his own long-neglected emotional bookkeeping.

Smart lay next to Libby for awhile, feeling the body heat radiate from her skin and listening to her measured breathing as he strained to catch the respiration of the old house itself. But it was totally silent, and Smart hoped this meant that the older Brimstons, too, had finally found peace.

He felt Libby's fingers stroking his neck and looked at her in the dim light. She was staring at his eyes, and now she gave him a warm smile. She pulled him toward her, and their lips met in a kiss that was as leisurely as it was full of a desire more delicious for its long denial. He brought his hand up under her nightgown and placed it on the mounded plain of her abdomen. Then he began to move his fingers in a gentle circular exploration that brought them lower and lower until they reached the dense tangle of curls the feel of which had never failed to quicken his pulse. He was kissing her all the while, her lips, ears, neck and swelling breasts, and she moved closer and clasped him to her and reached between his legs to guide him into her. That night they had each other again and again, like young lovers in the first discovery of physical passion; and the sun, when it rose hours later, only just caught them sleeping at last.

The radio alarm on the night table next to their bed suddenly came on, though it wasn't very loud. It had been more than enough to awaken them both the morning before, when they had planned to get up early to drive to the airport, but this morning only Smart awoke. In the excitement of their return and the hectic preparations for the cielidh they had forgotten to reset it, but there was no need to roust themselves out of bed so early today, thank God. Smart was about to turn it off when he heard a familiar gravelly voice: Lord Kenspeckle, who said he was filling in for the usual sunrise man. Smart liked the self-styled rajah of retro radio; he had a philosophical bent, and you never knew what he might say.

"I want to start off wi' a Stones song that has a message very appropriate to the beginning of each new day. It's a song about how you can't always get what you want. And you can't, you know. Try as you might, as we all might, a great muckle comes to naught in the grand scheme of things. But still, we have to try. Because, as the song points out, when you try sometimes, you might find ... you get what you need. It just might happen. What about you, dear listeners, rubbing the sleep out of your eyes at the dawning of the rest of your life? Do you think you'll find what you need today?" Smart turned the radio down low just as the beginning of "You Can't Always Get What You Want" began to fill the room. He loved that choral part but didn't want Libby awakened.

Smart looked down at his wife, whose beautiful face still showed a trace of the smile that had adorned it when her eyes had closed, and said to himself: *I've already got it. Everything I need is right here.* He thought about the Devil's room: Now that its tenant was gone, they could change it if they wanted to. But it might be best to just leave it, and its legend, in peace.

Then he turned off the radio, closed his eyes, and shed a tear of pure joy that trickled slowly down one cheek before he went back to sleep.

A Word About Joe Fegan

Among the Fegans, formerly of Dublin, it was well known that the men were more the storytellers of the clan while not necessarily the movers and shakers. Thus it was no surprise when this tale was found among his effects with a note that someone should try to do something with it if possible. — Jeff Durstewitz

Made in the USA
Middletown, DE
07 April 2016